A Masquerade of Muertos

Wisteria Tearoom Mysteries

A Fatal Twist of Lemon
A Sprig of Blossomed Thorn
An Aria of Omens
A Bodkin for the Bride
A Masquerade of Muertos

A Masquerade of Muertos

Patrice Greenwood

Evennight

Evennight Books/Book View Café
Cedar Crest, New Mexico

This is a work of fiction. All of the characters, organizations, and events portrayed in this novel are either products of the author's imagination or are used fictitiously.

A MASQUERADE OF MUERTOS

An Evennight Book
Published by Book View Café Publishing Cooperative
P.O. Box 1624
Cedar Crest, NM 87008

www.bookviewcafe.com

Cover photo: Chris Krohn
Map illustrations: Chris Krohn and Patrice Greenwood

ISBN: 978-1-61138-610-3

First Edition August 2016

for Pari
who gets all my weird stuff

Acknowledgments

My thanks to my wonderful publication team for their help with this novel: Doranna Durgin, Pari Noskin, Sherwood Smith, Leah Cutter, and Chris Krohn; to my infinitely patient consultants Ken and Marilyn Dusenberry; and to my helpful colleagues in Book View Café.

And as always, thanks to Mary Alice Higbie and the staff of the St. James Tearoom, for inspiring me to write this series, for making Wisteria White tea a reality, and for offering in their tearoom an incomparable haven.

Wisteria Tearoom
upper floor

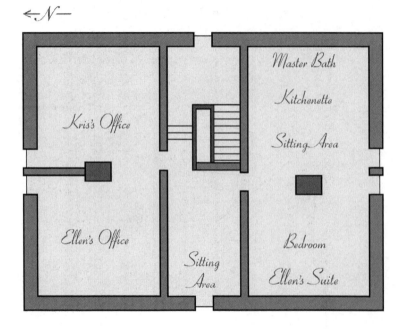

←N—

Kris's Office

Ellen's Office

Sitting Area

Master Bath

Kitchenette

Sitting Area

Bedroom

Ellen's Suite

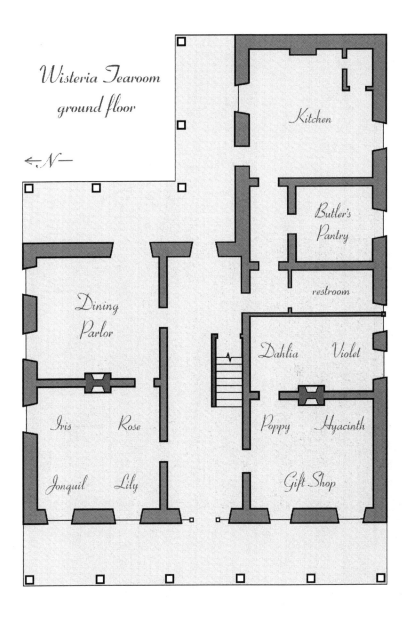

Wisteria Tearoom
ground floor

←.N—

Kitchen

Butler's
Pantry

restroom

Dining
Parlor

Dahlia   Violet

Iris   Rose

Poppy   Hyacinth

Jonquil   Lily

Gift Shop

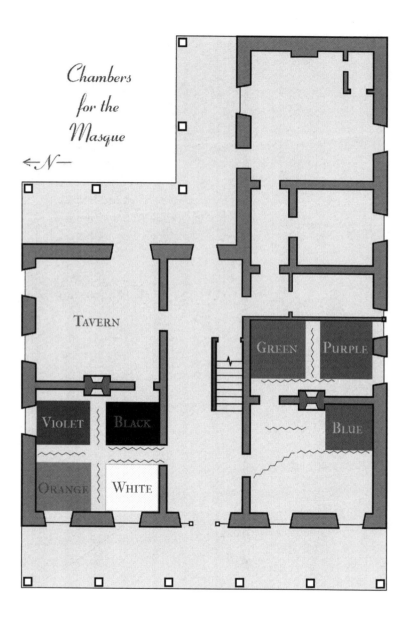

Chambers
for the
Masque

←—N—

...while the chimes of the clock yet rang, it was observed that the giddiest grew pale, and the more aged and sedate passed their hands over their brows as if in confused reverie or meditation. But when the echoes had fully ceased, a light laughter at once pervaded the assembly; the musicians looked at each other and smiled as if at their own nervousness and folly, and made whispering vows, each to the other, that the next chiming of the clock should produce in them no similar emotion...

—Edgar Allen Poe,
"The Masque of the Red Death"

THE DAY BEFORE MY AUNT NAT'S WEDDING, IT RAINED. We agreed, when we talked on the phone that morning, that this was a good omen. Rain is always welcome in Santa Fe. Neither of us voiced any wish for it to stop, although I privately hoped that we'd get sunshine for the wedding, which was to take place in my garden.

It was Friday, so the tearoom was bustling. The day flew by as I juggled final wedding details, tending to my customers, and preparing for a meeting that evening. Late in the afternoon I stood on the front *portal*, shivering despite my wool coat, watching workers set up a tent in the garden. I didn't want them to trample any of my flowers. The roses were big enough to be on their radar, but the smaller plants might go unnoticed.

The rain had dropped to a cold sprinkle tossed by a capricious breeze. Wet cottonwood leaves scattered over the lawn, and the wind raised a wonderful, autumnal scent from them into the air. It made me want to run up into the mountains and walk beneath the aspen trees, all cloaked in golden glory. I promised myself I'd do that soon, because the fall color was almost over. We should get some more pleasant days before the end of October, but the first snow could come any time.

The front door opened with a jangle of tiny bells, and my office manager, Kris Overland, looked out. "Ellen? Meeting starts in ten minutes."

"Yes, all right."

With a final glance at the workers, I eased past the café tables—unoccupied; too cold for tea outdoors that day—and retreated into

1

the comfort of the tearoom. The smells of piñon wood burning in the fireplaces and sweet bread baking in the kitchen combined to fill me with bliss as I hung my coat on one of the hooks in the hall.

In the parlors, the last few customers of the day murmured quietly over their tea. Or as quietly as possible; I recognized the strident voice of the Bird Woman—one of our regular customers, often a challenge—soaring out of the main parlor. She was expounding on the virtues of the Ouija board versus the pendulum.

The meeting, which Kris had arranged, was for planning an event on Halloween night. She and her friends had booked the entire tearoom.

I followed Kris down the hall to the dining parlor. Her burgundy velour dress hugged the curves of her hips nicely, its close sleeves extending past the wrists in a quasi-medieval touch. Rather sensuous for a business meeting, but though Kris's wardrobe was often striking, it was always in good taste. She stopped outside the door and turned to me.

"I'd like you to meet someone," she said, a tinge of color blooming in her cheeks.

In the parlor, a young man stood waiting at the far end of the dining table. He was tall, with honey-colored hair that brushed his shoulders and chiseled cheekbones worthy of a Tolkien elf. He wore black, as did a lot of Kris's Goth friends: in his case a long-sleeved black dress shirt (silk if I was any judge), open at the neckline to allow a glimpse of a silver ankh hanging on a fine chain, and black jeans. A pair of penetrating, warm brown eyes fixed on me and a slight smile grew on his lips, then he looked to Kris.

"Gabriel," Kris said, "I'd like you to meet my boss, Ellen Rosings. Ellen, this is Gabriel Rhodes."

"How do you do," he said with a small, gracious bow that would have caused heart flutters in a colder woman than me.

"Pleased to meet you, Gabriel," I said, nodding in return. "Are you here for the planning meeting?"

"Yes," he said with a chuckle. "I'm a little early."

Kris slipped past the table to join him, and he slid an arm around her waist. She leaned into his shoulder and smiled up at him.

Oh.

"I'll just check on the tea," I said brightly. "Back in a minute."

I crossed the hall, going through the short side hallway to the butler's pantry, where Dee, one of my servers, was preparing for the meeting. She brushed a wisp of blonde hair behind her ear as she looked up at me with a smile. "Don't worry, it'll all be ready."

"I'm not worried," I said. "Thanks for being willing to stay late."

"No problem. They're a fascinating group."

"That they are."

I went on through to the kitchen, more to keep out of Kris's way for a few minutes than to verify that the food was ready. I hadn't seen or heard a hint of Kris's romantic interests before, and felt curious about Gabriel.

Ramon glanced up from sprinkling sugar over a fresh batch of miniature *pan de muertos*. His hair was just long enough to be caught back in a tight ponytail, and with the hairnet over it, and his black T-shirt, he looked like a gang member at first glance.

"Julio go home?" I asked.

"Yeah. He left me to finish since I'm going to be in the meeting anyway. It's almost done."

I leaned over the work table to inhale the scent of the sweet buns. I could just catch a hint of the orange flower water and anise, and my mouth watered. I was tempted to sample one, but held off, knowing I'd probably have one at the meeting.

I had taken to calling it just *"pan"* since "bread of the dead" bothered me a bit, even in Spanish. At first I had objected to Julio's wanting to include *pan de muerto* in the October menu, as being perhaps a bit too morbid, but he'd talked me into it. I caved partly because I'd already nixed any sort of pumpkin-spice item from the menu, and I didn't want to restrict Julio's creativity too much.

To my surprise, the *pan* was a hit. No one commented about the traditional finger-bone decorations, which were kind of abstract anyway. Unless you looked pretty closely and thought about the name, they just looked like a variation on hot crossed buns.

"I'd forgotten you were coming to the meeting," I said to Ramon. "You're playing music for the party, right?"

"Yeah. Not so sure I should have let Kris talk me into it."

"They're paying you, aren't they?"

"Oh, yeah. The pay's good. Just not sure I'm up to the

company."

"But you're a Goth, too!"

"I thought I was. But I'm not like these guys." He shook his head. "They're really serious."

I smiled, remembering the night I'd caught Ramon and two girls sneaking around my lilac bushes, trying to peek into the dining parlor in hopes of glimpsing the tearoom's resident ghost. I'd been angry at the time, but I'd long since forgiven Ramon.

In the months since I'd gotten to know him better and hired him on to help in the kitchen, he'd blossomed. He was thinking about going to culinary school—Julio had told him about his own experiences—and he was working hard to learn all he could. He wasn't going to give up music, and I was glad because he was brilliant on the guitar, but the skills he was learning in my kitchen would help him find work when the musical prospects got thin.

He finished a tray of *pan* and moved it aside, replacing it with a second. This caused more delicious aromas to waft through the kitchen, and for the sake of my waistline, I decided to leave.

"I'm going to check on the parlors before the meeting. Rosa is still here, right?"

"Yeah. She wants to leave as soon as we're closed, though. Doesn't like the Goth scene."

Rosa, Ramon's sister, was about as sweet and gentle as a person could get. It was a toss-up whether she or Iz, the shy Pueblo girl who was my third server, was more shocked by Kris's friends.

"She can go as soon as all the customers have left. You too, Mick," I called to Dee's brother at the dish washing station.

He carefully set down a rose-covered teacup and took out one earbud. "Huh?"

"You can leave when the customers are gone. I'll take care of cleaning up after the meeting."

"Oh! Dee's going to load stuff as she goes, she said."

I nodded, and with a wave for them both, I beat it out of the kitchen before my willpower could crumble.

Hearing voices in the gift shop, I went up toward the front door and stepped in. Rosa was at the register, lovely in her lavender dress and white apron, ringing up a purchase for a departing customer. A young couple were looking at the china, and I smiled, thinking of weddings.

The alcoves adjacent to the gift shop were empty; the fires in the back-to-back fireplaces had died down to embers. I paused for a moment in Violet, looking up at the portrait that Julio had painted of Vi Benning. I still got a lump in my throat whenever I saw it.

We all missed Vi, one of my first servers from the day the tearoom had opened, who had been killed during the summer while she was an apprentice at the Santa Fe Opera. Someone—Julio, probably—had set a votive candle in a small glass on the mantel beneath the painting.

Not wanting the portrait to be damaged, I nudged the candle toward the front edge of the mantel, and resolved to find a fireproof coaster to put beneath it. The flame flickered, then stilled. I watched its light play over the canvas, glinting before settling.

With little daylight coming through the window, Vi's portrait was not well illuminated. Maybe I could hang one of those little halogen spotlights to shine on the painting. I added that to my mental list of things to do, and returned to the hall.

Silence made me wonder whether everyone had left. Then a piercing scream issued from the main parlor.

I dashed into the room, adrenaline cranking my pulse, and beheld a tableau:

Surrounded by her friends in a small semicircle, the Bird Woman lay on the floor right where all four alcoves met, her gaze fixed at the ceiling, her pink dress covered in blood.

I STARED, FROZEN IN HORROR. The ticking of my old mantel clock was loud in the silence.

Not again!

My first thought was that the tearoom wouldn't survive yet another murder on the premises. Especially the murder of the one person who reveled the most in the ghoulish reputation the Wisteria Tearoom had accumulated. Remorse held me stricken until I recalled that I had duties in this situation.

I knelt beside her—Mrs. Olavssen, I made myself call her in my mind—and lifted her wrist. Her flesh was warm.

I was trying to figure out exactly where all the blood had come from when the victim sat up, looked me in the eye, and laughed gustily.

"Gotcha!" she crowed.

Cold relief washed through me as her friends came to life, helping her to stand and sharing her laughter. I managed to put on a smile as I got to my feet, though I felt anything but amusement. A glance around the parlor reassured me that no other customers remained to be disturbed by the Bird Woman's antics.

"The look on your face," said the Bird Woman, chortling. Her bright eyes peered at me from beneath her feathery white bangs. "I punked you good!"

"You certainly did." I took a deep breath, trying to calm my thundering pulse.

Rosa arrived in the doorway, and Dee appeared a half-second later. Both were wide-eyed.

"It's all right," I told them. "Just a little joke."

"Margie's got a great scream, doesn't she?" said the Bird Woman, grinning at one of her friends.

"Yes, indeed," I said, playing along.

Margie, a thin, retiring woman with salt-and-pepper hair, smiled shyly. "I practiced."

I wondered what Miss Manners would say in such a situation. Something clever and kind, no doubt. Alas, I was unable to come up with anything. My pulse had not yet settled, and despite knowing it was unworthy, I was angry.

"Could I get a box for my leftovers?" asked another of the Bird Woman's friends.

Dee stepped forward. "Of course! Does anyone else need a box?"

The bells on the front door rang. Casting a grateful look at Dee, I went out to greet the newcomer. Rosa followed me.

"You OK, Ellen?" she whispered.

"I'm fine. It was just a prank."

Rosa's frown and pursed lips told me her opinion. I agreed, but now was not the time to vent.

Standing just inside the door was a lithe young woman in a black velvet cape over a long dress of something very slinky indeed, black as well, adorned here and there with sharp-looking bits of silver. It looked expensive, as did the pageboy hairstyle that angled downward from her jawline to frame her neck in two perfect points, the kind of cut that required frequent maintenance. The hair itself was dark red, perhaps with a hint of henna, though it was too subtle for me to be sure. She was petite, like a china doll, but tall, strappy heels brought her almost to my height. Her eyes were outlined in perfectly-shaped kohl. The entire effect of her ensemble was reminiscent of an Erté print.

"Good evening," I said. "You're here for the meeting?"

"Yes." She smiled, and suddenly looked attractive as well as striking. "I'm Cherie," she said, giving her name the French pronunciation. "Is Kris here?"

"Pleased to meet you, Cherie. I'm Ellen Rosings. Right this way."

I led her down the hall to the dining parlor, being careful to announce our approach by saying, "You can hang your cloak here, if you like. Weren't you at the opera tea this summer?"

Cherie nodded, draping her cloak over one of the coat hooks and revealing the shoulder-straps of her dress: silver chains, studded with more bits of dangerous-looking metal.

"Yes. So sorry about the singer; she was lovely."

Vi had sung at that tea, a bittersweet memory. I nodded, throat tightening, then turned toward the dining parlor. "In here."

"This is the room?" Cherie asked, pausing in the doorway to look around.

"Yes."

I knew she didn't mean the meeting room. She meant the room that had been Captain Dusenberry's study. The room in which he'd been murdered.

Cherie's gaze took in the long dining table set for tea with lace, china, and an arrangement of yellow and orange chrysanthemums, then rose upward to the chandelier. It was completely still. Disappointment crossed her face, then she looked toward the French doors and her stunning smile flashed out. "Hello, Gabriel. Kris."

"Hi, Cherie," Kris said, stepping forward. She and Gabriel had been looking out at the back garden, which was fast falling dark.

Something about the exchange of glances among the three of them caught my notice. Unusually intense? A wry curve to Gabriel's smile?

Distant bells announced the front door opening again. Rather than risk encountering the Bird Woman in the hall, I ignored it, trusting that Rosa or Dee would guide Kris's friends to the meeting.

"Brilliant idea for the theme, Gabriel," said Cherie, "but do you think you can pull it off?"

"Of course," Gabriel said. "I wouldn't propose it if I couldn't."

"But the ending. How will you manage it?"

He smiled, showing teeth. "With artistry."

Kris turned to me and said a little too brightly, "Gabriel's an artist. Did I tell you?"

"No. What kind of art?"

"Paintings, mostly," Gabriel said. "Some sculpture. I'm experimenting with different media, but I usually work in acrylic."

"Are you showing in town?"

"Yes." Pride and satisfaction rang through the word. It was a big deal for an artist, to be able to say you were showing in Santa Fe.

"Where?" I asked. "I'll go see your work."

"So you got it," Cherie said to him in a soft voice.

"I got it," he said with a nod, then turned to me. "White Iris Gallery."

"It's on Canyon Road," Kris added proudly.

Canyon Road. The Holy Grail of Santa Fe gallery-land.

"Congratulations!" I told Gabriel.

"It's just three pieces so far, but they're going to mount a full show next month," Kris said. "Gabriel's got some work in the Autumn Arts Exhibition as well. Are you going?"

"I hadn't planned to. It's this weekend, right? At Sweeney Center?"

She nodded. "You should see it. Oh, hi, Dale!"

Rosa ushered in a young man I recognized: slender and about my height, dressed in a black jacket over a gray turtleneck and jeans, with a mop of curling brown hair ruthlessly pruned to the top of his head, and kind brown eyes. He was Dale Whittier, a friend of Kris's who had recently applied for a job as a server in the tearoom. I hadn't yet offered it to him, but I probably would. We were going to need extra help for the holidays.

Behind him came a young woman whom I did not recognize, a few inches shorter than Dale. She was dressed à la Lolita, with a frilly skirt beneath a black corset, pink petticoat poofing out the skirt, and a black ribbon around her neck. There was nothing Lolita-ish about her curvaceous figure, and the corset's effect was amplified by a large tattoo of a raven adorning her cleavage. Her brown hair was pulled back into a high ponytail that fell in curling ringlets, and her earrings were long, silver crosses with pointed feet.

She stopped in the doorway, perhaps for effect. Her eyes widened like a little girl's and her mouth opened in a beestung "O," then she turned her head to look up at the chandelier. I began to think there was a discussion I had missed.

"Hello, Margo," Cherie said. "Dale, you look so mainstream. Are you feeling all right?"

Dale shot me a self-conscious glance. The dining parlor was getting full, so I slipped out to do a last minute check on the food.

"Mrs. Olavssen left," Rosa said, coming up to me. "That was a mean trick she played on you!"

I waved a dismissive hand. "No harm done."

"Well, it was in bad taste. After all you've been through…"

"Thanks, Rosa, but it's all right. She didn't mean to be rude."

"You're so good to forgive her," Rosa said with a rueful smile.

She took off her apron and put it in the laundry hamper in the little hallway outside the butler's pantry. In its place she put on a raincoat from one of the coat hooks there, pulling her hair free of the collar. "You sure you'll be all right?"

"Yes, Dee's here. And Ramon. Go on home and have a nice evening."

She glanced toward the dining parlor. "Same to you," she said, not sounding very hopeful about it.

Dee was in the pantry arranging food on two three-tiered tea trays, frowning in concentration behind her dark-framed glasses. Pots of tea sat ready under cozies.

"Can I help?" I asked.

"Just waiting for the scones. Go be the hostess."

"Kris is the hostess tonight," I said, picking up one of the teapots and setting it on a tray. "I'll take this on in."

The last two attendees had arrived in my absence and stood talking with Cherie and Margo: a tall, ethereal blonde dressed in layers of white gauze, looking like a dove in a flock of crows, and a devilishly handsome Hispanic man in a tailored black suit. Their body language—subtle touches, elbow brushes, frequent glances—suggested that they were a romantic couple. I edged my way past them and set the teapot on the sideboard.

"Ah, here's Ellen," said Kris, turning to the room. "Has everyone met Ellen?"

"I haven't," said the blonde, turning wide, pale blue eyes toward me in open curiosity.

"Ellen, this is Gwyneth Bancroft, and that's Roberto Chavez," Kris said.

"How do you do?" I said, shaking hands. Gwyneth's hand was cold, Roberto's almost hot.

"Shall we sit down?" I added. "The food is about to come in."

The group milled around the table, finding their names on the place cards. Gwyneth paused before taking her seat, looking up at the chandelier.

The crystals remained still. At last Gwyneth gave a little sigh and drifted into her chair.

Nine chairs pretty much filled the room. Kris had drawn up the seating chart, and had honored my request to be near the door in case Dee needed help with anything. The empty chair across from me was for Ramon.

I uncovered the teapot and poured: Assam, a rich and malty tea, at Kris's request. Dee came in, followed by Ramon, who had removed the hairnet and let down the ponytail, black hair not quite brushing his shoulders. They each carried a tiered tea tray, and as they set them near either end of the table a murmur of approval went up from the group.

Smiling, I filled my own cup and Ramon's, then returned the pot to the sideboard and took my seat. Roberto, seated beside me, picked up the printed menu by his plate.

Afternoon tea, which was technically what this was even though it was evening, was a substantial meal. I had skipped lunch, and was thankful to start passing the savories at my end of the table. I took a cucumber sandwich, a pumpkin fritter, and a cream-cheese-and-pistachio-stuffed date, then passed the plate to Roberto.

"Thanks for coming, everyone," Kris said from the opposite corner. She had placed Gabriel at the head of the table instead of herself, which was interesting. Kris was not the sort of person who generally deferred to others.

"And thank you for being willing to help with All Hallows Eve," she added. "It should be a smashing party."

Ramon shot me a glance as he slid into his chair. Gwyneth, beside him, gave him a winsome smile.

"Did everyone get Gabriel's email?" Kris asked.

I hadn't, but I supposed that didn't matter. My function at their Halloween party would be behind the scenes. Kris had suggested I didn't need to be there at all, but since the house was my home, I was not going to vacate for an evening party, particularly this one. I'd decided to help serve and keep an eye on things.

"Which email?" Margo asked, pausing with sandwich halfway to her mouth.

"The one about the theme."

I glanced at Ramon, who shrugged. Most of the others nodded. Gwyneth added a lump of sugar to her teacup.

"OK, then," Kris said, "I'll let him explain what he's got planned."

I watched her trade smiles with Gabriel. His gaze lingered on her just a second longer than necessary, then he turned his attention to the table.

"Has everyone read the story?" he asked.

"Story?" Gwyneth said. "There's a story?"

"'The Masque of the Red Death,'" said Kris.

"Oh, that."

"If you haven't read it, please do," Gabriel said. "It's the basis for the theme. It's not long."

It had been years, but I remembered reading it. Edgar Allen Poe, one of his more picturesque tales. A prince, fabulously rich, throws an elaborate party for his noble cronies while a plague rages outside the castle walls.

"So, we'll be using seven of the alcoves as the seven chambers of Prospero's abbey. The food will be finger food, like this," he said, taking a deviled egg from the tray in front of him, "a different item in each chamber, presided over by one of us. Here's a map." Gabriel handed a stack of paper to Cherie, who took one and passed the rest to Margo.

"These alcoves are pretty small," Cherie said.

"Yes. People will go through as they arrive, in shifts if necessary. Four at a time, probably. Since we can't have stained glass windows and braziers, we'll have candle lanterns with glass of the right color in each chamber."

When the maps came to me, I saw that it was our floor plan for the tearoom's ground floor. Kris had copied it, and Gabriel had made notes on the alcoves—white, blue, green, orange—and drawn in a crisscrossing traffic pattern. Seven of the eight alcoves were labeled with colors; the smallest, Poppy, would serve as an entryway.

"The final chamber is the one called Rose," he continued. "We'll decorate it all in black, and the lamps in there will be red." He glanced at me, watching for objections. Kris and I had already talked about what kind of decorations were OK and what I preferred they leave alone. I nodded.

"There's a mantel clock in that room already, so it's perfect," Gabriel said. He turned his gaze on me and I found myself straightening my shoulders. "The clock is accurate, right?"

"It keeps time pretty well," I said. "I can set it that day."

"And it chimes every hour?"

"Yes. Also on the quarter hours. It's the Westminster chimes, and at the top of the hour it's followed by gongs for the hour."

"Only the top of the hour matters. Ramon, when the gongs start, you pause, no matter where you are in the music."

"OK," Ramon said.

"And everyone stops what they're doing, wherever they are, and stands still until the chimes end. Then the music starts again."

This was beginning to sound familiar. I'd have to dig up that Poe story and read it again.

I cleared my throat. "I don't think the clock can be heard in the south side of the house," I said apologetically.

"I've got that worked out," Gabriel said. "I'll put a wireless mic under it and a speaker in the gift shop. I brought them with me tonight, to test."

Dee came in with fresh tea and started filling cups. Gwyneth offered hers with a charming smile. The one savory she'd taken—a deviled egg—sat untouched on her plate.

Gabriel went on, saying he wanted each of the people around the table to wear the color of one of the seven chambers. He assigned them all: white for Gwyneth (obviously), blue for Cherie, orange for Margo.

"I look terrible in orange!" she said, pouting.

Gabriel's brow creased slightly in exasperation, but his voice was gentle. "No, you don't."

"I *hate* orange!"

"I'll switch with you," Roberto offered. "You can be green and I'll be orange."

"Thank you, Roberto," Margo said, turning to him with a sudden, sweet smile.

"You still haven't explained how you're going to manage the ending," Cherie said, helping herself to a scone.

Gabriel looked at her, eyes narrowed a little in mischief. "You can't guess?"

I reached for my teacup and found it empty. Poe's story did not end well, as I recalled.

"Doesn't everyone wind up dead?" I asked in a small voice. "In the story, I mean."

"Yes, of course," Gabriel said. "We'll be doing that symbolically."

He signaled to Ramon, who stood and headed for the kitchen. Julio had said there was a special item for the party's menu but he hadn't told me what it was.

"We'll need someone to play the role of the stranger," Gabriel said, giving me a glance. "Someone who doesn't mind being in costume."

"I could do it," said Dee from the doorway. She had a teapot in her hands, and her eyes were bright with interest.

Gabriel gave her a long, speculative look. I felt a stab of worry; she was just twenty-one, and Gabriel's personality was decidedly magnetic.

"As the clock strikes midnight," he said, "the stranger appears in the blue chamber. The prince challenges him, and he makes his way through each of the chambers in turn until he reaches the black chamber. There the prince confronts him. In the story, the prince dies, and his followers tear off the stranger's mask, only to find nothing underneath the shroud. Then one by one they fall dead. What we're going to do is symbolize that. When he gets to the black chamber, the stranger will serve everyone this."

Gabriel gestured toward the doorway. Ramon came in past Dee, carrying a tray of small cordial glasses filled with a clear, bright red liquid. It didn't look like blood, but somehow it looked sinister. As Ramon passed the glasses around to the silent guests, I saw them sparkling subtly.

"We drink, then we all unmask," Gabriel said, raising his glass.

Ramon reached the foot of the table with two cordial glasses left. He gave one to me, took one for himself, and set aside the tray.

I was distinctly reluctant to taste what was in my glass. It was definitely glittering; someone had added some of the edible glitter that we used for decorating. I frowned, and sniffed at the liquor. A faint smell of spice reached me.

"What is it, Gabriel?" Gwyneth asked. She looked angry, and her voice trembled a little.

Gabriel smiled. "Cinnamon schnapps, and a little food coloring. Cheers."

We all watched in silence as he knocked back his glass. He set it on the table and regarded us.

I realized I was holding my breath. Gabriel's storytelling had affected me. I gave myself a mental shake and a silent scold.

Kris sipped from her glass, eyes on Gabriel. He smiled.

"Schnapps. Ugh," Cherie said. "Why not absinthe?"

"Because it's green, my dear. This is the Masque of the Red Death, not the Green Death."

"What about sloe gin? That's red," said Gwyneth.

"That's even worse!" Cherie protested.

"I agree," said Margo. "Not that I care for schnapps."

"You might as well just make it a Bloody Mary," said Dale with a wicked grin, prompting immediate, indignant protests.

Gabriel shrugged. "If you all object to schnapps, then it can be vodka. It's the color that matters."

"Or lack thereof," said Cherie.

Margo shrugged. "At least with vodka, you can choose from more flavors."

"Pumpkin spice vodka," Ramon murmured, making me grin. I sniffed my glass again, then took a sip. Definitely cinnamon-y.

"I thought cinnamon would be appropriate," Gabriel said. "Red death."

"So that's it?" Roberto asked. "We drink a shot of vodka and take off our masks?"

Gabriel nodded. "The enchantment ends at midnight. So does the story. The party can continue, of course."

Again, he glanced at me. Kris had asked about running late, and I'd agreed to it for an additional fee. I had drawn the line at two a.m. I'd have to get *some* sleep that night.

"So, you get to be the prince," Roberto said with an edge of bitterness, "and we're all supposed to bow down to you."

"Would you prefer to be Prospero?" Gabriel said, a clear note of challenge in his voice. "It doesn't matter to me."

The tension in the room cranked up a notch as they stared down. Finally Gwyneth's bell-like laughter broke it.

"Really, Roberto. It's Gabriel's idea, and he's clearly put a lot of planning into it. He should be the prince."

Roberto glowered at her across the table. Interestingly, rather than reacting meekly, she fixed him with a clear do-what-I-say glare.

"If you don't like the theme, you can always put forward an alternative," Gabriel said.

There was a long silence. Apparently no other themes were forthcoming.

"It's a charming conceit, I'll give you that," Cherie said. "I can't think of a better one."

"I think it'll work," said Dale, nodding. "We'll all be pretty stoked by midnight."

I grimaced, picturing forays into the garden for recreational smoking. I'd been explicit with Kris: no drugs of any kind on the property, no underage guests since there would be alcohol, no smoking in the house including vapor cigarettes, which I thought foul. She had promised me she'd make sure of these conditions, that anyone who smoked outside would use an ash tray, and that there would be no minors at the party. They'd ordered cases of champagne and red wine to go along with the menu that Julio had created for them, and there would be other drinks including absinthe.

I looked at Dale, hoping that it was the wine he'd referred to. Maybe I'd hold off on the job offer until after the 31st. He'd done well at his interview, but I couldn't deny being curious to see how he behaved at this party.

"So I can count on you all?" Gabriel asked.

Roberto leaned back in his chair and didn't say anything. Gwyneth smiled brightly. "Of course you can!"

A plate of sweets appeared under my nose, distracting me. I looked up at Ramon, who had taken the plate from the tea tray at our end of the table in order to hand it around. I chose a *pan de muerto* and passed the plate to Roberto.

The bread was soft, still warm, and went surprisingly well with the cinnamon schnapps. I sipped, getting used to the color. I would not be downing a shot, thanks, but as an aperitif it wasn't bad.

Gabriel started discussing the music with Ramon. The party would begin at nine o'clock. Three hours until the midnight unmasking, fairly long for a musical performance. Gabriel agreed to generous breaks, but insisted that Ramon be playing at the top of each hour, so that the music could pause when the clock chimed.

I hoped they were paying Ramon really well.

The others began chatting. Dale asked Gwyneth what her costume would be, which launched her into happy speculation. She leaned toward Titania, with Roberto as Oberon, which seemed to assuage his prince-envy somewhat.

Dee came around with fresh tea, and ended up standing at the far end of the table talking with Gabriel and Kris. No doubt they were discussing the "stranger" costume.

The Red Death was a fictional plague, but the made-up symptoms were vividly described in Poe's story. If I recalled correctly, the "stranger" wore a death shroud mottled with blood and a mask made to look like a victim of the Red Death. It would definitely be grotesque, and evoke emotional response. In this part of the country the idea of plague was never taken lightly.

Bubonic plague was present in the wild rodents of New Mexico, and there were usually a couple of cases every year. In bad years a handful of people would die. The worst cases were when tourists caught it and didn't show symptoms until they got back home; their local doctors had probably never seen the plague, and might not figure it out until it was too late. Modern medicine could cure bubonic plague, but modern medicine first had to catch a clue.

Feeling restless, I stood, picked up the empty tea tray, and carried it to the kitchen. Mick was putting away clean baking trays.

"I thought you'd gone home," I said to him when he had removed his ear buds.

"Nah, I stayed to give Dee a lift. I clocked out, though, don't worry."

"If you're working you should be paid."

"I've been reading," he said, showing me his phone. He'd found an ebook of "The Masque of the Red Death."

"Dee told me about it," he added. "Pretty creepy story."

"It is."

"Are they really going to reenact it on Halloween?"

"Apparently."

"Wow. Need extra help that night?"

I looked at him, recognizing vague apprehension as the source of my disquiet. "I just might," I said.

Going back to the dining parlor, I found that everyone was standing, intently discussing whether the dress code at the party should be historical or anything-goes. I found a tray and started collecting empty cordial glasses.

Before I had opened the tearoom, I really hadn't had much contact with Goths. The last few months had been quite educational, and so had this evening; I'd seen a side of Kris I had never expected. The softness in her eyes when she looked at Gabriel—that was completely new.

Gabriel listened patiently to all the arguments, then declared that the invitations would encourage historical dress, but not require it. Given the apparent variety of taste among just the group at the meeting, I couldn't help feeling that was wise.

Gwyneth and Roberto edged their way to the head of the table. I didn't hear what Gabriel said to them, but his nod was gracious. He really could have been a prince, I thought idly.

Ramon gave me an empty tray in exchange for the one filled with cordial glasses, and I began collecting china. As I reached for the teacup at Kris's place, I saw something black inside it and pulled my hand back with a sharp gasp.

Gabriel was instantly beside me. "Are you all right?"

Adrenaline flooded my veins, making me feel a bit unwell. I looked more closely at Kris's cup.

"Is that a black widow?" I asked, my voice wavering slightly.

Conversation ceased. Kris stepped to her chair, peered into the cup, and reached for it.

"Don't!" I said involuntarily.

She lifted the saucer, poked at the black object with her small, silver teaspoon, and declared, "It's plastic."

One of her sculpted eyebrows rose a fraction as her gaze swept the room. Someone chuckled.

"Really, what a foolish joke," Cherie said. "I didn't think any of us would stoop to baby-bat tricks."

Kris fished the fake bug out of the cup. "Someone is getting in the mood for trick-or-treat," she remarked, her voice cool. She tossed the spider toward Dale, who dodged amid sudden laughter.

The meeting broke up quickly after that. I helped Ramon clear, still recovering my calm, while Dee tagged along with Gabriel and Kris to test the microphone on the clock. I had a feeling Gabriel would like to say good night to Kris in private, so when we had moved everything out of the dining parlor I went to the gift shop to extract Dee.

A loud ticking greeted me, which I recognized as the sound of my grandmother's mantel clock, amplified. Gabriel stood looking at a pocket watch, flanked by Kris and Dee.

"Are you—"

I didn't get a chance to finish my question. The chimes began, deafening, making me flinch.

"Too loud!" Kris said, covering her ears.

Gabriel took out his cell phone. "I'll turn it down."

The clock's sound was suddenly damped. After the chime was finished, the ticking sound remained, much more subdued.

"Dee," I said, "I could use your help in the pantry. It was a pleasure to meet you, Gabriel."

His smile was warm as he shook my hand. "Thank you for letting us use your tearoom. I promise not to be a nuisance between now and the party."

A part of me wouldn't have minded him being a nuisance. I squelched that part firmly under a professional smile, and led Dee off to the pantry.

As we started sorting silverware from china, I asked, "Did he tell you about the costume?"

Dee grinned. "Yeah, it sounds pretty grotesque."

"I take it that doesn't bother you."

She shrugged. "I'm studying criminal forensics. I can't afford to be squeamish."

She sounded steady enough, but I was still concerned that she might be too attracted to Gabriel. Not that it was any of my business. I felt the spirit of Miss Manners hovering over my shoulder, ready to shake an admonishing finger at me.

Abandoning the subject, I took a stack of plates into the kitchen. Mick relieved me of them and shooed me out.

"We'll lock up," he said, nodding toward Ramon, who was wiping down the work table.

I thanked them, said goodnight, and returned to the hall. Kris was returning from the front door, where I gathered she'd let Gabriel out. We started upstairs together.

"Happy with the response?" I asked.

"Yeah. It's going to work. Gabriel's pleased."

"He's certainly an interesting guy."

She shot me a glance brimming with emotion, very unlike her usual cool demeanor. My worry alarm went off again.

"Have you known him long?" I asked.

"A couple of years," she said, smiling to herself.

We reached the top of the stairs, and Kris turned toward her office. I followed her and stayed by the door while she fetched her coat. The print of Ophelia hanging on her wall struck me: the help-lessness of a drowning madwoman rang a cautionary chord.

"I had no idea you were involved with anyone," I said.

"Oh, we just started dating. Gabriel was seeing someone else until last week."

"Oh?" Intuition prompted me to pry. "Was it someone who was here tonight?"

"Y-yes," she said, flipping off the light switch and stepping past me back into the upper hall. Moonlight lit the sheers on the west window with a pale glow.

My thoughts flickered over the women who had been at the meeting. "Which of them did he date?"

Kris turned to me, then gave a little sigh and a wry smile as she shrugged into her coat. "All of them."

I BLINKED. *"All* of them?"

Kris nodded. "Gabriel is very charismatic."

"Yes, I noticed."

"Don't worry—I've got my eyes open." She smiled. "I'm just going to enjoy my turn in the spotlight. I don't expect it to last. Gabriel's...not a long-term kind of guy, I think."

"Kris, you and I need to sit down together and have a nice long chat."

"Sure. Maybe tomorrow, after the wedding."

Oh, right. The wedding. I suddenly felt very tired.

"Ah. Yes," I said. "Well, we'll see."

"Would you like me to come early?" she offered. "I could help set things up."

"No, no. It's all under control. You're a guest, just come and enjoy the party."

She did not ask, at that late date, to bring Gabriel, for which I was grateful. Not that we couldn't have accommodated an extra guest, but it reassured me that she wasn't rushing into this new relationship completely without caution.

I myself had a date for the wedding: Tony. As Nat's maid of honor I'd be busy, but I hoped to get in a dance or two.

If Tony danced. I realized I didn't know.

There were a lot of things I didn't know about Detective Tony Aragón. Sometimes that worried me a little, but the man had saved my life. And he was a great kisser.

"I brought some black cloth to drape around Vi's portrait," Kris said, taking a length of georgette out of her coat pocket. "Is that all right with you?"

"Of course."

We went downstairs, and I ducked into the pantry to fetch a sandstone coaster before following Kris to the Violet alcove tucked behind the gift shop. She stood on a small footstool, carefully draping the sheer black cloth around the edges of the portrait's frame. When she stepped down, I slipped the coaster under the votive on the mantel.

Kris moved the footstool back to its place in front of a chair and stood gazing at Vi's portrait. "I wonder if Captain Dusenberry was there to meet her when she died."

The comment surprised me, but I treated it seriously. "I didn't know you believed in the afterlife."

She glanced at me. "Of course. Don't you?"

"I...hadn't thought about it lately."

"Ellen, you live in a haunted house!"

"True."

I glanced at Vi's portrait, disturbed by the idea that she might decide to hang around with the Captain. The last thing I needed was for the tearoom to become Ghost Central.

Of course, the Bird Woman would love that. So would Willow Lane, no doubt.

"Vi didn't die here," I said. "Probably someone she knew met her."

If you believed that the dead are met by a loved one. I wasn't sure, myself. Part of me (trying to be very practical) believed only what I could see, hear, or touch. But since the tearoom had opened, I had seen and heard a lot of inexplicable things.

I had carefully avoided thinking about whether the two women who *had* died in the tearoom recently were haunting it. For comfort, I reminded myself that I hadn't seen or heard anything to indicate they were. No new noises, no new mysteries. Only the occasional turning on of lights or music, and dancing chandelier crystals, that were Captain Dusenberry's trademarks.

"You're probably right," Kris said. "She was the sort of person everyone loved. I bet she had plenty of people to meet her." She stepped up to the mantel and adjusted the drape of the georgette.

"Miss you, Vi."

The candle's flame flickered as she stepped back. It could have been the movement of the air.

I followed Kris to the back door, said goodnight, and watched through the window as she got into her car and drove away. The kitchen was dark; everyone else had left. I headed upstairs and into my office, turning on lights as I went.

My list of things to do for the wedding was on my desk. I glanced over it, checked my phone for messages, then retired to my private suite across the hall for a hot bath, a book, and bed.

A gust of wind swept something—rain, or more likely leaves—against the west windows as I crossed the hall. I glanced that way in time to see a large, pale bird flying past in the moonlight.

An owl? It was gone before I could be sure.

Owls symbolized wisdom. Did they also symbolize death?

I decided not to look it up.

Saturday morning dawned cold and damp, with rags of cloud in the sky. I hurried down to put the "Closed for Private Party" sign on the front door. There was another one for the front gate, and as I hung it there I couldn't help thinking of Bilbo Baggins.

It was chilly, but the lack of clouds over the *Sangre de Cristo* Mountains made me hope for fair weather later. I paused to admire the dew glistening on the chrysanthemums along the white fence, then went back to my suite for a quick breakfast of tea, soft-boiled eggs, and a small mound of buttered toast.

When I came downstairs again, Julio was in the kitchen working on the food for the wedding. Nat and Manny had decided on a New Mexican buffet—quite a change from the tearoom's dainty fare—and Julio was plainly having a blast putting it together. He had two slow cookers full of tamales on the counter; rice, *refritos*, and red and green chile sauces on the stove; and on the work table, giant bowls of tortilla chips, plus a tray of cherry and apricot *empanadas*. As I came into the kitchen he was dancing to salsa music while he peeled avocados for guacamole.

"Morning," I said. "Anything I can do to help?"

"Nope. Want some *huevos?*"

"No, thanks. I already ate."

"*Bueno.*"

I eyed the *empanadas*, then resolutely turned away and went to the main parlor to start rearranging furniture, dismantling the four alcoves that were our normal setup and returning the parlor to being one open room. As I moved the lighter chairs, small tables, lamps and ornaments to the walls, I thought about Gabriel's plan to turn the alcoves into the colored chambers of Poe's story.

A Goth masquerade in my living room. Now that was a different way to spend Halloween.

I paused with an end table in my hands, realizing that it was almost exactly a year since I'd purchased the house. A year ago, all this had been a dream.

I set the table down and gazed around the room: a few beloved family pieces like my mother's piano and grandmother's mantel clock, the rest carefully chosen for nostalgia and comfort. We had worked so hard, Nat and I, my friend Gina, and others. So many people had helped make the dream a reality. I was so deeply grateful.

The morning went by with only three phone calls from Nat. The clouds blew away on a brisk breeze, and sun shone down, raising my hopes that the lawn would not be soggy. The flowers arrived, the cake arrived, and Mick arrived to help me move the heavier furniture, handsome in a dress shirt, dark vest, and tie, blond hair sleeked back into a neat ponytail. We lined up the credenzas along the wall of the main parlor for the buffet.

In the garden, the guys from the rental place were back, laying a portable dance floor under the tent. The roses had put out a late burst of bloom, a final glory before winter's sleep. The wisterias were turning, leaves mottled green and gold. Pansies clustered in the flower beds, and the dahlias, too, were still blooming.

On impulse, I picked a handful of pansies and put them in a tiny vase on the mantel in Violet, where a fresh votive candle was burning. Julio again, I thought, smiling.

Rosa and Iz arrived, wearing their lavender dresses but without the white aprons, as Nat had requested. They looked beautiful with their hair caught back in matching barrettes that Iz had beaded.

"You'd better change, Ellen," Rosa reminded me, pointing at the clock in the gift shop.

Half an hour. I dashed upstairs to put on makeup, brush hair, and don the traditional blue velvet dress that Nat and I had made. I added the concho belt that my father gave me for high school graduation, and my mother's squash blossom necklace. I paused to take in the effect of the full ensemble, which I hadn't worn before, in my bedroom mirror.

Very New Mexican. The blue complemented my complexion, heightening the color in my cheeks and making my hair seem a richer brown. I tried on a smile, then hurried downstairs.

Nat came in the back door as I reached the hall, already wearing her dress, patterned like mine but in dark red velvet instead of blue. She took off a scarf that protected a picture-perfect hairstyle.

"You look smashing!" I told her.

"Thank you, darling!" she said, giving my cheek an air kiss. "Did the cake arrive?"

"It's in the dining parlor. Julio and Mick will put it out when the ceremony begins."

Claudia Pearson came in behind Nat, classy as always in a tangerine sheath and matching pillbox hat with a net veil.

"I parked in the back," she said. "Is that all right?"

"Yes, that's fine. Thanks for giving Nat a ride."

"My pleasure."

"Go on upstairs," I told them both. "There's a pot of tea waiting for you in the sitting area. I'll come get you at ten minutes to one."

"Bless you," Nat said, heading for the stairs.

I found Manny out front, chatting with the minister and his best man. He grinned at me, dapper in his tuxedo.

"Hey, *chica azul!* Where's my *chica rosa?*"

"Upstairs, getting zen. You look grand, Tio!" I said, giving him a hug.

He chuckled. "You know Louie Cordova, right?"

"Of course! Nice to see you again," I said, shaking hands. "Can I get you gentlemen some tea or coffee?"

They declined, so I fetched their boutonnieres from the kitchen fridge, and returned to find Kris chatting with them. She was sleek and sultry in a plum-colored satin dress and a picture hat that would have done Scarlett O'Hara proud. I was silently thankful that she hadn't worn black.

The mariachis were tuning up on the back *portal*. Rosa was at the front gate, greeting the early arrivals and directing them to the tent. Butterflies began fluttering in my stomach, though I knew everything would go fine. My watch said twenty to one.

The roar of a motorcycle made me look up the street. The sight of a man in a suit on a bike is fairly rare; my pulse jumped a notch as I watched the black bike glide to a parking place near the corner. The rider got off, removed his helmet, and ran a hand through dark hair. Yes, it was Tony.

4

"THERE'S YOUR HEARTTHROB," Kris said.

I shot her a glance, but she was already sauntering away toward the tent. Tony, helmet in hand, approached with a smile.

"Can I stash this inside?" he asked.

I smiled back, glad to see him. "Of course."

We went into the gift shop and I tucked his helmet behind the counter. His suit was the one he'd worn on our first disastrous dinner date a few months earlier. Probably the only one he owned; his regular wardrobe leaned more toward jeans and a leather jacket.

"You look elegant," I told him.

"You look beautiful," he said, sliding his arms around my waist. "Mmm, nice velvet."

"Thank you." I rewarded him with a lipstick-preserving peck, and gently disengaged from his embrace. "I have to go get Nat. It's almost time."

"OK. Dinner after?"

"Um…sure, if you don't mind waiting while I wrap up the party."

"I don't mind." He nuzzled my neck, which tickled. I pulled away with a nervous giggle.

"Go find a seat," I said, squeezing his hands.

I couldn't believe I had actually giggled.

He went outside while I hustled to the kitchen to fetch the bouquets. Julio was moving tamales to a serving pan.

"Are you going to watch the ceremony?" I asked him, my arms full of flowers.

"Yeah, as soon as we have the buffet set up."

Upstairs, I handed Nat her bouquet of fiesta-colored roses: red, orange, and gold. "Time for a final beauty check. Do you want to use my mirror?"

She stood and took a deep breath. "You're my mirror. Anything out of place?"

I smiled. "You're perfect."

My watch said six minutes to one, so I ushered Nat and Claudia down to the Dahlia alcove, left my bouquet with them, and stepped outside, sidling over to where Manny and Louie were waiting behind a wisteria vine at the corner of the house. A light breeze stirred the mostly-golden leaves of the cottonwoods and pulled a few into the air to drift down atop the tent. Gina stood there, talking with Katie and Bob Hutchins and a man who looked vaguely familiar—probably Gina's current beau.

At a table inside the tent entrance, Iz stood supervising the guest book and a growing stack of presents. I stifled a small sigh, wishing more people knew the tradition of sending gifts to the couple at home rather than bringing them to the wedding, where the bride and groom would have no chance to deal with them. It was old-fashioned, I knew, but sometimes old fashions make sense.

As the mariachis began a slow march, Manny turned to Louie. "That's our cue, man." They bumped fists, then started for the tent.

I went in to fetch Nat and Claudia. We paused behind the wisteria until the mariachis struck up "Mexico Lindo y Querido," which Nat had chosen in preference to the customary march from *Lohengrin*. One last kiss for luck, and we walked out between the roses and into the tent. Claudia slipped into a seat while I continued down the aisle ahead of Nat.

Behind Manny, Louie, and the minister, rose bushes bloomed joyously against a taller row of lilacs. We stepped into place, the music ended, and the minister opened his book.

The service was generic, short and sweet. No elaborate phrases were needed; their delight in each other shone in their faces. It all went perfectly, and festive music accompanied us as we filed out to form the receiving line.

Loren Jackson and his sister Shelly were among the first. I liked him a lot, but not quite as much as he liked me. He was a counselor, and had helped most of my staff after Vi's death. He had honored the wedding with a nicely-tailored dark suit and a pastel green tie that matched his eyes. He lit up with a smile as we shook hands.

"You look wonderful, Ellen!"

"Thank you. So do both of you."

Shelly beamed beneath her pale blue picture hat. "That was a beautiful ceremony," she said. "Did you help write it?"

"No, no. They did it themselves."

My gaze traveled to the next guest, who was Tony. He looked a bit broody.

"Tony, have you met Loren Jackson?" I said.

"We've met," Loren said, turning toward him and smiling. "Good to see you again, Detective."

Tony hesitated, then shook the offered hand.

"And this is Loren's sister, Shelly," I added. "This is Tony Aragón."

"Hi," she said, a little wide-eyed. "You're a detective?"

"Yeah." Tony turned to me. "Can I talk to you?"

"After I'm free here, of course," I said. The line started moving again, and Loren gave Nat a hug.

"Is something wrong?" I said softly to Tony.

He shot another glance at Loren, then stepped closer, still holding my hand. "Why did you invite him?" he muttered.

"My *aunt* invited him to *her wedding*."

He didn't answer, and Gina, who was behind him in line, gave him a flashing smile. "No hogging the maid of honor, Tony."

Tony stepped back, and Gina promptly enfolded me in a Chanel-scented hug. Tony had no choice but to move on, taking the hand that Louie held out to him.

"Got to keep him in line, hon," Gina whispered in my ear. Aloud, she said, "You remember Rick?"

I shook hands with her date, a slightly lumberjackish-looking fellow with a dark hair and a nice smile. "Of course." Turning to Gina, I added, "You look splendid, as usual."

She took a slight bow, her calf-length dress of multicolored flowers swirling gently. "Thanks. I expect dancing."

"You shall have it," I promised. "I hope you're ready, Rick."

He grinned. "I've been training all week."

At last the guests had all been greeted, and the bridal couple followed them into the house to attack the buffet. I hung back to see that Rosa and Mick were moving chairs off the dance floor. Only a few shreds of cloud remained overhead. I shot a grateful glance at the sky, and headed for the house.

The tables on the *portal* were reserved for the wedding party and their families. Tony was at his seat beside mine, poking at his phone.

"What did you think of the wedding?" I asked, joining him.

He shrugged. "Nobody messed up their lines."

"Not your cuppa, eh?"

He looked out at the street. "I've been to too many weddings that ended badly."

I remembered a recent case he'd worked on: a gang fight that had broken out at a wedding and left two dead. I bit my lip.

Finding things to talk about with a cop was hard.

We seemed to do all right when we weren't talking. I thought of his hands on my back and felt myself blush.

"Are you hungry?" I asked.

"Not really," Tony said, frowning.

Behind me, a light voice said, a bit gushingly, "May we join you?"

Shelly Jackson was gazing at Tony with a plate of tamales in one hand and a champagne flute in the other. I seemed to have become invisible; she stared right past me.

"I'm sorry, these tables are for the wedding party," I said, standing. "But there are some others in the garden. May I help you find a shady one?"

"Oh. Uh, well…"

"We can manage, thanks," said Loren, shooting me a wry glance as he gently took his sister's elbow and guided her away.

I couldn't help it. I smiled. It was relief, and gratitude for his tact. Unfortunately, Tony saw it.

"Think I need a beer. They with Julio?" Without waiting for an answer, he stood and went into the house.

I sank into my chair, closed my eyes, and sighed. Part of me wanted to go after him. Part of me resented his assumptions; I shouldn't have to explain anything. I had told him that Loren was a friend. That should be enough.

"Tired, Ellen?" said Nat's voice. "Poor dear, we've been running you ragged."

I jumped up to help Nat settle herself at the table. "I'm fine."

"You should get some food," she said.

"I will." I hugged her shoulders and gave her a smooch on the cheek. "Can I get you anything? Champagne?"

"Oh, yes, please!" said Nat.

I took orders, then went in to fetch champagne for Nat and me, beer for Louie and Manny. The food line had gone down, so I delivered the drinks and went back to get myself a *tamal*, which was the proper name for what most Americans call a tamale. Julio had reprimanded me on that point during the menu planning.

Tamal is singular. Tamales is plural. Tamale is stupid.

Beside the *tamal* I put a token spoonful of rice, a dollop of guacamole and a handful of chips. What I really wanted was a huge chunk of the wedding cake. Bad sign.

Back at the table, Nat and Manny were snatching bites of food between conversations with well-wishers. When the mariachis started a waltz, Manny jumped up and reached for Nat's hand.

"This is our dance!"

They hurried to the dance floor, beaming like kids. Halfway through the music, Louie touched my arm. "Let's dance, OK?"

"Sure," I said, knowing that Manny had probably asked him to join in. It would signal the guests that they could dance, too.

Louie built custom adobe fireplaces, and it showed in his muscular frame. I was grateful to discover that he knew where to put his feet and how to guide me. Gina and her beau joined us, and by the time the song ended, the dance floor was filled.

"Thank you," I said to Louie. "You're a good dancer!"

He bowed, and escorted me off. I saw Tony watching from beside the lilacs, drinking a beer. The band was now playing a lively polka. I went over and looked at Tony expectantly.

"You looked good out there," he said. "You take ballroom dancing?"

"No, but my father taught me to waltz."

He nodded and took a swig of beer. Not catching a clue, today.

"Are you going to ask me to dance?" I said.

He tilted his head, glancing at the mariachis. "To this?"

"We don't have to actually polka," I said, gesturing to the floor, where about half the dancers were doing the old high-school step-right, step-left kind of dancing.

"Good, 'cause I wouldn't know a polka from a hiphop."

"Do you dislike dancing?"

He took a long time to answer, gazing at the dancers, his jaw working. Finally he looked at me. "It's OK."

I was ready to give up and return to my uneaten *tamal*, but Tony tipped up his bottle, drained it, and left it under a bush, then offered me his hand and actually smiled. We stepped onto the floor just as the polka concluded. The band struck up a slow dance, and Tony's smile turned to a grin as he slid his arm around my waist.

"This is more like it," he said, pulling me close.

Yes, it was. A whiff of beer combined with Tony's familiar smell to make me wish there weren't so many people watching. I sighed as the tension drained out of me, and put my free arm around his neck as we rocked back and forth.

"Were the mariachis your idea?" he asked.

I shook my head. "Manny's. He loves them. Nat does, too."

"Because…" He shook his head, and laughed softly as he gazed at the dancers.

"It's their wedding."

He looked at me, flashed a grin, then spun me under his arm. Caught off guard, I laughed.

"You *can* dance!"

"A little."

"I bet you broke hearts in high school."

"Nah. I was too moody. Usually I ended up with the broken heart."

I was silent, not thinking it prudent to pursue that line of conversation. We swayed gently and I closed my eyes.

This was good—this moment. If we could only have more moments like this.

The song ended far too soon. Somewhere in there I rested my head on Tony's shoulder; I had no idea when. As we stepped apart, he brushed his lips against my cheek.

"Can we go somewhere?" he whispered in my ear as we left the floor arm in arm.

"I have to stay until the party's over," I said.

"What if we just went upstairs for half an hour?"

I shot him a Look.

"OK, OK. Just a thought."

I steered us toward our table, where Manny and Nat had retired after three dances. "I think I need some more champagne."

"I'll get it," Tony offered. He saw me to my seat, picked up my empty flute, and disappeared into the house.

"You two looked cozy out there," Manny said to me, grinning. "Gonna give me a new nephew?"

Nat gave him an admonishing tap on the arm. I leaned forward to answer Manny.

"You're going to have to settle for just a niece for now."

He laughed, and raised his beer in salute. Tony returned with my champagne and a fresh plate with one *tamal*, red sauce, rice, and guacamole—exactly what I'd had before. He swapped this out for my cold plate and went off again to get food for himself.

He might not be Mr. Congenial, but he was certainly observant. That was a cop skill. His using it to be nice to me gave me hope.

CAKE, AND MORE CHAMPAGNE FOLLOWED THE MEAL. I was starting to feel a little tipsy by the time a sleek, black limousine turned the corner and glided up to the front gate, where it double-parked and turned on its hazard lights. Manny stood and, with a flourishing bow, held out his hand to Nat.

"Your chariot awaits, fair lady."

Nat put down her fork. "Manny! I thought you were going to drive us!"

He grinned. "I wanted to have too much alcohol for that. Better toss your bouquet, sugar. It's time to go!"

I hopped up, swallowing my last bite of cake, and hurried to gather the single females. A sweep of the garden netted Kris, Shelly, Gina, two of Manny's nieces, and a couple of others. I nudged Rosa and Iz into the flock for good measure.

Nat stood before the front door, framed by wisteria vines and watched by her adoring husband. She looked over the waiting maidens, and I saw her take note of my position before she turned her back to us. I almost stepped back, but there was no need. The bouquet sailed skyward and descended directly into Gina's arms.

Applause and cheers followed. Gina showed off her prize, grinning. I looked at her date, who wore a deer-in-the-headlights expression.

Nat and Manny headed down the path toward the limo. I caught up with them at the gate.

Nat turned to me, clasping my hand. "You'll take care of—"

"Everything." I hugged her. "Have a fabulous time!"

Manny claimed a kiss from me, then hustled Nat into the limo. It glided away to the cheers and waving of the guests.

Whew.

Tony was still at the table. I started toward him, but was intercepted by Loren and Shelly, both carrying plates of cake.

"Have you seen the Art Exhibition?" Shelly asked.

"We were wondering if it's worth a visit," Loren added.

"I haven't been," I said. "I'm interested in going, though. There's an artist whose work I'd like to see."

Shelly's face lit with eagerness. "Come with us! We're going tomorrow."

"Um, that sounds like fun," I said, "but—"

"We can all have lunch," she said.

All? I glanced toward Tony, who glowered from the table.

"I'll have to check. Can I let you know tomorrow?"

"Don't worry about saying no," Loren said quietly, with a glance at his sister. "If it's too much, after today, we'll understand."

"Thanks."

I disengaged politely and rejoined Tony. His mood had dropped back to sullen.

"He just can't keep away from you," he said.

"More like she can't keep away from you. She wants us to go to the Art Exhibition with them tomorrow."

"An art show?" He looked like he'd rather visit a funeral.

"Yes. I was thinking of going anyway, and we're closed tomorrow, so…"

"I can't. Promised to help my grandmother. Her dishwasher's leaking."

"Oh. That's too bad."

"What about Monday?" he offered. "I could go on my lunch hour."

"I think tomorrow's the last day."

His frown deepened. "You're going to go anyway."

"I'm interested in the show."

He drew breath as if to speak, then gave his head a small shake instead. He stared at my bouquet, still lying on the table. I saw a swallow move his throat.

"Tony, there really is no reason for you to feel threatened—"

"I don't feel threatened."

Right.

"Think I'll get some more cake."

I wasn't really hungry. I just wanted to be alone for a minute. I felt like Tony and I were going in circles.

With the departure of the happy couple, the guests began to trickle away. A few came in for a last crack at the buffet. I stepped across the hall and into Violet, where Julio's candle still flickered on the mantel. Here, in private, I allowed myself a sigh.

Looking up at Vi's smiling face, I wondered if things were any better where she was. Did this kind of misunderstanding happen in the afterlife?

Not that it mattered. I was here, not there, and if a difference of opinion between me and Tony was making me unhappy, the only real solution was to face it.

Deep breath. Onward.

Back outside, I found our table deserted. Looking for Tony, I kept getting waylaid by farewells: Gina and Rick, Claudia Pearson, Thomas Ingraham, the Hutchinses, Kris. Louie was talking with the minister, who looked about to depart. Mick had started collecting plates from empty tables, while Rosa carefully gathered champagne flutes onto a tray. I really ought to help; there was so much to do.

Maybe Tony had left.

I picked up the guest book and a few of the smaller gifts and took them inside, heading for the dining parlor. I met Tony coming out of it, looking extremely annoyed.

"There you are," we both said.

"I have to go," he added, frowning. "Got a call. I'm sorry."

"Let me put these down." I stepped past him to set my burdens on the dining table.

"I should be able to deal with it fast," he said. "Then I'll come back and pick you up for dinner. OK?"

"Sure. Take your time, I have plenty to do."

I made an all-encompassing gesture. Tony caught one of my hands and kissed it. "I'll be back soon, I promise."

Heart suddenly racing, I swallowed. "I'll be here."

Iz came in with an armload of gifts. Tony dropped my hand and backed away. "I'll call you."

I nodded as I watched him go, then realized my cell phone was upstairs in my suite. I'd get it in a minute, but first there were the gifts to be secured.

My staff, no doubt eager to finish and be free for Saturday night, were a whirlwind of efficiency. Julio had already put away leftover food from the buffet and was now disassembling what remained of the cake. He pointed to a box about ten inches square.

"That's the top layer. It goes in the freezer, right?"

"Right." I found a marker and labeled it, peeked into the box and saw that Julio had already wrapped the cake in plastic and foil. I would give it to Nat and Manny when they got home from Hawaii, to keep in their own freezer until their first anniversary. I stashed it in the industrial freezer, then helped Julio box up the rest of the cake. I saved a generous piece for each of my staff, labeled the boxes with their names, and pushed one into Julio's hands.

"You're done. I'll finish. Have a good weekend."

He grinned. "I'll be in early on Monday to make the sugar skulls for next Sunday. They have to dry overnight after they're molded," he added, "so if you don't mind having them in the kitchen…."

"No, that's fine. They won't be in my way."

Julio stripped off his chef's jacket and tossed it in the laundry hamper. This reminded me that it was time for me to change out of my velvet dress and into working clothes. I ran upstairs and hopped into jeans and a tee-shirt, thinking about the sugar skulls.

Julio had asked to hold a decorating party in the kitchen the Sunday before Halloween, and I'd agreed. Sugar skulls were a tradition for *el Dia de los Muertos*. This would give me a chance to see firsthand what it was all about.

I stuffed my phone in my pocket, then returned to the kitchen, peering out the south window at the garden. The wedding guests were all gone and the rental company's truck was at the curb.

"We vacuumed and swept," Rosa said as she and Iz came in. "Should we fold up the chairs from the tent?"

"No, the rental people will do that. Go on home," I told them, handing each a box of cake. "We're almost done. Have a great evening, and thank you."

"I wanted to ask you," Rosa said, hanging back. "Would you mind if I brought something to add to your *ofrenda?*"

"My *ofrenda?*"

"In Violet. For Vi."

"Oh." I hadn't intended to create an altar, but I could see how it might look like that with Julio's candle and my little vase of pansies on the mantel. "Of course you may add something if you wish."

She smiled. "Thanks. Goodnight, Ellen."

Mick and I restored the parlor to its normal state. The floral arrangements from the wedding now adorned the alcoves. They'd be good for a few days. Outside, the rental people were disassembling the dance floor. The lawn beneath was rather flattened, but looked like it would recover.

Long shadows crept across the yard. To the west, above the rooftops, clouds glowed golden. I sent Mick home with his box of cake, started a load of laundry, and checked the time. Quarter to six.

Maybe Tony had forgotten. Even if he hadn't, I could use a shower. As I trudged upstairs, mariachi music running through my head, my phone rang and displayed Tony's number.

"Sorry, this is taking longer than I thought," he said. "Do you mind a late dinner? I can get away by eight or so."

"I'm kind of wiped, actually. What about tomorrow night?"

There was a beat, during which I imagined him frowning, but his voice was resigned rather than angry. "Family night at my mom's. She'd probably be glad to have you over, but I should talk to her more in advance."

"Right. Another week." Good that he was thinking that way.

"Monday?" he said.

"OK."

"OK."

A silence followed. I was too tired to come up with pleasantries.

"Wish I could see you tonight," he said.

"Monday's not that far away. I'll be better company after I get some rest anyway."

"OK. I'll come at 5:30."

"Sounds good."

"See you then."

"Yes. Goodnight."

Nothing.

Well, he had almost said goodbye. That was progress.

At the top of the stairs I found a wash of orange light glowing all through the upper floor's central hallway, spilling in through the window to the west. Nat and Claudia's tea things from that morning sat on the low table. I took them downstairs. I'd wash them up in the morning, but I was done, done, done for now.

My maid-of-honor bouquet stood on the kitchen break table, reposing in a small vase. Rosa or Iz must have brought it in. I took it upstairs to my suite, where I trimmed the stems, then arranged the flowers in the vase. As I was doing this, I accidentally snapped the stem of an orange rose.

"Drat."

I set the rose aside and put the vase on my table. It was time for supper, but I was more tired than hungry. I'd been on my feet most of the day.

And I was still being haunted by the mariachis, a fragment of a song that I didn't know completely. I put on Chopin's Nocturnes to banish them, then started hot water running in the bathtub. A bottle of Malbec yielded its cork with a satisfying pop, and I poured myself a generous glass. The first sip tasted of pepper and berries.

On impulse I picked it up the broken rose and pulled off the petals, tossing them into the bath water. Then I lit three candles, stripped off my work clothes, and fetched my wine.

Sinking into the hot water, I let out a long sigh. Rose petals drifted around me, gently bumping against my skin. I took another swallow of wine and began to relax.

Really, the wedding had been a success. No disasters. No murders; no fights, even. Nat and Manny were blissfully happy.

I pushed it all out of my mind and focused on enjoying my bath. Not until the water had gone tepid and my wineglass was empty did I climb out and wrap myself in my fluffy bathrobe.

Leftovers for supper, another glass of wine, then wedding cake for dessert. I retired to bed, thinking of Nat and Manny. They were spending the night in Los Angeles, but soon they would be on a beach in Hawaii, and that's how I pictured them—walking hand in hand, barefoot, through the sand—as I drifted to sleep.

A clap of thunder woke me and I sat up, disoriented, half-dreaming about being pursued through a thunderstorm by mariachis. The battering of rain on the steel roof overhead proved the storm was real. A glance at my clock told me it was after nine, so I dragged myself up and put on a kettle for tea.

Stormy weather, good for baking or sitting by the fire with a book. Would it be odd to build a fire downstairs so I could enjoy the warmth of the chimney upstairs in my suite?

As I pondered this question, my phone rang. I grabbed it, feeling slightly let down when I saw that the caller was Loren.

"Good morning," I said.

"Morning, Ellen. Shelly and I are going to the art show at eleven. Would you like to join us, and maybe have some lunch afterward?" After the slightest of hesitations, he added, "Detective Aragón is welcome, of course."

"He's busy today."

"Oh."

A pause; I pictured Loren trying compose a sentence that politely expressed a degree of disappointment that he didn't actually feel. I couldn't help a silent chuckle.

"I'd be happy to join you, though," I said.

"Great! We can pick you up."

"Why don't we meet there? It's just around the corner from me."

"But it's raining."

"I have an umbrella."

"OK. Don't twist an ankle dancing in the gutters."

I laughed. "I won't. See you at eleven."

The call lightened my mood, and I hummed as I went downstairs to wash up the dishes from Nat and Claudia's tea. Halfway through drying them I realized what I was humming: a mariachi tune.

"Aargh!"

I turned on the stereo in the butler's pantry, filling the house with Beethoven. For breakfast, I treated myself to a couple of Julio's *empanadas*, which I hadn't had a chance to try the day before. They were delicious: flaky crust and tangy fillings, apple with just a touch of cinnamon in one, and cherry in the other.

By then, it was time to leave. I changed into jeans and a nice sweater, donned my wool coat and a hat, and stepped out the front door.

The thunder had stopped, and the rain was now little more than a drizzle. I didn't bother with the umbrella. The storm had knocked a lot of leaves down, turning the sidewalk into a pretty fall mosaic. Someone had a fire going, and the aroma of piñon smoke teased me as I walked north to the corner and crossed the street.

The Santa Fe Community Convention Center was hopping. Much expanded from Sweeney Center, the humble community auditorium it had been during my childhood, it was now a true convention center, tastefully designed in pueblo revival style. A banner reading "SANTA FE AUTUMN ART EXHIBITION" graced the front entrance. I went in and paid my admission.

"There she is!"

I turned and saw Loren and Shelly approaching, bundled in coats and scarves over jeans. Loren smiled. "How was the walk?"

I glanced toward the street with a bemused look. I'd walked perhaps fifty paces to get here; if it weren't for the height of the building next to my house, I could have thrown a rock into my yard from the sidewalk outside the convention center.

"Very refreshing," I said, smiling.

"You were smart. It took us five minutes to find a parking place."

I laughed. "Shall we go in?"

The main hall was like any big convention space, presently filled with booths of artwork. The door-keeper, an older woman with silver hair up in a bun and a festive, colored shawl, handed each of us a badge-holder on a lanyard, containing a diagram of the ballroom laid out with booths. "Here's your guide."

"Oh, that's clever," I said, looking at the map of numbered booths. "So I don't lose it."

"Right. The index is in your program." She gave each of us a folded page. We stepped aside to look them over.

The exhibition was a juried show. The index listed Gabriel Rhodes in a booth at the back of the hall. I started off in that direction.

"Don't you want to see the ones in front?" Shelly asked.

"I do, but I'm looking for a particular artist. I'd like to see his work first, then I'll go through the whole hall."

"We can keep you company," Loren offered.

"Up to you."

They followed, apparently by silent consent. The booths we passed contained everything from oil paintings to photography to textiles and pottery. Artists looked out eagerly, ready to sell.

The booth designated as Gabriel's was unattended, though a security guard nearby was keeping an eye on the entire row. I stood looking at the paintings, which impressed me more than I expected. They were stark and rich at the same time. Color was used sparingly, but what color was there was striking.

One painting, mostly white, was of a beautiful young woman looking forlornly downward while a dark, faceless figure in black robes with black feathered wings loomed behind her. The model for the woman must have been Gwyneth; the nose and hair were hers, and the ethereal, filmy garment was just the sort of thing she'd probably wear. But the look of hopelessness in her eyes was unfamiliar. I assumed that was the artist's interpretation. I glanced at the title: "Resignation."

I suspected Gwyneth had also modeled for an odalisque all in tones of gray—although her face was turned away in that piece—and for a very dark painting titled "Harpy" that was the most sensually attractive harpy I'd ever seen. Remembering Kris's assertion that Gabriel had slept with all of the women at Friday's meeting—or had she meant the women and the men both?—I felt uncomfortably informed about his relationship with Gwyneth.

What had happened to make Gwyneth transfer her affections to Roberto? Had Gabriel simply moved on?

Not that any of it was my business. I gave myself a shake and returned to admiring the artwork.

There were a couple of abstract pieces in Gabriel's display, and two small sculptures. His paintings were far more moving. My attention was caught by one titled "The Seventh Chamber." It was dark, with two asymmetrical patches of mottled red at the sides. At first I thought they were merely abstract, but then I realized they were windows: red windows, lit from behind by fires on pedestals.

That tickled my memory and I looked at the central figure of the painting, a man dressed as a Renaissance nobleman, illuminated by the red light from the windows. He stood in an attitude of despair, mouth agape beneath an elaborate, silver-trimmed mask, one hand drooping with a dagger about to slip from its grasp. Almost invisible against the dark background, a shadowy form robed in black stood opposing him. A tall, standing clock stood in the figure's shadow, its hands just discernible, pointing to twelve.

It was the climax of Poe's "Masque of the Red Death."

So Gabriel's fascination with the story was not just about the Halloween party. The painting was surely Prince Prospero realizing he was about to die in the moment before the Red Death took him.

I moved on, looking for comfort in some other picture. I didn't really find it. Gabriel's work was not about comfort.

On the last panel was a single painting of a nude—Gwyneth again, I was pretty sure, but her face was obscured by her hair—crouched amid the shattered remains of something that had been made of red glass. There was no blood, but the implication that blood would flow the moment she tried to move out of the disaster zone was strong. Her bare feet would surely be cut by some tiny unseen shard, or her hands if she used them to sweep an escape path. If she tried to jump clear of the glass, she might land on a piece with painful results. The painting was titled "Calculation."

"Interesting work," said Loren beside me. "Is the artist a friend of yours?"

"A friend of a friend. I just met him a couple of days ago."

"Ah."

Shelly joined us, gazing at "Calculation" with troubled eyes. "Kind of disturbing," she said.

I nodded. "Yes."

"It's meant to be," said a smooth voice behind us.

I turned and saw Gabriel smiling with satisfaction, dressed in cream silk and linen, his ankh just peeking out of his neckline. Kris was beside him, in a clinging black chenille sweater over spiderweb tights, more overtly Goth than anything she wore to work.

"Glad you could make it," Gabriel said to me.

"Me, too, but I just got here, so I haven't seen much yet. I came looking for you first."

"Merci du compliment."

"Your work is striking. I see why you were accepted into the White Iris. Allow me to congratulate you again."

He gave me a small, gracious bow. "Thank you."

I introduced the Jacksons, and Gabriel made Shelly giggle by bowing gallantly over her hand. As we stood chatting, Dale Whittier and a familiar-looking woman approached. For a second my mind dressed her as Lolita.

Right! One of Kris's friends. Martha, or Margaret? She'd been at the Halloween planning party.

"Hi, Dale," I said, then smiled at the woman. "Hello, again."

"Hi," she returned absently, looking at Gabriel.

He turned at the sound of her voice. "Margo! Thank you for coming."

Her face transformed with pleasure. "I wanted to see your latest stuff."

Gabriel welcomed her into the booth with a sweep of his arm. Margo stepped up to "Calculation."

"I haven't seen this one," she said.

"It's new."

Margo nodded, slowly smiling. Dale joined her.

"Have you any favorite artists in the show to recommend?" I asked Gabriel.

"Well, you must see Roberto's work, of course. He's two rows down." he gestured, and as far as I could tell his smile was sincere.

"Thanks. Are there others?"

"Let me mark them on your map."

"Perfect! Thank you."

I took off my lanyard and handed it to him. He slipped the map out, produced a pen, and began circling numbers. Loren had turned to watch, and I gestured to him.

"Kris, you remember Loren," I said.

"Yes, of course. And Shelly. We were all chatting at the wedding yesterday."

Shelly was staring at Gabriel, eyes wide. I wondered, uncharitably I admit, whether she was one of those women who specialized in falling for other women's partners. In my private thoughts I figured she'd be better off mooning after Tony than after Gabriel. Not that I wished her to do either.

Gabriel seemed to become aware of her regard, and an interesting shift occurred. He turned to face her, and his smile expanded. A new radiance rose around him.

"Are you fond of art, Shelly?" he asked.

"Kind of," she said lamely, taking a step back.

"Let me guess. Peaceful landscapes are more to your liking," he said, with a soft laugh.

Magnetism. That's what it was. No wonder he'd slept with whole roomfuls of women.

"These aren't easy to look at," she said, gesturing to his paintings.

"That's true," he said. "I didn't intend them to be easy."

"Peaceful landscapes sound nice," I said. "Think I'll see if there are any here."

"Oh, there are," Gabriel said, his eyes narrowing in amusement. "Here are my suggestions, but you probably won't find peaceful landscapes at any of them."

"Thank you." I nodded as he handed back my lanyard. "Best of luck with the show."

"Mark them for me, too!" Margo said, holding out her own lanyard to Gabriel.

"Good idea," Dale said, taking his off his neck.

I turned toward the next booth, and found myself facing Cherie. In a black velour dress with a plunging, lace-bordered neckline over net stockings and knee-high laced boots, eyes heavily lined with kohl, she looked more ready for a nightclub than an art show. Her sly smile acknowledged my reaction. She gave me a nod, then glided past me.

"Gabriel," she called. "I made it! Be proud of me."

Gabriel handed Margo's badge back to her and glanced at Cherie as he slid Dale's map from his badge. "Astonished, but proud."

"Tsk. What are you doing? Signing autographs?"

"Giving advice about what to see in the show."

"Ah!" She produced her own badge and held it out to him. "*Por favor.*"

Their fingers met on the badge holder, and a tiny tug-of-war ensued. Cherie released it with a grin, and Gabriel grinned back.

I shot a swift glance at Kris. She was watching, standing back.

Eyes cold, not smiling.

I stepped toward her, instinct prompting me to shield her, though there was no practical way that I could. She looked at me, then turned toward "Calculation." I stepped up beside her.

"Don't," she whispered. "I don't own him."

I pressed my lips together, swallowing my sympathy. Kris calmly fielded a question from an older gentleman in a tweed coat, providing him with one of Gabriel's business cards from a tiny ebony table.

My interest in antique furniture made me look closer at the exquisite little piece, no more than two feet by eight inches. It bore a filigreed rack holding Gabriel's cards, and a scattering of other business cards, presumably left by visitors. One of them drew my attention.

The card was plain white stock. It bore no type, only a hand-drawn image of a skull and crossbones.

I picked it up, looking at the back side. Nothing. The edge felt rough, as though it had been hand-cut. When the older gentleman left, I caught Kris's attention.

"Who left this?"

She took the card, looked at the blank back, and shrugged. "I don't know. Some baby bat, maybe."

She dropped it back on the pile, dismissing it.

"What's a baby bat?"

"A baby Goth. They do silly things at first, until they learn the culture."

I touched the card with a fingernail, drawing it away from the others. "Are pirates part of Goth culture?"

"Not really."

The skull and crossbones had other meanings. One that leapt to mind was a warning against poison.

"Kris—"

Her attention was back on Gabriel. His head was bowed over Cherie's map, and Cherie leaned in to see what he was writing. Just for a moment, I saw a crease on Kris's brow.

"Think I'll check out the next aisle," I said. "Want to come with?"

Kris shook her head and turned to straighten the cards in the rack, which were already straight. There was nothing more I could do.

Shelly and Loren followed me to the neighboring booth. We admired some photographs of wildflowers—lovely and quite safe—and a display of beautiful pottery with sumptuous glazes that shaded from sand to green. Farther down the aisle I spotted Gwyneth, talking to two men in what had to be Roberto's booth. She wore a floor-length beaded dress of creamy gauze, rather formal for the setting, but it set off her slender figure charmingly.

As I approached, Roberto slid from a tall stool and gave me a nod. "Nice to see you, Ellen. Thank you for coming."

He wore a dark green vest over a black shirt and jeans, with a stunning bolo tie: a single pale green turquoise stone, wedge-shaped and over two inches long, in a classic, silver shadowbox setting. His hair was caught tightly back from his face in a clubbed braid adorned with a sandcast silver lizard.

"I'm glad to have a chance to see your work," I said.

Where Gabriel's paintings were stark, Roberto's came close to being florid. Gwyneth was a frequent model here, too, but in Roberto's work she was never threatened; she was revered. The settings were lush and tended to woodland themes. Gwyneth was Titania, Galadriel, and Morgan le Fay. Against the dark greens and browns of the backgrounds, she glowed.

"These are splendid," I told Roberto, and meant it. His skill was excellent, and if his work was intellectually less demanding than Gabriel's, well, that was something of a relief.

Shelly seemed to think so. She stared raptly at Titania, and her brother watched with an amused expression. I sidled over to Loren.

He nodded, glancing at Roberto. "I gather the artists know each other?"

"Yes." I stopped myself from saying they were friends. Upon reflection, I wasn't sure it was true.

Some of the smaller paintings in Roberto's booth were darker. None of these featured Gwyneth. Instead they depicted soldiers with swords—either medievalish or Romanesque—and bits of hacked-up bodies. Nothing *too* gruesome, but more what I would have expected from an artist who identified himself as a Goth.

But even these pieces were less challenging than Gabriel's.

Roberto was talented, and his work was beautifully executed, but none of it was breathtaking.

The two men Gwyneth had been talking to departed, and she came over to me, smiling, holding out both hands as if I was an old friend. "You made it!"

"Yes. Gwyneth, I'd like you to meet Loren Jackson. Loren, this is Gwyneth Bancroft."

"And the fair Titania, yes?" said Loren gallantly.

Gwyneth giggled, plainly pleased. Roberto joined us, and I performed more introductions. Shelly gushed a bit at both Roberto and Gwyneth. They launched into a discussion of Gwyneth's costumes in the paintings. After a few minutes my interest waned, but the subject was by no means exhausted, so I drifted away toward the next booth, which was filled with beautiful woven shawls and scarves in a luscious rainbow of colors.

I ran my hand along a rack of shawls, reveling in the caress of chenille. From the dozens I found two that sang to me more than the rest: a shawl in shades of blue and green that reminded me of the sea, and a violet-lavender-fuchsia scarf. With one in each hand, I stood rapt, fantasizing just for a moment that I could actually afford to buy one.

"The purple one is more your colors, right?"

Loren stood on the other side of the rack, grinning at me. I lifted my chin.

"I love the colors on both. If the shawl were the colors of the scarf, I'd be in serious trouble."

Loren began to look through the rack. "Maybe we can find one like that."

"Oh, I hope not."

Reluctantly, I hung the two pieces where I'd found them and moved on to the next booth. Whimsical statues of animals, very colorful. Fun, but nothing I'd want in my home.

Loren tagged along, and with a glance back toward Roberto's booth, said, "So who was she with first?"

I considered pretending I had no idea what he meant. It would have been the polite thing to do, but since I was puzzled about Gwyneth and the two artists, I answered. "Gabriel, I think. I don't know why she switched."

"Roberto is safer," Loren said.

"Safer?"

"He's got her on a pedestal. He'd never hurt her."

"Gabriel wouldn't either. That is…" I picked up a *millefiori* giraffe and rubbed a thumb along its lacquered surface. "I don't *think* he'd hurt her."

Truth was, I didn't know. They were Goths, and I'd heard some scary things about Goths. They liked darkness, were obsessed with death. While I'd never seen or heard of Kris doing anything destructive, it was possible that some of her friends were into dangerous pursuits.

Not wanting to think about that, I decided to put more physical distance between myself and Kris's friends. My map was my guide as I left Loren patiently waiting for his sister. The booths that Gabriel had recommended all contained artwork at least as disturbing as his —more so, in a couple of cases. Giving up on his recommendations, I began going up and down the rows, glancing into each booth and stopping at the ones that caught my interest.

I soon found myself back in the land of Titania. Roberto was talking to a woman with ash blond hair and big, round sunglasses, bundled in sheepskin and alpaca as though it was the middle of winter. For a second she reminded me of Willow Lane, except that I didn't think Willow would ever wear shaggy boots.

Gwyneth hovered near them, vibrating like a moth, her attention glued to the furry woman. Roberto glanced at me, but didn't acknowledge me. Something was up.

To give them space, I stepped away toward the paintings that featured Titania. Now that I had leisure to examine them closely, I saw more details. Titania stood in the middle of a glade surrounded by her fairy court, a handful of white blossoms in her hands. She was bending to smell them, her eyelids gracefully drooping. Both she and the flowers glimmered, the brightest things in the scene.

Four smaller, separate paintings surrounded Titania, all thematically related. The next largest, about a quarter of the size of the main painting, was titled "Oberon." It was a self-portrait: very shadowed, very dark, but unmistakably Roberto, crowned in leaves, gazing directly at Titania across the gap in canvas.

Below this were a small pair of portraits, both fairies:

"Mustardseed," impish in gold and green, took me a moment to pin as Margo; "Cobweb" seemed to be a young man in a silver-gray tunic with wispy wings, but a closer look revealed it as Cherie. To the right of the main painting was "Puck," a very well-done portrait in earth-tones of Dale Whittier, looking remarkably at home in the shape of a satyr.

I paused to consider that for a moment. Puck was Oberon's servant. Did this mean that Dale was a follower of Roberto's?

More likely Dale happened to match what Roberto had in mind for the painting. They were friends; all of the models were part of Roberto's circle. Put it out of mind, I told myself, which would be easier said than done. Now I had a potential employee whose image in the guise of a satyr was burned into my brain.

Below "Puck," the smallest canvas was titled "Nick Bottom," a horizontal image of the ill-fated mortal in his ass's-head guise, asleep on the forest floor. He held one of Titania's glowing flowers—now purple with white edges, but still glimmering—clasped to his chest. Something about the long lines of his limbs rang a bell for me. I crouched to look closer, and noticed a honey-colored shock of hair forming Bottom's "mane."

With a small gasp, I straightened up. It was meant to be Gabriel, I was certain.

I was equally certain that Gabriel would not have posed for such a painting.

6

STEPPING BACK, I gazed at the whole group of *Midsummer Night's Dream* paintings, a little dismayed. What was going on with these people?

I glanced at the title cards, looking for dates. The paintings had all been done in the current year.

Activity drew my attention back to Roberto in time to see him shake the furry woman's hand. Gwyneth said something to her with a glittering smile. The woman returned a slight nod and departed. Undimmed, Gwyneth turned to Roberto, who was holding a business card.

I went over to join them. "Was that someone important?"

"Cecilia Brough," Roberto said.

"She owns a gallery!" added Gwyneth, beaming with delight.

"And I gather she's interested in your work?" I said to Roberto. "Congratulations!"

"Thanks. Nothing's settled, but she wants to come to my studio."

"That sounds pretty serious," I said. "What gallery is it?"

"Zafarano."

"I haven't heard of it. Is it on Canyon Road?"

Roberto's jaw tightened. "No. Galisteo Street."

"It's a very important gallery," Gwyneth said, watching Roberto with a tiny frown.

"Yes, near the Plaza," I nodded. "Very prestigious."

Though not, we all knew, as prestigious as Canyon Road.

"Oh, there you are!" Shelly's voice rang out from nearby.

I turned to see her hastening toward us. Loren followed with a lumpy package in his arms.

"What did you get?" I asked.

"A frog," Shelly said. "He's so cute! Let me show you."

She pulled back the paper and bubble wrap to expose the multicolored head of a frog that had come from the booth I'd seen earlier. I made admiring noises, then added, "Would you mind if we headed to lunch? I'm getting peckish."

Loren shot me a grateful look. Shelly looked up from re-wrapping the frog.

"Can we get back in after? I haven't seen everything yet."

I assured her that we could, and after saying goodbye to Roberto and Gwyneth, we headed off to deposit the frog in Loren's car before walking to lunch. There were many options; French, Italian, Indian, a zillion sandwich places and New Mexican cafés. We settled on Indian.

The sun was out, and the streets were less sloppy, though still wet. A bank of dark clouds hovered atop the *Sangre de Cristos*, and I silently resolved to be home by three-thirty. It wasn't monsoon season, when one could almost set one's watch by the rain that arrived right at tea-time, but the look of the sky made me cautious.

Soon we were sipping hot chai and enjoying the exotic smells of our upcoming lunch. I fell into musing about Roberto's gallery opportunity. He should have been thrilled, but there'd been an undercurrent of frustration in his manner. Disappointment that it wasn't Canyon Road, no doubt.

Gabriel was showing on Canyon Road. Roberto had cast Gabriel as Nick Bottom, the clownish human who suffers abuse at the hands of Shakespeare's fairies. Nick Bottom, whom Puck gave the head of an ass, and whom Titania loved, but only under the influence of a love potion.

And Titania was Gwyneth.

"Ellen?"

I looked up into Loren's kind eyes. "Sorry. Wool-gathering."

"That's OK. I just wondered if you had visited those booths that Gabriel recommended."

"A few. They're not my style."

He nodded. "Challenging."

"You said it."

"And he's close to Kris, I gather."

"At the moment, apparently."

"He's dating her?" Shelly said, and I had to stifle a smile. Her disappointment was not hard to deduce.

Note to self: do not wear heart on sleeve.

Loren picked up his chai and sipped. I found myself watching the fine lines of his face, wondering what he was thinking. Had he drawn the same conclusions I had? He had less to go on, but Roberto's *Midsummer Night's Dream* paintings were not exactly subtle.

He noticed me watching him and looked up with a smile. "So, I heard about the ghost tours. How are they doing?"

"Gangbusters," I said.

"Should I take one?"

"I don't know. How do you feel about ghosts?"

"Skeptical, I admit, but I'm willing to be convinced. Can the tour guide do that?"

"Willow? I wouldn't be surprised. She takes it very seriously."

"Does she do seances?" Shelly asked, brightening a little.

"Not that I know of," I said.

We talked about Willow and the tearoom for the rest of the meal. After lunch, I decided to walk around town a bit while Loren escorted Shelly back to the art show. I had seen enough, I realized, and I still needed to decompress after the wedding.

The sky was a patchwork of turquoise and white. No rain, but the smell of it was there, enticing with its promise of more moisture for a thirsty land. I walked toward the Plaza, then turned east, strolling up Palace Avenue toward the St. Francis Cathedral. (Basilica, rather. It's still the cathedral to me.)

The long *portal* along the front of the historic adobe buildings hid my view of potential rain. These were some of Santa Fe's earliest houses, a couple of centuries older than my mere Victorian. They were all connected—easier to defend that way—and many of them were organized hacienda-style around a central *plazuela*.

I glanced through the *zaguan* passage that led to the Shed, a favorite restaurant. It was closed on Sundays or I'd have suggested it for lunch. The small *plazuela* was empty and quiet, a state that was rarely to be found when the Shed was open for business. Moisture glistened on the leaves of the trumpet vines, and a few valiant petunias still bloomed in the planters.

Moving along, I saw a glint of light farther down the *portal* and wondered what it was. More leftover wet from the rain? But it was both dry and dark beneath the roof of the covered walkway.

The light had gone as quickly as I had seen it. I continued to where I thought it had appeared, and looked around for something shiny. Nothing obvious that could have caused it.

To the left, a narrower *zaguan* opened onto Hidalgo Plaza. I looked through, and followed an urge to step in.

Hidalgo Plaza was much larger than the little courtyard that housed the Shed and a handful of other businesses—about fifty feet square. The Hidalgos had been among the earliest Spanish settlers in Santa Fe, and the family had remained influential. A wisp of sadness brushed through me as I thought of Maria Hidalgo, with whom I was certain Captain Dusenberry had been in love. I needed to get back to my research about them. Nat's wedding had taken up all my spare time lately, but I was still determined to figure out who had murdered the captain when he had lived in my house.

I gazed around the plaza, trying to picture how it had looked when Maria had lived there. A second story had been added, almost certainly in the twentieth century. In which side of the compound had Maria's bedroom been, I wondered?

The *plazuela* was probably dirt, then, or perhaps a corner had been reserved for a kitchen garden while the rest was given over to stables and storage. Now a very expensive restaurant that served nouveau Southwestern cuisine had spread patio tables over a third of the space, and the rest was mostly garden, with tall trees, flowering shrubs, flagstone paths winding between beds of flowers and herbs, and even a little pergola draped in wisteria. I drew a deep breath scented with rain and green and let it out in a contented sigh.

From the corner of my eye another glimpse of light snagged my attention. It was gone by the time I turned my head to look. The way it appeared and disappeared was familiar.

Frowning, I walked slowly to the center of the garden, again looking for anything metal or glass that could have produced such a light. There were no fireflies in New Mexico, except in very rare places up in the mountains, and in any case the light didn't look like a firefly. It looked like sunlight, reflected from...what?

I *had* seen it before, I knew. But not here. The memory teased at the edge of my awareness, just out of reach.

I stood at the crossing of two paths and turned in a slow circle, surrounded by rosebushes and peonies, with a riot of thyme, mustard, and sage at their feet. The nearest shiny surface was a one of the patio tables, at least five yards away. It wasn't reflecting anything.

There wasn't much to reflect.

Looking up, I saw the sky was quickly filling. The puffy white clouds I'd seen minutes before had gone gray and ominous. A distant rumble growled among the peaks, warning of the storm to come. Time to go home and curl up with a cup of tea.

One final look around, turning in a circle again, this time focusing on the building. What had been the Hidalgo hacienda now housed more than a dozen shops. The garden was lush and romantic, and seemed almost to be trying to climb to the sky. Vines of honeysuckle twined around the pillars of the interior *portals*, and big baskets of flowers hung from the second story addition.

It was wrong for the period, that change, but it had been done so long ago that it was now a part of the place. Like so much of Santa Fe, Hidalgo Plaza had been reinvented, probably more than once. The upper floor fit, even though it was odd. A lot of it was private, but on the west side it housed shops, with stairs accessing it at either end made of big, heavy beams of wood, stained the ubiquitous dark brown of all the exposed wooden pillars and beams.

The light gleamed from the upper story, right between two pillars.

With a little gasp of frustration I glanced at the sky. The sun was hidden. The light must have come from another source.

There was nothing across from there to cast a light. The second story on the east side was featureless except for a few small windows.

A car headlight, maybe?

It was a long shot, but the only other thing I could think of was someone standing on one of the rooftops with a flashlight—an even longer shot. I turned to gaze again at the space where I had seen the light gleam. Maybe someone upstairs had lit a cigarette.

Wrong kind of light, I thought as I climbed the stairs. I walked to where the light had appeared, hoping to find a shop window, maybe with one of those intense halogen accent lights inside. Instead, there was a blank wall between the two pillars. To one side was a shoe shop, to the other a soap place that smelled so strongly of lavender I didn't have the fortitude to go in.

Frustrated, I looked out over the plaza, stepping to the wooden railing, which was far too low for current safety rules. I felt a moment's vertigo and took a step back.

Maybe it was all the dark wood, coupled with the storm clouds. Maybe it was remembering Maria's sad story—she had never married, and I suspected it was because she had been forbidden by her family to marry her true love, Captain Dusenberry—that made me shiver with a wave of sorrow.

Home. I wanted to be home, with a fire and a pot of tea and a book that would take me away from the real world and promise me a happy ending.

Hurrying down the stairs, I didn't slow until I reached the ground. A more overt crack of thunder quickened my pace again as I turned west, and by the time I stepped out from beneath the *portal* it had begun to rain.

I tugged on my hat and deployed my umbrella, hastening past the Palace of the Governors, where tourists bent to admire the wares of the Indian vendors despite the weather. The last couple of blocks I kept my gaze on the sidewalk except where I had to cross streets, and went up the back way to my house as it was closer.

Wind and rain had set the lilacs thrashing. I scurried up the driveway to the back door.

Safe inside, with the door locked behind me, I breathed a sigh of relief. Quiet enfolded me, the rain a distant patter on the upstairs roof.

The hall was shadowed; storm-darkened daylight coming in the little windows called "lights" that surrounded the door was inadequate to penetrate more than a few feet. I flipped on the switch for the hall lights, welcoming their brightness.

The dining parlor door stood open on my right, taunting me. Nat and Manny's wedding gifts: I had meant to take them to Nat's house that day. Not going to happen in this storm, though. It would have to be Monday.

Could I do it in one trip? I stepped into the parlor to try to estimate whether the presents piled on the table would all fit into my car. There was enough daylight coming through the French doors that I didn't bother turning on the chandelier, but I did glance up at it.

A single crystal drop swung, and a glint of light from the hall shone out from it.

I stood stock still. *That* was the light that I'd seen in Hidalgo Plaza.

7

CAPTAIN DUSENBERRY HAD BEEN SENDING ME GLINTS OF LIGHT as I walked around Santa Fe. I hadn't known he could do that. And as far as I knew, he'd never left the house before, at least not since I had bought it.

"Why?" I whispered, watching the crystal's swing grow smaller and smaller until it stopped.

Had he been trying to tell me something about Maria? Pointing out some feature of Hidalgo Plaza? But I was pretty sure the upper story where I'd last seen the light hadn't existed in his day.

The crystal was now perfectly still. A gust of wind spattered rain against the French doors.

I needed tea, and some time to sit and think.

Upstairs, I shed my wet coat and hat and left the umbrella in the hall to dry while I put on my kettle and lit every candle in my suite. A fleeting wish for a warm chimney was doomed to be unfulfilled; I didn't feel like going downstairs to build a fire. Instead I switched on the little electric space heater I'd bought the previous winter and put on my favorite raggedy sweater and my sheepskin slippers.

Sheepskin. Reminded me of the fuzzy woman, the gallery owner who had approached Roberto. He had kept cool, but Gwyneth's excitement had betrayed how much the opportunity meant to him.

The kettle whistled, interrupting my musings. I set the tea brewing and leaned against the counter in my kitchenette while I waited, enjoying malty whiffs of Assam.

The lights in Hidalgo Plaza troubled me. The feeling that it was important, that Captain Dusenberry was trying to tell me something, stayed with me. Maybe I should consult Willow about it.

Except that was a slippery slope that I had managed to avoid. Mostly. Talking with Willow about the captain, I had so far maintained the stance of listening to her opinions with an open mind, but not committing to much myself.

Captain Dusenberry was the ghost—or spirit, as Willow always said—of the man for whom my house had originally been built. I had acknowledged that much. He had made his presence known in the house ever since I had opened the tearoom. He could move crystals on the chandelier in the dining parlor, which had been his study and was the room where he had been murdered. He could turn on lights and the stereo system. He had, a couple of times, played music on the piano.

This was the first time he had followed me out of the house, and the first time he had manifested light out of nothing, as far as I knew. Somehow he had recreated the glint of light on a chandelier drop. Very clever of him.

But why?

I was no closer to answering that question. If I asked Willow for help in understanding, I would be acknowledging that she could communicate with the captain.

Would that be so terrible? I had already tacitly validated her by going in with her on the spirit tour and tea combination that we had been running all month—very successfully, I admitted. Every tour we scheduled had sold out quickly, even the second batch of dates we had added. Tourists and locals alike were delighted to walk around Santa Fe with Willow, visiting the haunts of several well-known spirits, and concluding with tea in my dining parlor and a talk about Captain Dusenberry from a local reenactor.

It was Halloween. People liked that kind of thing around Halloween.

The timer went off, and I retired to my favorite wing chair with a steaming mug of tea. Wind moaned among the tree branches outside, and the rain was still hitting the roof and windows in sharp, intermittent gusts.

There wouldn't be any dire consequence if I acknowledged that Willow could communicate with ghosts. It wasn't as though I'd be giving her a public endorsement. Why did I feel so reluctant?

Maybe because I didn't want to share the captain.

I curled deeper into the chair, cupping my tea with both hands. I still hadn't told anyone about the ribbon-tied bundle of papers I'd found beneath the floor in the dining parlor: letters to Captain Dusenberry from Maria Hidalgo. They were my secret treasure, and while I knew they belonged in the museum, I wasn't ready to give them up.

If only I could find Maria's stash of letters from the captain. Then I'd have a fuller picture.

Was that what the captain had been trying to tell me? Was he directing me to Maria's room at Hidalgo Plaza?

I shook my head. It didn't make sense. The light had appeared in the garden, and then upstairs on the balcony, not near any room that would have been there during Maria's time. And anyway, it was pretty unlikely that any of Maria's personal papers had survived. She would have burned them, or asked a family member to do so upon her demise. Anything that was left would probably be in the state archives, and I'd already looked there.

Unless, of course, they were in the possession of some private citizen who was unreasonably hoarding them. I acknowledged a twinge of guilt, and promised myself I would hand over the captain's letters to the museum soon.

So assuming that there was no stash of papers to be found in Hidalgo Plaza, what could the captain's lights mean?

A puzzle. One that Willow might be able to help me solve.

I took a mouthful of tea and luxuriated in the feel of it on my tongue, the tingle of caffeine on my palate. I'd leave the puzzle until tomorrow. Willow was probably working. Weekends were good for tourist activities, though I hoped for her sake that Willow wasn't having to lead a tour in this weather.

The next morning I woke to the distant sound of salsa music: Julio was at work in the kitchen. I rolled out of bed and made myself a breakfast of tea, soft-boiled eggs, and toast. The storm had passed, and the sun was shining on the wet garden. I dressed and went downstairs to find the kitchen counters overrun with rows and rows of small, white skulls.

The smell of sugar hung in the air. Julio glanced up at me from the work table, where he was up to his elbows in our largest bowl. An unopened ten-pound package of sugar stood nearby.

Julio carefully slid a filled mold onto a cardboard rectangle which already held five skulls, gave it a tap, then lifted it off, leaving a sixth skull behind. He dropped the mold into the bowl, wiped his hands on a towel, and turned down the music.

"Morning, boss."

"Good morning. This is quite a production!"

"We might have a dozen or more people here for the decorating. I don't want to run out. Don't touch," he warned as I peered more closely at the skulls on the counter. "They'll crumble. You can handle them tomorrow."

The skulls were flat on the back, each about four inches long, comprising perhaps half a cup of sugar. I'd seen full skulls, but those probably took more work to make and put together.

"Are they edible?" I asked.

"Sure, if you don't mind a little meringue powder. But would you want to eat one?"

When I was a kid, yes, I would have, but Julio was right. I was past the age when consuming a giant lump of sugar sounded like fun.

"Guess not," I said. "Well, I'll leave you to it, unless you need help?"

"Nah. Thanks."

I crossed the hall to the dining parlor, then realized I didn't have my keys. Dashed upstairs to get them and caught sight of my laundry basket, which I grabbed. Returning to the dining parlor, I started piling gifts into the basket.

It took six trips to move all the presents. The back seat of my Camry was stuffed to the windows, and the trunk and passenger seat were also full, but all the gifts were in. After letting Julio know I was going out, I drove sedately to Nat's house.

The hills north of town smelled of damp piñon. The sun shone brightly in a sky of brilliant blue, untroubled by a couple of token puffs of cloud. I drew a deep breath of the fragrant air as I got out of my car, grateful for the beauty of the day. Nat had a splendid view of the *Sangre de Cristos*, and today they were splashed with gold: the aspens were in full fall color. I felt an urge to run up there and walk beneath those magical trees.

However, there was my laundry basket on the passenger seat, full of giftwrapped packages. I carried it to the front door of the old adobe house and fished Nat's key out of my purse. There was still a gash in the heavy oak of the door from where Tommy Swazo had stuck a knife into it. Repressing a shiver, I opened it and carried the presents inside.

I loved Nat's house. Funky and old, made of adobe and local pine, it held many fond memories for me. Growing up, I ran tame in the place. Our families spent a lot of time together. Things had changed—Uncle Stephen was gone, and my cousin Alice had left for college three years before I graduated from high school and never returned—but the echoes of happy times still lived here.

As I was bringing in the third load, my phone rang. It was Tony. My heart gave a happy little flutter as I answered.

"Bad news," Tony said. "I can't do dinner."

"Oh, no! Still working?"

"I've got a meeting at six."

"Are you free now?"

"For a couple hours. Lunch?"

"Lunch would be fine. Actually…I've been wanting to go look at the aspens. I can throw a picnic together. What do you think?"

"As long as I'm back by two. Waiting on some lab results."

"Give me about forty-five minutes," I said.

"OK."

As usual he didn't say goodbye. I put the phone in my pocket and finished unloading the presents, then locked up and drove home, stopping at a cheese shop on the way for a baguette, fontina, cheddar, smoked gouda, and some olives.

Julio's car was still in the driveway. Through the open kitchen window I heard his boom box playing something slow and sultry.

I went in, and found every horizontal surface in the kitchen—the counters, the work table, even the break table in the corner—covered with sugar skulls. Julio stood at the dish washing station, cleaning up the bowl and utensils he'd used.

"Wow," I said, taking in the mass of rounded white shapes. If I hadn't known they were skulls I would have thought at first glance that it was a snowball-manufacturing operation.

Julio turned off the water and set a measuring cup in the drying rack. "I ran out of room, so there are a few in the dining parlor. Hope that's OK. I covered the table first."

"That's fine."

"I'll come in early tomorrow and put them away before work."

As he took off his apron and donned a jacket, I spotted the skull mold on the corner of the work table and picked it up. It was clear plastic, very light—probably a candy mold. It fit into the palm of my hand.

"Sounds good," I said. "Are we set for Tuesday?"

"Yes, and Ramon's going to make scones for the rest of the week. We'll be fine."

"You've done a great job training him."

Julio held out his hand for the mold, and I gave it to him. "He's got a lot to learn still, but he's willing," he said.

"That's the most important step."

Julio grinned and switched off the music. "*Hasta mañana, jefa.*"

"*Mañana.*"

I saw him out, then peeked into the dining parlor. My lace tablecloth sat carefully folded on the sideboard next to the flowers that had graced the table during the wedding. The dining table was draped in a plain cotton cloth, and half a dozen pieces of cardboard filled with sugar skulls sat on top of it.

I glanced at the chandelier, but apparently the captain had no opinion about the skulls. Leaving the parlor door open to make sure they would dry, I collected some leftover wedding cake for my picnic, then went upstairs to get away from all the sugar. From the depths of my storage cupboard I unearthed my mother's old wicker picnic basket, and smiled.

I hadn't been on a picnic in ages. Definitely since before my father died. This would be fun.

I made a virtuous salad with tart apples and toasted walnuts to go with the bread and cheese, and to compensate for the cake. No wine; instead I made a thermos of tea and packed a couple of bottles of sparkling water. Paper plates, utensils, cups, napkins, a small trash bag, and a blanket to spread on the ground, and my basket was full.

I was just finishing when I heard steps on the stairs, and came out of my suite in time to meet Kris.

"What's with all the skulls?" she asked.

"That's for Julio's decorating party. Didn't he invite you?"

"Oh, that. Yes, he did."

"I wasn't sure you were coming in today."

She took off her coat, revealing a long, knit tunic in black and purple chevron stripes over black leggings and ankle-high suede boots. "Payroll this week. Also, I wanted to bring you this."

She handed me a small envelope. I followed her into her office and borrowed her letter opener, a replica of a dagger with a dragon twined around the hilt. Inside was a folded note and a check.

Dear Ellen,

Thank you for letting us use your delicious house for our All Hallows celebration. Here is the deposit we negotiated, rounded up a bit to cover the advance purchase of the wine. I look forward to meeting you again.

—Gabriel Rhodes

The signature was an ebullient flourish, not what I would expect from the artist who had painted what I saw at the show. I handed the check to Kris.

"More work for you. Good of Gabriel to be so prompt."

She smiled. "He's a man of honor."

"Is he? That's good to hear."

She tilted her head up with a quizzical smile. "You don't trust him?"

"Do you?" I said, thinking of the other women.

"I trust him to be who he is. Don't worry, he won't hurt me."

"Has he hurt others?" I asked, then mentally whapped myself. I was being too nosy. I could feel Miss Manners frowning.

Kris laid the check on a stack of paperwork, then answered quietly. "He has never acted with the intention of hurting someone that I've seen. But a person can fling herself against a stone pillar and hurt herself."

"Ah," I said, and let it drop. "Well, I'm going out for a couple of hours. I may be out of cell range, so if you can't reach me don't panic."

"OK. Ellen?"

I paused in the doorway and looked back. Kris wore a small smile.

"Thanks for caring."

I smiled back, then left her to her work and crossed the hall to put on a warmer (and prettier) sweater—dark teal with a cowl neckline—and collect a sun hat and my picnic basket. As I reached the foot of the stairs, the front doorbell rang.

Tony was waiting with hands shoved in the pocket of his jeans. Beneath his leather jacket, he wore a heather-gray Henley that clung rather nicely to his torso.

"Hi," I said. "I thought you would come to the back."

"I was on Guadalupe Street." His gaze traveled my form, then he nodded. "Nice sweater."

"Thanks. Would you like to park your bike in the driveway?"

He glanced over his shoulder toward the motorcycle parked at the curb in front of my gate. "It'll be all right there. You driving?"

"Yes." I hefted the basket. "Come on through."

As I closed the door, he slid his arm around my waist, demanding attention. I was happy to give it to him, along with a lingering kiss. The basket kept us from getting closer, which was probably just as well since time was limited.

We walked down the hall to the back door. Tony looked into the dining parlor. "What's that?"

"Just a project of Julio's."

He stepped into the parlor and flipped on the light switch, then stood gazing at the sugar skulls for a few seconds. "You going to serve those to your guests? Kind of big for sugar cubes."

"They're for decorating," I said. "Julio's going to host a party next Sunday. I'm sure you'd be welcome," I added, going out on a limb a bit. Julio's opinion of Tony was guarded.

"Thanks, but I don't do art. I'd just make a mess."

"That could still be fun."

He gave me a wry look and switched off the light. We went out the back door and climbed into my car. Tony kept quiet as I negotiated traffic. Soon we were driving into the foothills. I rolled my window down, enjoying the crisp breeze.

"How's your mom?" I asked.

"Oh, fine."

"Did you get the…was it the washer? Fixed?"

"Dishwasher. *Abuela's*. Yeah."

I hoped Tony wasn't in a monosyllabic mood. That always made conversation a strain.

"It just needed a new hose," he added.

Oh, good. A whole sentence.

"So you're handy with fixing things? How about light fixtures?"

He shrugged. "Electrical's a pain. You'd be better off hiring a pro."

"OK."

"Gonna replace that chandelier?"

I felt his gaze on me and glanced over at him. The dark eyes were giving me a cop stare, except that I saw the laughter tightening the outer corners of his eyelids.

"Never," I replied loftily. "That chandelier is a pathway of communication with the spirit world."

"You've been hanging around with that Willow lady too much."

Or not enough. I smiled.

"Actually, I want to add an accent light to shine on Vi's portrait."

"Oh."

"I showed it to you, didn't I? Julio's painting?"

"Yeah."

We passed Ten Thousand Waves, Santa Fe's amazing Japanese spa, and I thought about suggesting we visit there some time, but decided against it for the moment. Soon we passed Hyde State Park, and began to see aspens here and there. I was heading for higher ground, up by the ski hill where the aspen groves were bigger.

"So did you go to the art show?" Tony said.

Ah. I smiled. "Yes. It was really great. So many talented artists."

"Did you go with that counselor guy?"

"His name is Loren. I met him and his sister at the show, and we had lunch."

I waited. Would Tony explode? If he did, that might just be where I drew the line.

The road got steeper and the pockets of aspens got bigger. I began to look for a place to park.

"I'm not good at art," Tony said.

"It's OK."

"I mean I'm not interested in it either."

"I'm not interested in football. That doesn't mean we can't be close."

That evoked a soft laugh. "You were miserable at that party I took you to."

"Not miserable. But certainly a fish out of water." It would have helped if I had known anyone else there, but they were mostly Tony's old high-school buddies, and I'd gone to a different school.

"We don't have to have everything in common," I said. "We have enough."

"Yeah? Like what?"

"Murder victims?"

Bad time to be sarcastic. Tony fell silent again, and when I glanced at him I saw his mouth was set.

We rounded a curve and came to a hillside splashed with gold. A small pullout provided parking. I stopped the car and got out, drinking in a deep breath of mountain air.

Tony reached out a hand to carry the picnic basket. I gave it to him, and we climbed the hillside. Leaves crunched beneath our feet, sending up the wonderful smell of autumn. Whenever I walked among the aspens, I always imagined myself in Lothlorien.

We found a spot in dappled sunlight, right in the midst of a stand of tall aspens. Their leaves rustled in a constant waterfall sound, and now and then one drifted gently down to the ground. I spread the blanket on a patch of mostly-dry grass and started unpacking the food. Cheeses and olives on a small cheese board, and I offered Tony the baguette.

"Where's yours?" he said.

"We're sharing. Just tear off a hunk."

He did so, pulling off one end and handing the loaf back to me. "I feel like a cave man," he said, gazing at the bread in his hand.

I laughed, relieved. "Try this. It's fontina," I said, cutting him a slice.

He sniffed it, then took a cautious nibble. He nodded approval and took a bigger bite along with some bread.

"Tea or fuzzy water?"

"Tea."

I agreed with his choice; it was chilly up here despite the sunshine. I poured into paper cups for us both, and we ate in silence for a while. Picking through potential topics of conversation, I found nothing brilliant, so I fell back on a safe, customary standby: work.

"Are you still working on the case that called you away Saturday?"

That got me a dark look. "Yeah."

"I'm not trying to be nosy."

He leaned back, chewing a mouthful, then washed it down with some tea. "My job isn't fun to talk about. Sorry. It's cleaning up other people's messes, with a lot of boring paperwork thrown in."

"Don't you swap stories with your colleagues?"

"Yeah, but the stories are mostly pathetic. Or morbid. You wouldn't like them."

"I can still sympathize."

He took an olive and ate it. I dished up salad for us both and handed him a plate, afraid to try a different subject. So far I'd just made things more awkward.

"The thing is, I don't want to put that on you," he said.

Looking up, I saw concern in his eyes. That was better than a defensive wall. Progress.

"How can I support you, then?" I asked. "That's all I'm trying to do."

He glanced up at the aspens. "Tell me about paintings. Or flowers. Something good. Your life is about good things."

The implied converse broke my heart. Tony looked back at me, his expression almost pleading. I could do as he asked, but that would be avoiding the undercurrents of this conversation.

"And your life is about doing good," I said softly. "That's harder."

Our gazes held for a long moment. A tingle went through me, not sexual, but intimate. As if we were looking into each other's souls.

"I just want to keep you safe," he said, almost whispering. "I don't want the bad stuff to touch you."

"Thank you. But if you build walls between us, they'll keep us apart."

I held still, hoping he'd answer, wanting to preserve whatever connection we had just made, but it was insubstantial, like cobwebs. Tony picked up his fork, and the moment had passed.

All right. Talk about something good. I thought about my day.

"I've never decorated sugar skulls," I said. "Have you?"

"Nah. Angela's the artist in the family."

"Is she? What kind of art does she do?"

"Different kinds. She's always crocheting something, and she scrapbooks. In school she loved art classes. *Abuela* still uses an ashtray she made."

"I like your sister," I said. "I'd like to get to know her better. Do you think she'd enjoy decorating skulls?"

He gave a skeptical shrug. "You could ask."

"Is *el Dia de los Muertos* a big deal in your family?"

"Not really." He ate a bite of gouda, then added, "Mama lights candles for Dad and *Abuelo*. That's about it."

I nodded. The defensive wall had come back, though not as solid as before. I got the feeling I should avoid asking about his family life too much.

I drank some tea. Why did talking to Tony feel like tiptoeing through a mine field? It shouldn't be this hard.

The salad was gone, and the cheese was mostly gone. I got out the cake and served Tony a piece.

"What about Christmas?" I asked. Christmas had to be safe. "Do you have any family traditions?"

"Yeah. Midnight mass. *Abuela* still insists on going. When we get home we have cocoa and bizcochitos, and we get to open one present. The rest of the presents are opened after breakfast on Christmas morning."

"We did presents on Christmas morning, too, when I was growing up."

Tony tilted his head. "Not any more?"

"Well, my parents are gone. Now I get together with Nat for

brunch, and we exchange gifts then. Though—I don't know. It may be different this year, now that she's married again." Smiling, I shrugged, trying to shake off a moment's insecurity. "We'll see. I'll still go to the Plaza on Christmas Eve, and walk up Canyon Road to look at the *farolitos*. Do you like to do that?"

"That's for Anglos."

Rich Anglos, I heard behind the tone. I cut a bite of cake to hide my annoyance.

"Not necessarily."

"We always thought it was a tourist thing. We'd go to *Las Posadas* instead."

I nodded, remembering the candlelight procession of Joseph and Mary looking for a place to stay, with crowds of people singing as they followed the couple around the Plaza and watched at each stop where they asked for shelter. "When we were little, our parents would take us to that. I loved booing the devils."

"You don't go any more?"

"It's so crowded these days. Like Zozobra."

He nodded. "Like everything."

"Progress, I guess."

"Mm."

We finished the cake and drank the last of the tea. I packed up the remainder of the food and set the basket aside, then lay back on the blanket, staring up at the aspens. Golden-white towers reaching up to the incredibly blue sky. I sighed with pleasure.

Tony stretched out beside me. "OK, that's gorgeous," he said.

I turned my head to look at him, glad to see the frown was gone. He still looked care-worn. There were lines of weariness etched into his face.

"Worth taking the time?" I said softly.

He turned his head to meet my gaze. "Yeah."

I smiled, and he moved closer for a kiss. One kiss became two, became more. We twined around each other and my heart began to race. Tony's hands moved over my body, sending flashes of lightning joy through me. Then, abruptly, he stopped.

"We should go," he said, his voice rough.

"In a little while," I said, and nipped his ear.

"No, I'm late." He kissed me again, then pulled away.

I sat up and looked at my phone. Quarter to two.

Damn.

He was watching me with a hungry look that had nothing to do with food.

"But you want to stay, right?" I asked, smoothing my hair.

"Yes."

"So let's get together again soon."

"Yes."

I demanded one more kiss, then got up. We folded the blanket and walked back to my car.

At home, I parked and headed for the back door, sorting through my keys. Tony stood looking at the car.

Oh. Yes. The bloodstain was gone from the driveway, but the memory would still be there.

"Tony?" I said softly.

He turned, giving his shoulders a shake. I opened the door and we walked up the hall to its counterpart, sunlight shining through the front door lights. I set the picnic basket down.

"Thanks for taking the time to see me. It was nice."

I reached for the doorknob but Tony intervened, catching me in a tight hug. I hugged him back, gave him the kisses he wanted.

"I have to go back to work," he said hoarsely, catching my hand and kissing the palm.

"OK. Call me?"

"Yeah."

One more kiss, then he reached for the door. I followed him out to watch him stride down the path to the gate, and shivered a little in the chill.

"Bye," I said softly.

He got onto his bike with the unconscious grace of a lifelong horseman. The engine started up on a low growl. Tony made a U-turn in the empty street, then cruised to the intersection at Palace Avenue and turned the corner out of sight.

8

THE NEXT FEW DAYS PASSED QUICKLY. A thousand small tasks needed attention, many of which had been on hold while I dealt with the wedding. In addition, the holiday season loomed.

I called Tony's sister, Angela, and got her voicemail. She was in college, I knew, and also cared for their grandmother. I left a message inviting her to come decorate sugar skulls on Sunday, then double-checked with Julio (yes, belatedly) that it was all right to ask a friend.

"Hey, it's your house," Julio said as he kneaded a mound of *pan de muerto* dough. "Sure, ask whoever you want. I'm just glad you're giving us the space."

"Should we have some snacks? I could make tea..."

"No, no, no. Not on your day off. You leave the snacks to me. I put it at one o'clock so people would have lunch before coming."

The first shipment of holiday merchandise arrived on Tuesday. I was not in the mood for Christmas; in fact, I resented its intrusion into autumn, which was my favorite season. Business demanded that I attend to it, though. I helped Kris sort through the goods and get them ready for sale, but I insisted that we would not put out holiday merchandise until after Thanksgiving.

"People like to shop early," Kris said, glancing up at me under sculpted, dark brows as we stood among stacks of boxes in the storage closet behind her desk.

"We have plenty of things they can buy. I just don't want holly and candy canes all over the place for two months."

She resumed checking off inventory on packing slips. Sometimes Kris's silences shouted louder than a dozen howler monkeys.

"This is our first Christmas," I said. "Let's see how it goes. If it's a mistake, we'll reconsider for next year."

Having put my foot down on the merchandise issue, I then caved on the subject of advertising. Our first holiday ad—tastefully designed by my pal Gina's advertising firm—would appear the week before Thanksgiving, announcing extended hours for December and encouraging early reservations.

Three more boxes arrived in Wednesday's mail. The smallest was addressed to Kris, so I put it on her desk and took the others into the storage closet. As I opened one and examined the ornaments inside, I became aware of a weighted silence in the outer office.

Looking out, I saw the small box standing open and Kris regarding a life-sized skull sitting on her desk. I put down a china teacup ornament and stepped out to join her.

"Is that something for the party?"

"Search me," Kris said. "I didn't order it."

"Is there a packing slip?" I leaned forward to peer into the box, but all I saw were wads of black tissue paper.

"No. The cancellation is from the Santa Fe post office."

The back of my neck prickled. "Maybe we should contact the police."

She shook her head and picked up the skull, turning it in her hands. "It isn't real. It's resin."

"It could be construed as a threat."

Kris swiveled her chair to face me. "No, it's an insult." She held the skull out toward me. "No lower jaw, see? It's a Death's Head. In Shakespearean times, that was a symbol for a bawd or a rake."

"I don't get it."

She shot me a wry glance. "Someone is calling me a whore."

I couldn't help a small gasp of outrage.

"Probably one of Gabriel's exes, is my guess," Kris added. She held it at arm's length. "It'll make a nice paperweight."

"Kris, I don't like this."

"If it bothers you I'll take it home."

"I mean I don't like that someone sent it to you."

She tilted her head, narrowing her eyes as she addressed the skull. "And why here, instead of my place? What do you say, Yorick? Is it because they didn't know my mailing address?"

I took a deep breath. "I need tea."

Escaping into my office, I poured myself a cup of Oolong from the pot on my credenza. Kris trailed after me.

"Don't worry about it, Ellen. It's just drama."

"Do Goths often send each other skulls?"

She grinned. "Probably more often than you think."

I took a swallow of tea, then gestured to the pot, offering to pour for Kris. She shook her head.

"Thanks. I've had my quota for the day."

"Let me ask Tony about that skull."

She gave me a skeptical look. "He's a homicide detective."

"Yes, but he might have some advice."

Kris didn't quite roll her eyes. "Don't bother him. If it makes you feel better, I'll keep the box. Then when I turn up dead, you can have it checked for fingerprints."

"Not funny."

She smiled. "Sorry. Really, it's OK. This isn't a threat."

"If you say so."

"Let's put away the rest of that merchandise," she said.

We did, but I couldn't help glancing at the skull on Kris's desk now and then.

Friday arrived on the wings of a howling wind storm. I half-expected a call from Willow, canceling her tour for that day, but I had apparently underestimated the determination of the spirit-watching crowd. When four o'clock came they arrived, with cold-reddened noses, bundled in coats, scarves, and hats which they shed on their way down the hall to the dining parlor.

The group included the Bird Woman, back for her third time on the tour. I put on a friendly smile for her and the others as they shuffled into the parlor.

As Willow passed, I touched her arm. "I'd like to talk to you afterward, if you have time."

She nodded and followed her charges in to tea while I went upstairs to alert Mr. Quentin, the reenactor who gave a talk about Captain Dusenberry as part of the tour. He waited quietly in the sitting area by the front window, a slightly stocky gentleman in his mid-forties, rusty-colored hair and beard with a few threads of silver, reading a book by the light of a mica-shaded table lamp. His Union army uniform, spectacles, even the book in his hands were authentic recreations and looked well-used, not donned merely for the occasion, but lived in.

I paused, watching him for a moment before intruding. Captain Dusenberry had probably looked very much like he did. Though Mr. Quentin was not here to portray the captain, he did help people understand what that 19th-century gentleman's life had been like.

"They're here," I said, stepping forward.

Mr. Quentin nodded, consulted a pocket watch on the end of a chain, then resumed reading. The group would have twenty minutes to enjoy their tea before he went down to address them.

I retreated to check on the tearoom, and met Iz carrying an empty firewood sling. "Didn't Mick fill the rack?" I asked.

"Yes, but we've gone through it all, and now he's backed up."

"Let me get it," I said, reaching for the sling. "You don't want to smudge your apron."

The firewood was stacked out back, against the fence that ran along the driveway. I put on my coat and brought in two loads of wood, one for the main parlor and one for the south parlor, where four smaller alcoves shared the back-to-back fireplaces.

Peeking into Dahlia, I saw that both it and Violet were empty. I filled the firewood rack, then paused to look at Vi's portrait.

Yes, it definitely needed better illumination, although there was a candle again, casting flickering shadows on the painting. I noticed a small card propped up behind the candle and picked it up. On the front was a picture of Jesus surrounded by sheep and doves. On the back was a prayer titled "Comfort for those who Mourn."

This must be the offering Rosa had wanted to leave. Prayer cards were mostly a Catholic custom, though I'd seen them at a couple of Protestant funerals. I read the card, then replaced it behind the votive. The prayer was pretty generic, so I didn't think it would offend anyone who happened to be curious.

It did add to the appearance of an altar, though. Well, if anyone complained I'd move the offerings. So far no one had.

Three logs were left in the sling. As I carried them to the dining parlor, bits of the prayer rolled around in my head.

Though invisible to us, our dear dead are not absent.

Hm. Guess I really couldn't deny that.

As I slipped into the dining parlor, hoping to avoid disrupting the tour group, the Bird Woman's voice rang out. "But how many times have you *seen* Julia Staub?"

Willow fielded this with grace. In the role of a chamber-maid, I pretended disinterest as I unloaded the wood into the rack. The fire had died down, so I gave it a poke and added one log, then beat a retreat as Dee came in with a fresh pot of tea.

I looked into the kitchen, where Julio was wrapping up for the day while Mick heroically tackled a mound of used china. "Grocery list for tomorrow?"

"Right there." Julio pointed to a slip of paper held by a magnet onto a small whiteboard mounted by the door. "I'm out."

Willow's tour group had another hour; Mick and Dee were staying to look after them. I headed up to my office and met Mr. Quentin—or Lieutenant Quentin, as he referred to himself in his presentation—on the stairs. He had donned his haversack and ammunition pouch, and carried his replica rifle carefully with the barrel upright. The upstairs chandelier cast a halo around him for a moment as he descended, making me pause.

…our dear dead are not absent.

As I reached the upper landing, I met Kris coming out of her office, also headed home.

"Payroll's on your desk," she said over her shoulder.

"Thanks."

I stepped through the doorway shared by our offices, and couldn't help glancing toward her desk. The skull was nowhere in evidence.

Retiring to my desk with a cup of tea, I wondered what Captain Dusenberry thought of Mr. Quentin's presentation. We'd hosted more than a dozen tour groups already. I'd heard the talk myself twice. It was thought-provoking, especially since I knew more about the captain than anyone else.

I opened the lower drawer of my desk where I had stashed Maria's letters, protected by a carved teak box. I had read them often enough to know them almost by heart, and I knew that handling them risked damaging them, so I left them where they were and locked the drawer.

Soon, I told myself. Soon I'd give them to the museum.

Remembering the lights in Hidalgo Plaza, I turned to my computer and sent off an email to my contact at the State Historical Archives, asking for any information about the plaza's physical characteristics—maps, inventories, letters—during the late nineteenth century. If I got very lucky, there might be a mention of Maria's rooms.

I signed the payroll checks and locked them in Kris's desk, then tidied my own desk, sorting through the stack of papers "to file" that never seemed to go away. It included Gabriel's diagram of the seven colored chambers for their party, and the lanyard with the map of the art show booths. Interesting juxtaposition. I laid them both in front of me and mused about Gabriel and maps. Maps were so technical and dry, not what I'd expect to be interesting to an artist.

Maybe they weren't. Maybe the elusive thought tickling at the back of my brain was just the coincidence that Gabriel had touched both of these maps. I was about to toss them, then thought perhaps I should keep the diagram for the party. In the end, I shoved them both to the bottom of the "to file" stack.

I finished my tea, locked my desk, and went downstairs. Mr. Quentin had just concluded his talk and stood in the hall chatting with the guests as they put on their coats. I moved past him, thanking the guests, working my way toward the dining parlor where I hoped to find Willow.

"Hey!"

The harsh whisper accompanied a tug on my sleeve. I turned to find the Bird Woman peering up at me. She wore a heavy fuchsia cable-knit sweater over jade green slacks and pink sneakers with lights that blinked red every time she moved her feet. Her feathery silver hair must have been charged with static, perhaps by her sweater; wisps of it stood straight up from her head, swaying gently.

"Mrs. Olavssen. What can I do for you?"

"You can get me that soldier's phone number," she said in a conspiratorial whisper.

"Soldier?" I glanced toward Mr. Quentin. "You mean the reenactor?"

"Yeah. He's really hot!"

I squelched an impulse to laugh, even as I felt a pang of sympathy for Mr. Quentin. "I'm afraid I don't have it. Would you like to write your number on a card, and give it to him?"

"OK," she said, taking a lime green scarf off a peg. "But you give it to him. I don't want the girls to know."

I fetched one of the tearoom's business cards and a pen from the gift shop and handed them to her, then looked into the dining parlor. Willow stood talking with Margo, who was dressed in a loose, forest green sweater over a black velvet broomstick skirt and boots.

"Hello, Margo" I said with a smile. "I didn't know you were taking the tour."

She smiled and shrugged a shoulder. "Dale said it was really good."

"Well, I hope you enjoyed it," I said, glancing at Willow.

Immaculate as always in a black turtleneck knit dress and a necklace of turquoise heishi, Willow seemed unconcerned. Probably she was used to both Goths and skeptics. I imagined that they, along with rabid enthusiasts, comprised the bulk of her clientele.

"The ghost didn't shake the chandelier," Margo said.

"That's pretty rare," Willow said.

"But you've seen it?" Margo looked from Willow to me.

"I've seen it," Willow said, moving toward the door. She held out her hand to me. "Thank you, Ellen. The tea was wonderful as always."

I smiled and nodded as we shook hands. Poor Willow had been served this same menu with each tour group, and had another half-dozen tours scheduled. Usually she just drank tea and maybe had one sandwich and a scone.

"I have a couple of questions for you, if you have time," I said to her. "If not, I can call you tomorrow."

"I have a little time," she said. "Just let me tidy up."

She headed for the restroom, and I turned to help Dee, who had come in and started to collect the used china. Margo lingered by the sideboard. I carried one of the tea trays to the pantry and returned for the other, and she was still there, looking bored.

"Anything I can help you with?" I asked.

She shrugged one shoulder and gave a lopsided smile. "No, I'm just waiting to see if...you know. Anything happens."

"It could be a long wait," I said, trying to keep my tone kind.

Margo looked back at the chandelier. I traded a glance with Dee as I took away the second tea tray.

The Bird Woman was lying in wait for me when I returned to the hall, now bundled in a very puffy, bubblegum pink, down parka. Her head looked tiny, peeking out of the neckline above the lime scarf. She pressed the card I had given her into my hand.

"Slip it to him after I'm gone," she whispered.

"All right," I whispered back.

She beamed, pulled a chartreuse fake-fur hat à la Russe down on top of her free-flying hair, and clomped along the hall toward her friends by the front door, heels and toes both blinking. I glanced at the card in my hand, saw a long-ish message scrawled on it in spidery handwriting, and hoped she hadn't written anything too outlandish. I couldn't bring myself to be so rude as to read it.

The last few guests were putting on their hats and gloves. Mr. Quentin was nowhere in evidence. Deducing that he had gone upstairs, I hurried up and found him donning his large, pale blue woolen overcoat.

"Thank you, Mr. Quentin. Another successful event."

He smiled. "My talk seems to be especially popular in nasty weather."

I returned the smile, then swallowed. "One of the guests asked me to give you her number. She was...very impressed, I believe."

He accepted the card with a small bow and tucked it into his pocket, much to my relief. Maybe he'd forget about it for a few days. Or months. Years.

We went downstairs together and found Willow waiting in the hall. Mr. Quentin bade us both a courteous goodnight and left by the back door. I locked it, and since the hall was otherwise empty, I glanced into the dining parlor.

Margo still stood looking up at the chandelier. I cleared my throat.

"We're closed, now," I said gently. "Thank you for taking the tour."

She slowly came out of the room. I switched off the chandelier as she reached the hall, and pulled the parlor door shut for good measure. Margo donned a heavy black coat and a dark plaid scarf, and followed me to the front door, where I said good night and locked the door behind her.

Turning to Willow, I heard a distant clink of china from the kitchen. "Thanks for staying. This won't take long. May I offer you a glass of something? sherry, or wine...?"

"Thanks, but no. I'm having dinner with friends."

"Ah. Well, I won't keep you. Let's sit somewhere more comfortable. Do you have a favorite alcove?"

"I heard you redecorated one of them."

"Oh, yes. Violet. Used to be Marigold."

I led her through the gift shop and back to Violet. The fire there had settled to coals. Willow stepped up to the fireplace, peering at Vi's portrait.

"That's a stunning likeness," she said. "It really captures her spirit."

"Thank you. Julio Delgado painted it."

"Your chef?"

I nodded. "They were friends."

She looked back at the painting, then took in the votive candle, the prayer card, and the small vase of marigolds with which I had replaced the faded pansies the previous day.

"Nice of you to honor her," she said, and moved to one of the wing chairs. "So, how can I help you?"

I took the other chair. "I had an unusual experience a few days ago."

"Oh?"

"Yes. I saw...well, a glint of light. It was just like the way light shines off the chandelier." I nodded toward the dining parlor, and she nodded back. "Only I saw it outside, in Hidalgo Plaza."

"Really?" Her gaze intensified a degree. "Maybe it was a reflection."

"I checked. There was nothing reflective in the area. Actually, I saw it in three different places. As if it was leading me along."

Willow's brows rose. "And where did it lead you?"

"To the balcony on the west side of the plaza. The spot didn't seem significant. There wasn't a door or a window right there."

"And yet you felt the light led you there."

"Well…yes. So I wondered if it could be Captain Dusenberry." I felt my cheeks getting warm. "Is that something he'd be capable of doing? Making a light out of thin air?"

"Not out of thin air, exactly, but yes. That would be a fairly simple manifestation."

"Is there a way to tell if it was the captain or…or someone else?"

"I would trust your instinct on that," Willow said. "You're pretty well acquainted with the captain."

I nodded, feeling a little silly, but glad that Willow hadn't dismissed my story. The light in the room wavered; we both looked up at the votive on the mantel, which was flickering. After a moment it stilled.

"If…if you went there with me, do you think you might be able to, um…sense anything?" I asked.

"I don't know, but it's worth a try."

"I'd pay you for your time. I don't want to impose."

She waved a dismissive hand. "You've done me plenty of good, Ellen. I'd be glad to go there with you. I don't know of any activity in Hidalgo Plaza so now I'm curious, but it'll have to be another day."

"Of course." I stood. "Maybe next month, after you're finished with the tea tours."

Willow smiled as she rose. "Or maybe we can find half an hour next week. I know you're busy too, but the sooner the better with this sort of thing. Let's both check our calendars and find a time that works."

"Yes. Thanks, Willow. I didn't know what to think." I gestured for her to precede me out of the alcove.

"Do you know of any reason the captain would be interested in Hidalgo Plaza?"

"Maybe," I said as we reached the hall. I felt reluctant to share what I knew about the captain and Maria, though if anyone could sympathize it would be Willow. She might even be able to get more information. "We could talk about it when we meet."

"All right." She put on her coat and a lavender cashmere scarf, then turned to me with a smile. "Well, see you at tomorrow's tour."

"See you then. Good night."

I let her out the front door and locked it behind her, then walked slowly back toward the kitchen to check on Mick and Dee. The dining parlor door was still closed. I opened it and looked in.

All was still in the dim light, softened by lace curtains, that came through the French doors. Dappled shadows lay across the table. The chandelier was quiet.

Waiting for something.

Was that my imagination, making up a story to account for my feelings? With a small sigh, I left to finish the last of the day's duties.

When Dee and Mick had gone and I had the house to myself, I opened the calendar on my computer and looked for a day when I could go to Hidalgo Plaza with Willow. The coming weekend was out; I was short-staffed on Saturday so I'd have to help out in the tearoom, and Sunday was Julio's skull-decorating party. Monday was the only possibility, unless Willow had time in between tours. From Tuesday through Halloween she was doing at least one tea tour a day, usually two, and who knew how many other tours sans tea were on her plate. I sent her an email suggesting November first if Monday wouldn't work for her.

November first. *El Dia de los Muertos.* Ironic if that turned out to be the best time for pursuing a ghost.

The next couple of days were uneventful except for phone calls. Nat called from Hawaii, bubbling with happiness. Gina called to gossip: she was having a lovely time with her beau, but did not expect a proposal despite having caught Nat's bouquet in his company. No, she couldn't decorate skulls; they were going to a concert.

Angela, however, was delighted to be asked to the decorating and called to accept. She had made arrangements for her grandmother in order to be free. I felt a moment's pang that her arrangements might inconvenience Tony, but then thought better of it. If he was still working, then he wouldn't be available to help Angela.

Tony called to say he was again working through the weekend; he wanted to see me but didn't know when he'd be free. I told him we could always talk on the phone if he didn't have time to meet. The suggestion didn't thrill him (conversation had never been his strong suit), and for a long moment's silence I imagined him struggling with an impulse to question me about whether I'd been seeing anyone else. If he had, I was prepared to give him a gushing description of Mr. Quentin. Fortunately, he didn't.

Sunday started early with Julio sneaking into the kitchen. I woke, aware of his presence despite his best efforts to be quiet, and rolled over to look at my clock. Seven a.m.

I sighed, knowing I wouldn't get back to sleep. I put on a kettle, dragged on some clothes, and went down to say hello.

The smells of Julio's coffee and fresh-baked bread greeted me as I reached the kitchen. On the counter stood a row of plastic storage boxes filled with sugar skulls, three gallon jugs of apple cider, a giant package of paper plates, and two grocery bags. Julio was at the work table, dumping powdered sugar into the largest bowl. He had on jeans and a black T-shirt adorned with an elaborate, giant sugar skull.

"Sorry," he said, looking up as I came in. "I tried to be quiet."

"I demand compensation in the form of coffee."

"Help yourself. There's *pan*, too, if you're not sick of it."

"I have been very virtuous in refraining from gobbling *pan,* so I accept. What are you making? I thought people weren't coming until one o'clock."

"Icing for decorating. I have to make all the colors, and put it in bags. Gonna take a while." He gestured to a small box, which I picked up to examine. It contained a dozen different colors of professional food coloring.

I poured myself a mug of coffee and took a *pan* off a tray on top of the range. The bread was warm, crusted with sugar, soft and delicious. The aroma of oranges filled my senses with each bite. I pulled tiny pieces off of the bun and nibbled them between sips of coffee, trying to make the treat last.

Julio mixed his icing with an expert hand. Where I would have scattered powdered sugar everywhere, he kept it all confined in the bowl, gradually adding more water until he was satisfied with the consistency. He then scooped a blob of icing into a smaller bowl and reached for the box of colors.

Having finished my *pan*, I washed my hands and topped up my coffee, then drifted back to the work table.

"Can I help?"

"Sure. You want to tint some icing?"

"If it will save you time."

"It will, thanks. Have you worked with this stuff before? It's pretty potent."

I nodded. "We have some toothpicks somewhere…"

Julio produced a box and handed them to me, then scooped more icing into a separate small bowl. I chose a jar of blue coloring and opened it carefully so as not to get it on my fingers. With a toothpick, I extracted a small dab of the coloring paste and smeared it into the icing in my bowl, then used a fork to stir it in.

We passed a contented hour mixing colors. Julio made extra purple and red, and a triple batch of black ("Goths," he said), then started spooning the colors into small bags for piping. There were dozens by the time we had used up a third big batch of icing.

"I think that'll be enough," Julio said, surveying the rows of colors. "If we start running out, I can mix up more."

"Were you planning to use the dining parlor?"

Julio shook his head. "Don't want to make a mess in there. I think we can all fit in here. There's the break table, and the stools."

Four stools, to be precise, at a height for working at the work table. The break table had room for four at best.

"How many people are coming?" I asked.

"I'm not exactly sure, but at there'll be least ten."

"It's a pleasant day," I said. "We could use the back *portal*, too. There's the café table, and we can bring another one around from out front."

"Good idea! Thanks, boss!"

We executed this plan, resulting in seating for a total of fourteen. Julio returned to the kitchen and started unloading a grocery bag, pulling out celery, carrots, and jicama.

"No," he said when I again offered to help. "It's your day off. Go relax, read a book or something. Shoo."

It was too lovely a day for staying indoors, so I collected my garden shears, hat, and gloves and went out to deadhead the rosebushes. Leaves crunched underfoot; the cottonwoods were now dropping theirs in earnest. The wisteria leaves were falling as well.

To my relief, the lawn showed only minimal damage from the wedding. I tidied all the roses, then the dahlias (done for the year), then the marigolds. Clipped a new handful of pansies for Violet, then grabbed a quick shower and a bite of lunch before one o'clock.

When I heard voices below, I headed down. The smell of hot cider with cinnamon reached me on the stairs.

Rosa and Ramon, wearing T-shirts and jeans, stood in the kitchen chatting with their cousin. Julio had set out stacks of paper plates on the work table and break table, along with platters piled with sugar skulls. Through the kitchen windows I could see a similar setup on the tables out back, with a couple of skulls weighing down each stack of plates.

Julio offered me a paper cup of hot cider. I inhaled the steam and warmed my hands, letting it cool before risking my tongue. Plates of chips and salsa, sliced cheeses and apples, and a relish plate with dip stood on the counter. The only sweet item, and it wasn't all that sweet, was a tray loaded with *pan de muerto*.

A tall, slender blond man in a navy long-sleeved tee and khakis came in the kitchen door. It took me a second to recognize him: Julio's roommate.

"Andre," I said. "Good to see you."

Dee arrived next, in jeans and a floppy, forest-green sweater, followed by Dale and Margo. Had Julio invited them? I watched him serve them cups of cider and decided it must have been Kris. Dale had on a dark sweater vest over a collared shirt, a touch dressy for the occasion; he must be trying to impress. Margo wore a tight-fitting black T-shirt and jeans. After introductions, they moved away and chatted together by the dish washing station. I wondered briefly if they were a couple, but the body language wasn't there.

At the sound of the back doorbell, I looked out the window and saw Angela Aragón in a pale yellow sweater and faded jeans. Her dark brown hair brushed her shoulders. Her expression was pensive, as mine has been in my college days. Rather than go around through the pantry to the back door, I opened the kitchen door and beckoned to her.

"We're all in here. Come on in!"

Angela stepped in shyly and looked around, eyes widening. "Wow, what a huge kitchen!" She gave me smile so much like Tony's that it made my heart jump a little.

"Not that huge for a restaurant. Have you met my chef?" I said as Julio offered her a steaming cup of cider. "Angela, this is Julio Delgado. Angela Aragón."

Julio's chin lifted slightly as a look of understanding flicked across his face, then he nodded and smiled. "Welcome," he said.

"So you're the one who makes all the wonderful food here," she said, smiling back.

"And this is Andre," I added. "He's also a chef."

Andre shook hands with her. "Hi."

I introduced her to the others, then Julio called for everyone's attention. "We might as well get started."

Dee, Rosa, and Ramon, who were sitting at the break table, shushed themselves and turned to listen. Julio put a skull on a paper plate, then picked up a sack of green icing and some scissors and snipped the tip off the sack.

"Let me open these for you; it's easy to cut off too much. Use a plate for working on. You can test the icing on the plate first, and practice designs on it." He squeezed a green curlicue onto his plate. "Get a fresh plate for each skull; there are plenty. There are some pictures of examples on the tables. Don't worry if you haven't done this before—the idea is to remember the people you love who aren't here any more. If there's no one like that for you, just have fun."

Andre climbed onto a stool at the work table and took a skull from a heaping platter. Dale and Margo drifted over to the other side of the work table while Julio started snipping icing bags for the group at the break table.

"There's more room out back," I said to Angela. "Shall we sit out there?"

She nodded, smiling, and followed me outside. Just as we were settling at a cafe table, Cherie came hurrying up the driveway, her fringed purple burn-out shawl swinging with each stride. Under it she wore tight jeans and a beige camisole.

"I'm late, sorry," she said.

"They're all in the kitchen," I told her, indicating the door.

She hurried through it, and Angela and I seated ourselves. A breeze rustled through the trees and sent leaves drifting down.

"I'm glad you could come," I said. "I've been hoping we could get better acquainted."

"Me, too," said Angela.

I sipped my cider. "Tony says you're artistic."

"Well, maybe 'crafty' is a better word. I like to make things, but I'm not all that good at it."

"That's just a matter of practice."

I picked up one of the example pages, four color photos of different skulls, each almost completely covered with intricate designs. A couple of the skulls had names on the foreheads, presumably of the honorees.

"Wow, these are elaborate!"

"Have you done this before?" Angela asked.

"No. Have you?"

"Once, in middle school art class. We used poster paints instead of icing. They kind of melted the sugar, but it was still fun."

I picked up a bag of pink icing, then chose a blank skull. "So, you're in college?" I asked.

"Community college. I'm studying nursing."

"What led you to that?"

"I'm pretty sure I can get a job," she said. "There's a shortage."

"But do you like nursing?"

She shrugged. "Beats waiting tables. Oh! I didn't mean—"

"Don't worry," I said. "I understand, and you're right, waiting tables is hard work. I try to make it a good job, here, but the tea-room is a bit different from most other restaurants."

Angela's cheeks were red. "I'm sorry. That was rude of me."

"No, it wasn't. I'm not offended. Table service isn't the sort of job people want to make a career of. I know that; I figure I'll have to hire new servers every two or three years."

I took a swallow of cider. It was the perfect temperature. Angela followed my example, her embarrassment fading.

The crunch of tires on gravel made me look up. Kris's black Scion was approaching up the driveway. She parked, and she and Gabriel got out. Kris wore a loose black sweater over a burgundy broomstick skirt, and Gabriel had on a sage green shirt over stone-washed jeans, the collar open to display the silver ankh on its chain.

"Sorry we're late," Kris said as they joined us.

"It's my fault," Gabriel added.

I introduced Angela and offered to fetch them some cider. As I stepped in the kitchen door, I almost collided with Julio.

"You need icing opened," he said, brandishing the scissors.

"Yes. Kris and Gabriel are here. I'm getting them some cider."

He nodded and went out, and I headed for the slow-cooker that held the cider. At the break table, Cherie chatted happily about fashion to Dee, Ramon, and a dubious-looking Rosa. At the work table, Andre was piping orange flowers onto a skull with a swift and steady hand, while Dale squeezed out tentative blue polka dots and Margo sat frowning at a skull, a bag of black icing in one hand.

I ladled up two cups of cider and returned to the patio table, where Angela was talking shyly with Kris while Julio snipped the tips off of icing bags. Gabriel held out a black bag to be opened, and after a couple of test squeezes onto the plate, commenced circling the eye sockets of a skull with precise lines.

"Need anything else?" Julio asked.

"Not now, thanks," I said, picking up my pink icing and giving it a tentative squeeze. A thin line squiggled its way out, and I wiped it on my plate.

Julio went back into the kitchen, and we all started decorating. This, I discovered, was trickier than it looked. My attempt to give my skull pink lips ended in its looking clownish, so I turned up the corners for a big clown smile, then piped yellow and orange flowers all over the skull, practicing until I had better control. I put two big globs of green in the eye sockets and called it done. Setting that plate aside, I took a fresh one and a second skull.

Before I began, I glanced at what my companions were doing. Angela was making a meticulous portrait of a man, with black hair and mustache and brown eyes. Kris's skull was an exercise in pointillism, an abstract of red and black. Gabriel's, all in black, was an eye-buzzing striped affair that followed the contours of the skull and somehow managed to be extremely dramatic.

Deciding to do something softer than these, I picked up a bag of lavender icing and carefully drew small flowers on the cheekbones and chin of my skull. Lack of errors built my confidence; I swapped the lavender for brown and piped curling hair around the face and over the top of the skull. It was too dark, but the color I had in mind wasn't among our choices. I settled for piping some orange highlights over the brown, then I picked up the violet icing.

Very carefully, I piped irises in the eyes, then eyelashes. Brown eyebrows, pink lips (successful this time), and I was nearly done. I glanced at Angela, who was gazing at her handiwork, a bag of blue in her hand. She had added "Papi" across the forehead in that color.

Noticing my gaze, she smiled. "Blue was his favorite color. I want to put more on there but I don't know where. I think it's done."

Gabriel glanced up from his work, giving a single nod. "White space is good."

Gabriel had made a crisscross pattern on one skull, and now I saw it was becoming a harlequin mask with exaggerated, three-dimensional facial features. He was carefully building up layer upon layer of icing, working on other skulls while waiting for each layer to dry.

"Gabriel, that's amazing," I said as I watched him apply another layer of bright green to a diamond on one cheekbone.

"Just takes patience," he said. "That's ninety percent of most art."

"But the inspiration is the hardest part," I said.

"Not the hardest. Ideas are easy. Making them real...I said it took patience. I didn't say that wasn't hard."

Angela gave a tiny sigh, looking at her much simpler efforts. "Patience and talent. You have a gift."

"Well, he's a professional artist," Kris said.

"But even that is a matter of patience," Gabriel added. "Lots and lots of practice. Years of it."

Angela tilted her head. "You're an artist, and you came here to spend your free time making folk art?"

"To experiment. I've never tried this medium. And I can use these." He gestured toward his skulls. "A seasonal display with the art I have showing. That could be fun, right?" he asked Kris.

"Have to talk to the gallery owner, but she might go for it."

His answering smile was so warm, I wondered if he would actually stay with Kris. She had a solid head for business, something that could be very helpful for an artist. She was obviously fond of him, too, even if she was able to look at their relationship with cold, objective speculation. I found myself hoping Gabriel would stick around, at least for a while. Kris hadn't confided in me, but I suspected she had been through some hard times.

Gabriel finished the green and set the sculpted skull aside, then looked at me. "We'll need to provide you with appropriate attire for All Hallows' Eve. Are you and Kris about the same size?"

"More or less," Kris said.

"I have a plain black dress I thought I'd wear..."

Gabriel smiled, eyelids drooping slightly. "Plain will never do. You are like a fine gem; you deserve a setting that will complement you." He tilted his head, as if contemplating a blank canvas.

"I'm just going to be helping in the kitchen and the pantry," I said, suddenly self-conscious.

"Ah, but you are part of the masque. You must be properly dressed. Don't worry, we can find something for you."

Unnerved at being the object of his artistic evaluation, I picked up my purple icing bag. To my relief, he let the subject drop.

I glanced at Angela, wondering what she thought of this. "Are you doing anything for Halloween?"

"I usually go over to *Abuela's* and give out candy. She has trouble getting up, so it's hard for her to answer the door, but she loves to see the kids' costumes."

"Does she get a lot of trick-or-treaters?"

"Yeah. There are bunches of kids in her building. I wear a clown nose and a rainbow wig, and a polka-dot dress. They love it!"

I smiled, then glanced at Gabriel and Kris. They were apparently uninterested in trick-or-treaters and rainbow wigs. Gabriel was working on a new skull, and Kris was just finishing one.

Angela leaned back, sipping her cider and gazing at the skull memorializing her father. Tony's father, too. I wanted to know more about him, to ask when he had died, but that seemed intrusive. Leaving her to her thoughts, I picked up the violet icing again and contemplated my own white space.

There was room for a name across the forehead, but I felt reluctant to do it. Instead, I gave the skull a widow's peak in the form of a "V," then piped an "i" below it. "Vi," vertically, could be taken for design rather than lettering. I liked it.

A feeling of satisfaction filled me. The skull didn't look anything like Vi, really, but it reminded me of her. She had been pretty, ebullient, feminine. I still missed her.

I put the icing back in the center of the table and picked up my cup. It was empty.

"Anyone want more cider?" I asked, getting up.

Angela nodded and handed me her cup. Kris glanced up with a quick smile and a shake of the head. Gabriel kept on working.

"I'll set these over here," I told Angela, picking up her finished skull and mine of Vi. I moved them to the smaller table along with my clown skull, then took our cups into the kitchen where I walked around the tables, admiring everyone's work.

Dee's skull was a study in anatomy, with vivid colors creating shadows and details, somehow making the little skull more realistic despite the rainbow hues. Rosa had covered one skull in orange and yellow flowers and was starting on a second. Ramon's skulls reminded me of Mexican wrestling masks. Cherie's seat was empty; maybe she'd gone to the restroom.

A line of plates holding finished skulls sat on the counter. It was pretty easy to guess which ones were done by Julio or Andre: the works of art. The more amateur skulls were harder to peg. One was one violet and black, with flowers, dots, and crosses; another Egyptian-looking, the eyes filled in black that drew to a point at the outside edges of the face, and three black "X"s across the mouth, reminding me of the stitchings on a mummy.

I frowned at that one. Three "X"s meant poison. Was it some Goth thing? I'd have to ask Kris.

Turning to the work table, I saw both Julio and Andre wielding the icing bags with precision and beauty. Andre's skull was all light colors: yellow, pink, pale blue, and lavender; rows upon rows of tiny, uniform dots. Julio was creating a fantasy in orange latticework, worthy of a wedding cake. Beside him, on another plate, was what I suspected was a portrait of Vi, much better than mine.

I suddenly wanted to add decorated petit fours to the tearoom's offerings, but I knew Julio wouldn't have the time. Maybe I could hire someone part time, and offer them for special occasions. I'd have to ask Kris if we had room in the budget, since we were adding two seasonal part-timers already.

Turning to the break table, I saw that Margo's efforts were like mine: wobbly, sometimes blotchy, but improving. She sat frowning at a fresh skull, red icing in her hand.

Dale had covered one skull in astrological symbols, and was now working on a second one that was some kind of demon with red, uptilted eyes and green, twisted horns drawn on the skull top. He glanced up and I gave him a quick smile, then fetched the cider and headed back outside.

Dale hadn't mentioned his job application. I really must make a decision on that soon.

As I edged my way through the screen door with two full cups of cider, I saw Gabriel and Cherie talking over by the lilac bushes, voices hushed, faces intent. Kris was decorating a new skull in shades of black and lavender, studiously ignoring them.

Gabriel took one of Cherie's hands in his and placed something in it, covering it with his other hand, keeping hold while he spoke to her with an earnest expression. I leaned toward them slightly and the screen door slipped from my control, banging shut.

Everyone looked up at me. Cheeks burning, I turned my gaze to Angela, smiled, and joined her at the table, setting her cider before her.

"That's a nice skull," I said, avoiding looking toward the lilacs. Angela's skull had *"Abuelo"* on the forehead in careful letters. "Your grandfather?"

She nodded, then reached for her cider. I glanced up as Gabriel stepped onto the *portal*, a stray breeze lifting his hair away from his neck and making me think of male fashion models with their open necklines, all collarbone and smooth skin. He slid into his seat and picked up the bag of green icing. Kris looked at him, but said nothing. Gabriel began adding to the crisscross of lines on his current skull.

The screen door banged again. I glanced that way and saw Cherie's shadow in the kitchen through the screen.

None of my business, I reminded myself. I took a sip of cider, then returned my attention to the sugar skulls.

Emboldened by my success with the skull for Vi, I decided to make one for my dad. Staring at a blank skull on my plate, I wondered how to honor him. He had loved the outdoors, and skiing, and good wine and cheese. None of these suggested decorations that I could imagine using on a skull. I ended up going very simple, just his smile and a suggestion of hair.

At three-thirty, Julio made coffee, then brought around the tray of *pan de muerto* and suggested people start moving their finished skulls onto a single, clean plate for each person. Margo, who had warmed to the game as the day went on, needed two plates for her seven skulls. There were lots of crosses with elongated, pointed ends. A favorite image of hers, apparently.

Looking over the all the skulls, I was impressed. The skill levels varied, but everyone had done really creative work. A sudden desire to capture it all sent me darting upstairs for my camera.

"Does anyone mind if I take pictures?" I asked when I returned to the kitchen.

"Sure, go ahead," said Andre, picking up yet another blank skull. Beside him, Margo looked annoyed, but didn't say anything. I was beginning to think "annoyed" was her most common expression.

Since no one protested, I proceeded to photograph each plate of finished skulls in the kitchen, then went outside to document the plates that had accumulated not only on the small café table, but on the nearby benches as well.

"You don't mind, do you, Gabriel?" I asked belatedly. "I want to remember all this wonderful creativity."

"Of course not," he said.

"Just don't use them in an ad without getting permission," Kris added.

I looked at her, a little surprised by the remark, then realized she was thinking not of her own work, but of Gabriel's. He grinned.

"My business manager speaks," he said.

"Well..." Kris said, with a shrug.

Gabriel kissed her, disarming her. I turned back to the café table, hiding a smile.

9

AT FOUR, I DECIDED THERE MUST BE TEA, since I'd gone for Julio's coffee instead that morning. I brewed up some Wisteria White and offered it around. The decorating was winding down, and guests gathered their handiwork to go home. Plastic wrap, held above the plates by sections of paper-towel tubes, protected the skulls.

Angela was the first to say goodbye. "I have to get back to *Abuela's*, but this has been so nice. I had a really good time. Thank you for inviting me."

I smiled, and on impulse gave her a quick hug. "Thank you for coming, though it's Julio's party, not mine. Will you come and have tea with me next week? I'd like to talk more."

She nodded, smiling. "I'd like that, too."

"We'll compare calendars." I waved as she headed for her car, an older model Corolla.

Rosa and Ramon left soon thereafter, with Dee following. Dale and Margo took off, leaving me alone in the kitchen with Andre, who had started tidying up the counters. I realized I hadn't seen Cherie for a while. Maybe she'd gone home early.

"Where's Julio?" I asked.

"Showing his painting to Gabriel," Andre said, gathering used plates.

I stepped into the hall and found Julio, Gabriel, and Kris heading toward me. Gabriel was saying, "—got to have a portfolio together, that's number one. Take high-res photos of your best work and make high-quality prints. I can recommend a photographer if you want."

Julio nodded. "Thanks, man."

They shook hands as Kris took her coat off a hook and swung it around her shoulders. She gave me a hug, gave Julio a bigger one, and headed out with Gabriel, plates full of skulls in their hands.

Julio had collected the unused skulls—about two dozen—into a plastic box. Andre was putting leftover snacks into containers.

"I'll leave this for the staff, if that's OK," Julio told me, gesturing to the food.

"Sure, they'll make it go away," I said. "It was a great party, Julio. Thanks for including me."

"Thanks for letting us do it here," he said, grinning as he carried the ceramic insert of the slow-cooker to the dishwashing station. "Did you make a skull for Vi?"

"I did. Thank you, I'm really glad I got to do that."

"I did one, too. Want to put them in Violet?"

"Oh. Sure, why not?"

I fetched my skull from my plate and followed Julio up the hall and into Violet. When I saw the mantel I caught my breath.

A length of lace now covered the wood. On top of it sat the votive holder on its coaster, the prayer card, my vase of pansies, a garland of pink silk roses that ran the length of the mantel, and three decorated skulls propped against the chimney. I recognized Kris's black-and-lavender work and Rosa's yellow and orange marigolds. The third skull was pale blue and lavender with touches of yellow, very swirly.

"Who did that one?" I said softly, leaning forward to take a closer look.

"Dee," Julio said. "Here's mine."

He placed his skull to the right of Rosa's, then put a fresh candle in the votive holder and lit it. I swallowed. There was now no pretending that this was anything less than an *ofrenda*.

Slowly, I propped up my skull next to Dee's, then touched the lace.

"Rosa brought that," Julio said. "And the roses."

"They're lovely. She didn't have to go to such trouble. She hardly knew Vi."

"She's Vi's successor, though. She wants to honor her."

I let out my breath in a gentle sigh, looking up at the portrait. The candle's flame made shadows dance across Vi's face.

"This is why you wanted to decorate skulls," I said.

"Partly, yes."

Turning, I saw a hollow look on Julio's face—a look I knew well. He immediately changed his expression, reaching up to straighten the votive which was already perfectly straight.

"I miss her, too," I said. "I'm going to get a better light for the painting."

He met my gaze, eyebrows tightening with sorrow. "Thanks."

We left in silence, walking slowly back to the kitchen. Andre had put away all the food and was swapping out the kitchen trash.

"You don't have to do that!" I said.

He grinned. "It was full. Lot of paper plates gooped up with icing."

"We'll stick it in the dumpster," Julio said. "Can I leave the extra skulls here for now? And the leftover icing—it's all in the fridge."

"Sure," I said slowly. "Actually, I might do another skull or two."

"Have at it."

Julio tucked the box of skulls into a shelf under the counter, then grabbed his jacket and headed out with Andre and the trash. Silence fell over the house. I looked around the kitchen, which showed almost no signs of the creativity explosion. The slow-cooker was still on the counter; its insert was drying in the rack.

A satisfying day, all in all. As I thought about the *ofrenda* in Violet, it occurred to me that I wasn't quite finished.

I took out the box of blank skulls and grabbed a couple of paper plates from the stack of leftovers that was on the same shelf. I put a blank skull on a plate and gazed at it for a while, then poured myself a cup of Wisteria White. Fortified by the tea, I opened the fridge and chose a half-dozen colors of icing, then sat down at the break table to work.

I gave the skull pale blue hair, big brown eyes, and red lips, then drew a triple line of yellow dots along the jaw. It didn't really look like a necklace, but I knew what it represented: lemon agate heishi.

Setting that skull aside, I got a fresh one and gave it black hair with some stripes of white, brown eyes, and red lips. Realizing I needed more colors, I went back to the fridge, then I carefully crowned the hair with pink roses, and put a couple more on the cheeks for good measure.

The third skull took a little more thought. I decided an abstract design would serve best. I gave it black hair and brown eyes, then used green, blue, and violet to make blocks of color on the cheeks and forehead. My lines were a little shaky, but that didn't matter. I knew what it stood for.

The fourth skull was the hardest of all. I didn't know the person it represented—much—and I certainly didn't like him. But I wanted to make a skull for him. It would give me closure. After staring at a blank skull for a while, I picked up the red icing.

Red is my least favorite color, but it was the right color to use. It represented anger and hate. Those were the things I remembered about the man who had died in my driveway—the man who had tried to kill me there. I made the eyes red and drew a down-turned mouth. With black, I added frowning eyebrows and a patch of hair.

I put the skulls on fresh plates: Sylvia Carruthers and Maria Garcia on one, Daniel and Tommy Swazo on another. Almost done.

I set a blank skull on a clean plate, and picked up the brown icing. Hair, eyes, brows, and mustache, all brown, and owing more than a little to Mr. Quentin's example. I didn't know if that was correct, but it felt right. A touch of pink to the mouth, just a line, because I didn't want it to look like lipstick, but I managed to give it a slight smile.

Not much to it, but something about the smile made it feel real. With the pale blue icing, I drew a "D" on the forehead.

"There you go, Captain," I said softly.

Setting down the icing, I looked out the kitchen window and realized it was dark. I put away the blank skulls and cleaned the table, then carried my skulls upstairs, where I arranged them on the low table by the front window.

I collected two candles and a box of matches from my suite and went back to the hall, where I placed the candles on either side of the skulls and lit them. Sitting on the sofa, I gazed at the five skulls.

Four of those people had died this year: two of them in the tearoom, one out in the driveway, and one in my Aunt Nat's driveway. To them, I sent a silent wish for peace.

To Captain Dusenberry, whose skull was in the center, I sent peace as well, and also gratitude. I considered him a friend, or perhaps even a family member, I realized to my surprise. I definitely felt affection for him.

Looking up at the pitched ceiling above me, I wondered what this space had looked like in his day. The walls hadn't changed that much. The dormer windows at the front and back of the upper hall were the same, just as the doors framed by lights on the ground floor beneath them were the same.

In my heart, I thought of it not as my house, but as *our* house.

Smiling at myself, I got up and went to my suite to find something for supper. As I stepped through the door, the hall chandelier behind me came on.

I turned to confirm it. Yes, the light was on—and a single crystal drop was swaying back and forth.

I smiled. "Good night, Captain."

October drew to a close in a frenetic rush. Willow called Monday morning to say she couldn't meet that day.

"The first, then?" I asked.

"That's Sunday. Monday would be better for me. Say, ten-thirty?"

"Got it." I added it to my calendar. "See you tomorrow, then. Are you sick of the tea food yet?"

"No, it's a nice break, especially when it's cold."

"Well, just one more week."

"Yes…for now."

Did that mean she wanted to do this again next year? I'd be willing. It had given our bottom line a nice boost.

I used the rest of my day off to get caught up on my personal life: laundry, housekeeping, bills, even cooking. I made a giant pan of lasagna in an attempt to duplicate Nonna Fiorello's secret recipe. The seasoning wasn't quite right, but I was closing in on it.

"Less rosemary," said Gina as we shared the results in my suite Monday evening.

"Really? I was wondering about less basil."

"No. More basil, if anything. Nonna loves basil."

I smiled. "How was the concert?"

"Good, but the chairs at the art museum were uncomfortable,

and we couldn't see the string quartet."

"Oh, when you said it was at the museum I thought it was the history museum. They have a nice auditorium."

"No such luck." Gina stabbed a forkful of salad. "How was the skull thing?"

"It was fun, and…quite satisfying."

Gina tilted her head. "Satisfying?"

"Yeah. It was a good thing to do. I made a skull for my dad, and for my mom and my uncle."

"Hm. Sounds morbid."

"It wasn't. If anything, it was the opposite."

"This whole Day of the Dead thing. I don't get it. Dancing, partying skeletons. It's weird."

"It's supposed to represent happy memories, I think. And help us think about the dead in positive ways, instead of continuing to grieve."

She fixed me with a speculative eye. "Is that what it's done for you?"

"I think it has," I said, nodding.

My plate was empty. I sipped my wine—a nice Malbec that Gina had brought—and thought about the skulls. "You want to see them?"

"Your skulls? Sure." She scooped up the last bite of her lasagna, grabbed her wine glass, and stood.

I led her out to the sitting area by the front window. I had put out fresh candles that morning—two tall, white votives in clear glass, the seven-day kind. I had also brought my other skulls up, except for the one that was in Violet.

"Impressive," Gina said, standing in front of the table. "These can't all be members of your family…."

"No. That's Dad, and that's Mom, and that's Uncle Stephen. Those are the only family members."

"Who are all the rest of these, then?"

"You can't guess?"

She frowned, gazing at the collection. She started to shake her head, then bent closer to look at the Captain's skull.

"D? D for Dusenberry?"

"Got it in one."

"But I don't have a clue about the rest."

I sat on the love seat. "This one is Sylvia Carruthers."

"Sylvia! Omigod. Then that yellow stuff is her necklace."

"Right. And this one is Maria Garcia."

Gina's eyes narrowed. "I don't know her."

"The Rose Guild. I told you about her. She was Julio and Rosa's grandmother."

"Oh, yes."

"And these are the Swazos. Daniel and Tommy."

"I never saw either of them. Just pictures on the news."

"Well, these don't look like them, any more than those look like Maria and Sylvia. This just represents how I think of them."

"You didn't do the opera singer. What was his name?"

"Victor Solano. He died at the Opera, and I didn't really know him."

"And Vi. You didn't do one for Vi."

"Yes, I did. It's downstairs in Violet. Several of us did skulls for her. Do you want to see?"

She turned and gave me a long look. "Yes," she said finally. "Let's get more wine, though."

We refilled our glasses and carried them downstairs. Gina stood looking silently at the *ofrenda* for a couple of minutes. Someone had added a small photograph of Vi in her tearoom server's outfit: lavender dress, white bibbed apron, lavender ribbon through her auburn curls. Smiling, of course. Vi had almost always smiled.

"It's a shrine," Gina said at last, in a quiet voice.

"Part of the tradition," I said. "It's called an *ofrenda*. I didn't plan it; it just sort of developed."

"What do the customers think?"

"No one's said anything. Of course, the skulls were only added yesterday." And the lace, and the roses…

"I want to add something. Is that OK?"

"Of course."

Gina put down her wine glass and reached up to the back of her neck, unfastening a chain that I hadn't noticed. She drew it out of the neckline of her red business suit dress. Dangling from the chain was a tiny, gold cross.

"That looks valuable," I said.

"Not terribly. It's plate, not solid." Gina slid the cross off of the chain, which she put into a pocket, and stood holding the cross in her palm and gazing at Vi's portrait.

"I'll always remember you fondly, *sorella*."

She laid the cross beside the votive, then picked up her glass and raised it in a silent toast. I joined her in drinking to Vi.

"Who made the other skulls?" she asked after a moment.

I told her, one by one. She nodded, looking thoughtful.

"This is more serious than I thought."

"Decorating sugar skulls?"

"Yes. I wish I had come, now."

"There are some skulls and icing left, if you'd like to make a couple. They're in the kitchen."

"Not tonight. I have to get up early. Maybe tomorrow night?"

"Sure."

We went back upstairs and finished the wine with dessert (dark chocolate mousse), after which Gina headed home. We promised to touch base about the skulls, though I suspected we'd both be too busy to get together.

That night I slept poorly, troubled by strange dreams full of symbols I couldn't interpret. When I woke, I didn't remember much: a hair-raising image of Gabriel drinking from Kris's mysterious new skull paperweight, and a vague memory of running around trying to get rid of vampires, but instead of a cross all I had to wave at them was an ankh.

As I was going through my photos of the sugar skulls and mulling over these delightful recollections, Kris came in with the morning's mail. "No boxes, hooray!" she said, handing me a short stack of business envelopes. "There's a letter from *New Mexico Magazine*. Maybe they want to do a feature on us."

I glanced at it, then set the mail aside. "Kris?"

She paused in the pass-through between our offices, looking back. "Yes?"

"Grab some tea and sit down. I want to talk."

She blinked, then did as I asked, leaving her own larger stack of mail on her desk. Stirring a spoonful of sugar into her favorite black corset cup, she avoided my gaze.

"I've been thinking about the skull."

That made her look up, with a chuckle. "Which one?"

"The one you got in the mail."

"Oh. I took it home."

"That's not what I'm worried about. I'm worried that you got it at all. Remember the card with the skull and crossbones that someone left at the art show?"

She shrugged. "It didn't mean anything."

"Things that don't mean anything by themselves can mean something when they're added together. Remember the black widow in your teacup at the planning meeting?"

She looked up at me, paying attention now. "It was just a joke."

"Maybe. Or maybe it was a warning."

I turned my flatscreen monitor so she could see the picture I'd taken of two sugar skulls, both Egyptian in style, one with three "X"s for a mouth. "I don't know who made this," I said. "Do you?"

She shook her head. "I didn't see it at the party."

"Someone in your group has poison on their mind."

"Or just death," she said, a trifle defensively. "Most Goths think about death a lot."

"I think this is more specific," I said.

"This is part of our culture, Ellen. We talk about this stuff a *lot*. It doesn't mean we're homicidal."

"It doesn't mean you're immune, either."

She leaned back in the guest chair and crossed her arms. "Well, there's nothing I can do about it. I don't know who's behind these little messages. It could be more than one person."

"I'd like you to talk to Gabriel about it," I said, "and I'd like you both to consider canceling your Halloween party."

"We can't do that! We've been planning it for months!"

"Kris—"

"People are making costumes. They've spent a lot of money. This is our biggest thing of the year!"

"But is it worth the risk? If someone is really making threats, and might carry them through?"

Kris set her jaw stubbornly. "I know what Gabriel will say. He'd never cancel."

"Then do you mind if I consult the police?"

Her eyes flashed. "And have them crawling around during the

party? No!"

"I just want to ask them to check that box that the skull came in for fingerprints. You did keep it?"

She was still. "Actually, no. I tossed it."

"Well, maybe they could check the skull."

"Gabriel and I have been messing with it. They probably wouldn't find anyone else's prints, at this point."

I sighed. "I don't suppose you still have the card from the art show."

She shook her head. I didn't ask about the black widow. I remembered seeing her throw it away.

"Look," she said, "print that picture out, and I'll ask around and find out who made that skull. OK?"

"All right." I sent it to the printer, but I wasn't satisfied. "Let me know who it was, please."

She nodded, accepted the printed page, and retreated to her office with her teacup. I turned my monitor back around and looked at the skulls. One with "XXX" for a mouth. The other had an upside-down ankh on its forehead.

I glanced toward Kris's office. Had she noticed that?

The week was nutty busy. Willow's tours were scheduled every day, with extras on Wednesday, Thursday, and Friday. The waiting list was a yard long. If we could have swung it, we would have crammed in a couple more, but we were stretched to our limits as it was.

The one good thing about this was that I didn't have time to be unhappy about how little of Tony I was seeing. We talked on the phone most evenings, but phone conversations had never been our strong suit. Too many long silences. We did better in person.

The night before Halloween, he called late. I was getting ready for bed, and would have let any other caller go to voicemail, but I spat out my toothpaste and snatched up my phone.

"Tony! Hi!"

"Hi, gorgeous. Want to go to dinner tomorrow night?"

"Tomorrow?"

"Yeah. We just wrapped up the case."

"Oh, that's great! Congratulations!"

"So I'm finally free for a real date. How about The Old House?"

"Oh, Tony, I can't—not tomorrow. It's Halloween."

"And you're planning to go trick-or-treating?"

"I've got a private party in the tearoom. What about the night after?"

Long silence. *Dammit.*

"Yeah, OK," he said, sounding disappointed. "Seven?"

"Seven would be great. I'm sorry—"

"Don't be sorry. We've got a plan."

"Right. Yes." I tried to banish insecurity.

"Can't wait to see you, babe," he said, in a voice that sent a zing to my loins.

"Me neither. Lo—looking forward to it!"

Dead air.

Had I really almost said, "Love you?"

Heart pounding, I put my phone aside and carefully applied fresh toothpaste to my brush.

10

HALLOWEEN STARTED WITH THE SMELL of *pan de muerto* rising from the kitchen to haunt the upper story. I had been good all week and refrained from having any *pan*, especially because of the lasagna, but that morning the smell had my mouth watering before I got out of bed and I caved. As soon as I had tea brewing and was dressed for work, I went down to the kitchen to beg for bread.

Julio was just removing a batch from the oven. He saw me and grinned. "Give me a minute. I need to sugar them."

"Can I help?"

"Yeah, put that next batch in."

I carried two big sheets of *pan* to the oven while Julio plied the sugar shaker. Ramon arrived and Julio set him to making the "bone" decorations for yet another batch.

"Lots of *pan* today," I said.

"We've got Kris's party on top of two tours on top of a full house," Julio said. "You know we're booked solid today, right? Plus people will probably want to buy some to take home. We sold three dozen over the counter yesterday."

I gave Julio a big smooch on the cheek. "You're my hero."

He glowered at me, but I caught him smiling. He slid two pieces of hot *pan* onto a plate and held it out to me. "Get out of here if you don't want to be put to work making finger bones."

"Julio?"

He looked up, and I licked my lips. "Could you make sure no one but you handles the food and drink for tonight?"

"They're bringing their own booze," he said.

"Well, I mean those vodka shots, especially. And all the food."

105

He frowned. "You expecting trouble?"

I gave a helpless shrug. The truth was, I was still worried. Kris hadn't said anything about the skull photos, and her mood through the week had been more bristly than normal. I knew she would dismiss my concerns if I brought them up again.

"It's Halloween," I said. "I just don't want any pranks to ruin the party."

"Sure," he said, frowning thoughtfully.

"Thanks."

I beat it upstairs and hid in my suite to gobble my bread and tea. By the time I came out, Kris was there. All black, today: a clingy knit dress and knee-high suede boots that were much better suited to the chilly, breezy weather than my dress. In honor of the day I had unearthed an orange chiffon number, vaguely Audrey-Hepburnish, that I'd worn as a bridesmaid a couple of years earlier, just before my father had died. Together, Kris and I looked like a page out of one of those magazines you see by the checkout at the grocery store.

"Happy Halloween," I told her.

She gave me a wry smile. "Thanks."

"Do you need to leave early?"

"Actually I'm going to stay. I brought my gown, and one for you." She nodded toward a garment bag hanging on the door of the closet behind her desk. "I'll be helping with the decorations before I change. Is there tea?"

I nodded. "I'll get you a cup."

From then on it was pretty much non-stop until we closed. We had discontinued regular reservations after three o'clock, and the last tour group would come in at four, so the house should be empty by six, which was when Gabriel planned to arrive.

Dee had wanted all the servers to wear *calavera* makeup for Halloween, but I'd said no. Her second choice was cat's ears, which I permitted. Rosa and Iz went along, donning pairs of black, pointy ears that blended with their hair. Dee wore white ears, along with penciled-on whiskers which I chose to ignore. She offered me a pair of striped ears, but I declined. I was in Proprietress mode and didn't think the cat ears were suitable. Besides, they clashed with my dress.

I was on my feet most of the day, and spent a lot of it in the gift shop. I happened to be there when Willow's second group of the day—the last scheduled tour, hallelujah—arrived for their tea.

Several of the customers that day had come in costume, but nothing approached the glory that blew through the front door in Willow's wake: the Bird Woman, in full Wicked Witch of the West regalia, including bright green skin. She had on red-and-white striped stockings, a pointed hat a good two feet tall, a black cape that threatened to drag the umbrella stand down the hall after her, and she carried a really quite excellent prop broom. As the door closed behind the group she spotted me standing in the doorway to the gift shop and uttered a shrill cackle that silenced every conversation in the tearoom.

"I'll get you, my pretty! And your little dog, too!"

"What an amazing costume," I said, gently herding the Bird Woman down the hall after the tour group. "Do come in, your tea is waiting. May I hang up your cape?"

She agreed to this, for which I breathed silent thanks as I hung it on one of the hooks in the hall. This was her fourth—no, fifth?—time taking the tour. Multiple visits to the tearoom in a month were not unusual for the Bird Woman, but this had to reflect her continued interest in Mr. Quentin. In a state of mild trepidation, I went upstairs to alert him.

"They're here," I said. "Last time."

He consulted his watch, then nodded and smiled. "It has been a pleasure," he said.

After making sure he had everything he needed, I went back to the kitchen, where Julio was switching over to preparing food for Gabriel's party. Ramon had gone home to change and collect his guitar. Mick was at his station, keeping the china at bay. With everything there under control, I returned to the gift shop, where I oversaw the cash register while the servers tended to the last few customers of the day.

"I love your tribute to Miss Benning," said an older woman who had been sitting in Violet with a couple of friends, as she paid for her tea and a half-dozen *pan* to go.

"Oh—thank you," I said.

"Such a lovely voice. Such a tragic loss."

"Yes."

Two other groups departed, leaving only the tour group

remaining. I turned the front door sign around to "CLOSED" and locked it, then went upstairs. Mr. Quentin was just picking up his rifle, and gave me a precise nod as he squared his shoulders and headed down to the dining parlor.

I stepped into Kris's office. "All clear except for Willow's group. I've locked up."

She nodded. "I'll do the receipts. Gabriel should be here in half an hour. Are you going to change now?"

I glanced at my orange chiffon, feeling slightly reluctant to put on the quasi-medieval, floor-length black gown that Kris had brought for me to wear during the party. It *was* chilly, though, and the velvet would be much warmer.

"Might as well," I said.

"I'll lace it up for you," Kris said, following me across to my suite, where the gown was hanging in my closet, silently arguing with my collection of Victorian styles.

Actually, I thought as I moved it from the closet to one of the posts of my canopy bed, it fit more with my bedroom décor than the Victorian dresses. My suite was more Renaissance; the Victoriana lived downstairs in the tearoom.

"Underdress first," Kris said, reaching beneath the black velvet to extract a swath of shimmering gold. The fabric was light and silky but opaque, a dark gold with an almost-metallic sheen. She gathered it up while I took off my chiffon. I stepped out of my shoes, and Kris slipped the underdress over my head. It slid coolly over my arms and shoulders, falling to brush my ankles. The sleeves were long and close-fitting, with points that came down past my wrists.

"Now the gown. You might want to put the slippers on first."

I stowed my work pumps in the closet and took out the black velvet slippers, embellished with a pair of gold Celtic knotwork pins, that Kris had helped me find for the occasion. The gown was hers, but we didn't wear the same size shoes, so I had sprung for the slippers and Kris had provided the pins from her jewelry collection.

Properly shod, I held out my arms and Kris slid the sleeves onto them. The velvet was rich and warm. I stood still while Kris tightened the lacing in the back, which started at the waist and went up to the neck.

"Not too tight," I said.

"No, but if it's loose you'll be uncomfortable."

"How do you manage to get in and out of this by yourself?"

"I'm not usually by myself," Kris said, and left the rest to my imagination.

After a few minutes of tugging and tucking, she pronounced me dressed, except for the hair. I took down the Gibson-girl style and brushed it out, then Kris tied a gold ribbon that matched the underdress around my forehead. A small, jeweled pin sat centered over my brow. My phone fit into a clever pocket in one of the sleeves that Kris showed me.

"Oh, and the kirtle." She produced a length of gorgeous brocaded trim, gleaming with gold thread in a knotwork design, and tied it low around my hips, with the ends dangling in front.

"Perfect," Kris declared, and stood me in front of my full-length mirror.

A fairy-tale lady gazed back at me: not a princess, but a woman of warmth and mystery. The simple hairstyle made my eyes look big. Instinctively, I raised my chin and straightened my shoulders.

"Do you need help getting into yours?" I asked.

"Not yet. I'm going to help decorate first."

We left my suite just as Mr. Quentin was collecting his belongings. He paused to admire my attire as Kris ducked back into her office to collect her decorations.

"We are stepping even farther back in time, I see," he said.

"It's for a private party," I said.

"You look very fine."

"Thanks. How did the talk go?"

"Pretty well. That witch was a little unnerving. She looked familiar. Not like Margaret Hamilton, but like I've seen her before."

"You have," I said. "She's a regular customer, and she took the tour more than once."

"Ah. That accounts for it."

Briefly, I struggled with myself. The Bird Woman would have wanted me to remind him of her phone number, but with the memory of her witch costume uppermost in his mind, it might not be the best timing. Before I could resolve the question, Mr. Quentin made it moot by departing.

Kris emerged with a shoulder bag and a small rolling suitcase, and we went downstairs. She headed into the main parlor and I paused in the hall, waiting for Willow who was herding her stragglers out of the dining parlor. Rosa stood at the front door, seeing the tour party out and listening to the Bird Woman, who had buttonholed her.

I looked at Willow. "Congratulations. The tours were a huge success."

She smiled, taking her coat off a hook. "Same to you."

"I bet you're looking forward to a break."

"I am. And also to exploring Hidalgo Plaza with you." She put on her gloves. "Have a wonderful evening. You look splendid."

"Thanks."

I watched her go up the hall, but not feeling inclined to face the Wicked Bird Woman of the West, who was still talking Rosa's ear off, I didn't accompany her. Instead I retreated to the pantry. Dee passed through with a tray full of china from the tour group. Grabbing another tray, I went into the dining parlor and gathered the rest of the china, being careful of my gown.

"Let me do that!" Dee said, returning.

"Don't you need to change?"

"It won't take me long."

She shooed me out, and I wandered into the main parlor to help Kris. She had her suitcase open on the piano bench and was removing large pieces of gorgeous fabric: brocade, jacquard, silk. My inner dressmaker drooled.

"Shall I start taking out the knickknacks?" I asked.

"Sure. But leave the tributes to Vi. Gabriel wants to see them."

I nodded, and began collecting ornaments from the alcoves in the main parlor. Vases, statuettes, table lamps, and lace were all to be banished, along with the low tables and the smaller chairs, which would line the main hall and provide places for the guests to wait for their turn to go through the seven chambers. Fortunately, the hall was wide enough to accommodate the furniture without violating fire code.

Rosa stepped into the parlor. "You look beautiful! Do you want me to help?"

"No, I can manage, and you already stayed late. Thanks for listening to Mrs. Olavssen. Did she drive you crazy?"

A slightly pained expression crossed Rosa's face, then she shook her head. "I think she's just lonely, you know? She was talking about going to the mall to scare the kids trick-or-treating."

And I bet she will, too.

I thanked Rosa again and sent her home. With my arms full of Victoriana, I made my way slowly upstairs, careful not to trip on my long skirt. I set my burdens on the credenza in Kris's office, then collected a couple of empty boxes for the next batch.

Dale and Cherie arrived and started moving the small furniture while I continued to gather the Victorian décor. I was beginning to feel amazed at just how much of it there was. It had accumulated gradually over the last few months.

As I was starting up the stairs with a full box, Cherie stopped me. "Here, this will help." She caught up the sides of my skirt and tucked them into my belt, raising the front hem several inches above the floor. "Now you won't have to worry about tripping."

"Thanks," I said, heading upstairs with an easier step.

When I returned, Gabriel had arrived. I found him closing the drapes over the windows in the main parlor. He paused to admire my dress, smiling appreciatively.

"Now *that* looks magnificent. You should always wear your hair down."

I gave a nervous laugh. "Thanks."

Over the next hour, the tearoom was gradually transformed from its customary cozy Victorian norm into an eerie, quasi-Gothic labyrinth. Kris's fabrics draped cleverly from the picture-rails to suggest high walls, passages, and arches, and defined the colors of the "chambers." Gabriel had brought a multitude of folding stools that stood four feet high and took up very little space. Some became stands for the colored glass lanterns in each of the chambers, while others were topped with trays to hold the platters of food that Julio was preparing.

The dining parlor was the designated beverage room. Here, too, the lace was banished in favor of a brocade tablecloth and more of the candle lanterns. There was a giant, shallow steel bowl in which a smaller bowl had been frozen, with an inch-thick layer of ice between them. *That* was a nifty trick and I wondered who had done it; it must have taken a big freezer. The inner bowl held a chilled, non-alcoholic punch, with a pear cider base. Another bowl that looked very much like a cauldron sat on a rack over a trio of tea-lights, not yet lit. It was destined, Kris told me, to hold mulled wine, which was heating in the kitchen.

In between these two, centered on the dining table beneath the chandelier, was an incongruous bit of Victoriana. It looked like an oddly-shaped epergne, or an elaborate lemonade server, comprising a silver footed stand holding a beautiful glass jar with four little faucets around the sides. It was filled with ice and water.

"Pretty fancy water dispenser," I said to Kris as we set out two dozen gorgeous glass goblets etched with filigree designs.

"It's a fountain. For the absinthe," she said, laying out a row of tiny, silver, slotted spatulas.

"I thought there wasn't going to be absinthe."

"Cherie insisted. But the drink at the end is still cinnamon schnapps."

She brought out an ornate silver bowl supported by three winged fairies, filled it with lump sugar, and set a pair of tongs shaped like bird's claws on top.

"The sugar is for the absinthe?" I asked.

Kris looked at me, tilting her head. "You've never had it?"

"No."

She picked up one of the goblets and pointed to where the etched design stopped, about an inch above the bottom of the bowl. "Fill with absinthe up to here. Then lay a spoon over it." She picked up one of the little spatulas and set it across the top of the goblet, then placed the whole under one of the spigots of the fountain. "Sugar on top, and trickle water through until the sugar dissolves and the glass is full."

"Oh," I said, nodding. "Who filled it?"

Her head snapped up and her eyes narrowed. "I did. I brought the sugar cubes too."

I nodded and smiled, though my brain was busy imagining ways that the sugar, or any of the open liquor bottles, for that matter, could be compromised.

"Want to try it?" Kris said.

"I do, but I'd better not tonight. The dress is enough of a challenge."

Her eyes narrowed in amusement as she returned the spatula-spoon and the goblet to their places. I heard the back door open and went out to see who had arrived.

Ramon, in black jeans and a long-sleeved black T-shirt, stood holding the door open for Margo, whose arms were full of shopping bags. She, too, was in all black with jeans. I started to feel like I was surrounded by stage crew. In a way, I supposed it was true.

"That wind sucks," Margo announced as Ramon closed the door behind her.

"Don't you mean it blows?" Ramon said with a deadpan expression.

That made me laugh despite my concerns. Margo raised her chin and headed into the dining parlor. The joke lessened my pique that Ramon was allowed to wear blacks when I had to dress up. This vanished altogether when Gabriel came down the hall toward us.

"There you are!" he said to Ramon. "I have your houpelande in the restroom."

Ramon held his guitar case out to me. "Could you watch this for a minute?"

"Why don't I put it by the stairs?"

"Sure. Thanks."

Dale had already set up a discreet microphone and a brocade-draped folding chair against the south wall near the foot of the staircase, and Gabriel had brought his small mic to amplify my mantel clock in the main parlor. Dale had magically hooked up both to the house stereo. Point in his favor, if I wound up offering him a job. Someone who knew his way around a sound system would definitely be an asset.

I set Ramon's guitar case on the floor beside the draped chair, then peeked into the main parlor. Draperies formed a tunnel from the hall to the center of the room, where four archways gave access to four of the colored chambers. The orientation was not that different from the normal arrangement of the alcoves, but the atmosphere was completely changed. Even with the canister lights still on—and they'd be off during the party—the chambers felt mysterious.

Lily was now swathed in white, with glints of silver here and there. Next to it, Jonquil was draped in orange. Iris was now lush violet, with Kris's "Death's Head" skull placed defiantly on top of the piano.

Rose was draped entirely in black. I stepped in, and noted that Gabriel had moved the mantel clock from the center of the mantelpiece to the end that was part of Rose. It was just visible past the edge of the drapery passage connecting the two chambers. The candle lanterns, not yet lit, were very red. A black brocade drapery arch framed the door into the dining parlor, which was usually kept locked but was open for this party.

Hearing a step, I turned to find Kris looking in. She smiled.

"What do you think?"

"Very effective. I wonder why Poe didn't have a yellow chamber, though."

Kris shrugged. "Or why he had both purple and violet, but not indigo. There are lots of theories, but they're really just blowing smoke. Poe didn't say, so we'll never know."

The sound of Ramon's guitar being tuned wafted in from the hallway, muted by all the cloth.

"Why is Iris the violet chamber, instead of Violet?" I asked.

"Because of the sequence," Kris said. "The violet chamber is next-to-last, and we wanted Rose to be the black one."

"We couldn't have them east-to-west, unfortunately," Gabriel said, joining us, "but that's a minor detail. Where's Dee?"

"Helping Julio," Kris said.

"I've got her costume, and I need to do her face." Gabriel turned to me. "I don't suppose you have a vanity in the house?"

"No, but there's my bathroom."

"Excellent! If you don't mind?"

"Just let me tidy it up a little."

I hurried upstairs to make my suite presentable and lock up my purse. It wasn't that I distrusted Gabriel, but this way I wouldn't worry if I was called back downstairs. There were already people I didn't know well in the house, and soon there'd be a lot more.

Dee came up, still wearing her lavender dress and the cat's ears. She had taken off her apron.

"Gabriel said I should change up here."

"Yes, come on in."

"He doesn't want anyone to see the costume underneath until

midnight," she added. "Wow, your bed is beautiful!"

"It is indeed," Gabriel said, coming in behind her with a garment bag over his arm. "So you are a Goth at heart!"

"I wouldn't go that far," I said. "It's probably got too many colors to be Goth."

"But they're the right colors. Jewel-tones, and the brocades are rich." He stroked a curve of the bed's drapery. "Very elegant. And those candlesticks are magnificent!" He gestured to the two carved wooden candle stands, four feet high, that flanked my bed.

"Thanks. They were a gift."

"May we have them downstairs? In the dining parlor?"

"Oh—I guess so."

"You really do shine in this setting," he added, smiling at me as he hung the garment bag from one of the bed posts. "How shallow of us all to assume you only cared for Victorian. Dee, you can start by washing off the whiskers."

"Oh!" She put a hand to her cheek, then pulled off the cat's ears. "Sorry, I forgot!"

"I'd have you wash your face anyway. I need a clean canvas."

Gabriel set a tackle box on my dresser and opened it to reveal a rather impressive makeup kit. The sight took me back to my theatre days in high school.

I led Dee to the bathroom and returned to find Gabriel poking through the tackle box, taking out brushes. "So you're going to paint her face?"

"Yes. She'll wear a veil over it until midnight."

"Are you planning to photograph your work?"

He flashed me a smile. "Oh, yes. It will be documented."

Dee came out, rubbing her face with a towel. Gabriel opened the garment bag and removed a length of pale, shimmering fabric, which he handed to her. He turned to me as she headed back into the bathroom.

"Would you mind making sure no one comes in? I don't want the surprise to be spoiled."

"Not at all," I said.

He moved to the head of the bed and put a hand on one of the carved candle pillars that Tony had given me. "Maybe we could move these while she's changing."

"Sure."

I collected the one from the other side, and we took them down to the dining parlor, where Margo was setting out bottles of wine.

"Hello, Margo, love. Drinks under control?"

Margo started, then nodded, going back to the bottles. Gabriel placed his candle stand beside the fireplace, then frowned.

"On second thought," Gabriel said, gazing around, "it's going to be crowded in here. These might be better by the windows."

"Yes," I said, relieved that they'd be in a place where they were less likely to be knocked over. I was pretty sure they were indestructible, but the candles were a potential fire hazard. The two windows in the north wall were recessed enough, due to the thick adobe walls, that the candlesticks should be safe.

As we headed back to the stairs, we found Ramon tuning his guitar, resplendent in a blue velvet tunic with wide sleeves that had zig-zag edges. So much for his escaping the dress-up.

I double-checked that he wasn't blocking access to the stairs, then followed Gabriel back to my suite. Dee's voice called from the bathroom.

"Is it safe to come out?" she called.

Gabriel turned to me with a slow smile. "Can you keep a secret, my lady?"

"Of course."

"Then I'd like you to watch. Yes, come on out," he called.

I had already decided to stay and chaperone Dee. She was over twenty-one, but just barely, and Gabriel's charm was so powerful.

She emerged, hair pulled back into a bun, and I gasped. She wore a skin-tight bodysuit, silvery-colored, that was painted with an exquisite rendering of a skeleton. It was not like commercial skeleton suits that I'd seen, white bones on a black background. This was all shadow and shade. The only part of the fabric that had no paint was the bones themselves. Gabriel had used shading to create a background and the details, but left the majority of the "bones" unpainted, which made them look ethereal. He had created the illusion of a heart inside the chest cavity, the only touch of red in the piece. It was eerie and exquisite and disturbing.

"Do you like it?" he asked.

"It's marvelous!" I said. "I was expecting a shroud."

"The story describes a shroud, yes, and we have one." He reached for the garment bag and took out a cloud of pale pink, lacy gauze, which he draped around Dee. "Like so."

It suggested a shroud, though the color was odd. The skeleton painting glowed through it, looking even more ghostly.

"Pink?" I asked.

"Yes. You'll see."

"Well, the skeleton is amazing!"

"Thank you. Please keep it to yourself. Not even Kris has seen it yet."

"I will."

"Good." He took the shroud off of Dee again and tossed it onto my bed. "And now, the face."

Never mind chaperonage; I was delighted to watch Gabriel at work. We all crowded into my bathroom, where the light was better. Gabriel gave Dee a wide hairband to put on, then commenced applying a white base for the makeup. With a half-dozen brushes, he added detail in shades of gray and cream and, to my surprise, silver. He matched the painting on the bodysuit perfectly, painting neck bones that continued the skeletal design. He magically hollowed Dee's cheeks and eye sockets, and made her face look incredibly skull-like. In addition to the gray shadows and sculpting, he added patches of the silver, dappled at random over the "bones" of her face.

Dee sat patiently, perfectly comfortable with Gabriel painting her face. Had she sat, or stood, the same way as he painted the bodysuit?

I glanced at him. So seductive. Had he made a pass at Dee? I hoped not, because if he'd been unfaithful to Kris I'd have to throttle him out of loyalty.

But Dee didn't show the agitation I would expect if she'd been seduced by this man. She was also pretty level-headed, and she was fond of Kris. She wouldn't try to steal Gabriel, I thought.

And Gabriel was completely intent on his work, not flirting with her at all. Maybe that was due to my presence, but he seemed all business. Focused. An artist at work, nothing more.

I had no idea how much time passed, but eventually I realized I was getting stiff from standing in the corner out of the way. I eased my weight from foot to foot, reluctant to leave.

Gabriel put down his brush. "That's good," he said, and dusted powder over the makeup to fix it.

From a small box, he produced a wig that he carefully placed on Dee's head, over the hairband. It was white with blood-red tips: a page-boy cut that ended right at her jawline. The effect, on top of the skeletal makeup, was striking.

"Good." He turned to me, radiating such a glow of delighted accomplishment that I almost gasped. "You like it?"

"It's magnificent," I said, nodding.

He beamed at me, then turned to clean his brushes. I now understood why every female who got near him—with the possible puzzling exception of Dee, who was busy admiring herself in the mirror—fell under his spell. He was attractive and sexy under normal circumstances, alluring when he flirted, and devastating when he was happy in his art.

Gabriel carefully cleaned his brushes and packed everything away, even wiping the counter clean. I watched, amazed at how unconscious he seemed of the impact he'd had on me, and equally amazed that Dee didn't seem affected.

We returned to my bedroom where Gabriel draped the shroud around Dee, pinning it in a few places to keep it from slipping. He took about a dozen photographs from various angles, then brought out a black, hooded cloak which completely concealed the "Red Death" costume. Inside the hood was a black veil with eyeholes, so that Dee's face was hidden. Because her eye sockets were black, her eyes seemed to float inside the hood. I couldn't decide if it looked more like a burqa or one of the Nazgûl.

"Comfortable?" Gabriel asked.

Dee nodded.

"Good." He gathered his makeup box and the garment bag, and we all went downstairs.

Dee slipped into the side hallway, heading for the kitchen. Gabriel, on his way to the back door, was buttonholed by a vision in blue—a naiad, perhaps—the watery gown clinging to her slender form, preposterously high spiked heels of a matching blue and glinting with blue gems, and a mask/headdress with a pair of slender horns curving upward through a forest of peacock feathers.

"Gabriel," said the vision, "You'd better get dressed."

I recognized the voice; it was Cherie.

Gabriel paused to bow. "I'm just on my way to do that."

He continued down the hall and I turned to Cherie, instinctively trying to distract her, though I wasn't quite sure why. "Do you have everything you need?"

She turned toward the gift shop, and I followed her in. Most of the shop was blocked off by screens, and Poppy had been converted into an entryway for both Hyacinth and Dahlia. Hyacinth, the smallest of the alcoves, was now the blue chamber.

"It's going to be dark, and my lamps are blue," Cherie said. "Could we get a little more light in here?"

I peeked into Hyacinth. Even without furniture, it would be cozy for more than three or four people.

"The fire will give some light," I said, looking at the coals in the grate. "Gabriel wants to keep them going, right?"

"Yes, but that won't reach people's faces," Cherie said. "We should be able to see each other's masks."

"I have something that might help."

I scurried upstairs to my suite and unplugged a small, stained glass lamp in the shape of a peacock's tail from my dresser. I took it down and installed it on the mantel. When I switched it on, it cast a blue-green light through the alcove.

"Oh, that's better!" Cherie said. "Thanks!"

"Why do people have to come through my chamber to get to yours?" said a female voice nearby. "He should have switched the order!"

"They would have had to go through anyway, on the way out," said a voice I recognized as Dale's. "You're not the only one, the other room has two crossovers."

I stepped out into Poppy and turned toward the east alcoves, where I saw draperies forming two arches side by side. The right hand one led to a short drapery passage passing the fireplace on the way toward Violet. The fire there was also down to coals. I'd have to build them all up. The left-hand arch showed a green drapery that angled left; I peeked around this and saw Margo and Dale standing in Dahlia, which was now the green chamber. Margo wore an emerald velour dress with black fur trim edging the low-cut bodice and a high, double-pointed princess hat from which floated a stiff black veil.

Hennin. The word came into my head, a ghost risen from my theatrical past. That was the name of the hat. Except that the points of a hennin were usually straight, and Margo's coiled like the horns of some African antelope.

As for the dress, I was pretty sure that the women who had worn the style hundreds of years ago did not have tattoos. Margo had several, most noticeably the raven erupting from her cleavage, the effect of which was exaggerated by the tightly-laced bodice.

Dale was trim and dashing in a rich purple brocade tunic over black tights. He smiled as I looked in.

"You look great, Ms. Rosings."

"Ellen, please," I said. "Thanks. So do you."

He made a swooping bow, taking off a beret-like hat with a big, purple ostrich feather. I couldn't help smiling.

"I'll get some more firewood," I said, backing out into the hall, where I almost ran into Kris, who was heading for the stairs. "Off to change?" I asked.

She nodded and slipped past Ramon, who had set his guitar aside on its stand and sat idly rubbing his fingers. His hair was down, and I saw that he was letting it grow out. It already brushed his shoulders.

"Will you be warm enough here?" I asked him.

"Should be, thanks, if the fires are going."

"I was just going to fetch some more wood."

"Want a hand?"

"Sure, if you don't mind."

We collected the two wood slings from their home in the kitchen. The smell of the food made my stomach growl. Julio was piping salmon mousse into a gazillion tiny profiteroles, so I left him alone. Once the party started I'd come beg for scraps.

At the back door, Ramon turned to me. "Let me bring it in. You don't want to get your dress dirty."

He took one of the slings and headed for the firewood stacked along the driveway. I waited, traded him the empty sling for the full one, then carried the wood to the rack in Hyacinth. Ramon was at the back door with the other sling when I got back. It took two more swaps to fill all four of the firewood racks.

"Could you bring in one more load?"

"Sure."

I put the other sling away, glancing at the kitchen clock. Twenty after eight. The party would begin at nine.

I added wood to both fires on the south side of the house, poking and coaxing them back to life. I eyed the drapery walls critically, decided they wouldn't be a danger as long as the screens were over the fireplaces, and checked that the fire extinguishers were in place.

The *ofrenda* in Violet was still on the mantel in all its splendor; Gabriel had been delighted with it and insisted it be left as it was. It had accumulated more mementos in the last few days. Someone had clipped Vi's photo and bio from the summer's opera program, which brought a lump to my throat. There was also a fresh piece of *pan* on a tiny, blue-and-white plate.

I checked the fires on the north side, finishing with Rose, now the black chamber. The fabrics here were not ornate, unlike those in the other chambers. No brocade, no rich textures, just black velvet. Even the floor had been covered with a black rug. All the furniture had been moved out, leaving Rose looking quite austere with only the candle lamps on their stands and a third stand for food.

Stepping through the draped archway into the dining parlor, I saw that the fire there was already rebuilt. A shadowy form rose up from beside it as the mantel clock began to chime, and my heart gave a heavy thump.

I TOOK AN INSTINCTIVE STEP BACK even as I realized who the black-draped figure was. "Dee!"

The clock's chime, amplified by the house sound system, ceased. "I thought you were going to be hiding until midnight," I added.

"I am," said the shadow. "I just thought I'd help with the fire. I'm not banished until eight."

"Well, thanks." I unloaded the last of the wood into the rack, then held out the sling. "Want to stash this back in the kitchen?"

"Sure."

She slunk across the hall as a knock fell on the front door. I started toward it, but Ramon was two steps ahead of me and had it open by the time I arrived. A flutter of white drifted in, followed by a festive figure in orange and black, carrying a large cardboard box.

"Are we late?" The lady in white peeled off her outer layer, which proved to be a gorgeous hooded cape. It was Gwyneth, looking more ethereally lovely than ever in translucent layers of iridescent white that shimmered and floated with every movement. Her golden hair was piled on her head, white gems twinkling among the curls.

"No, we're on time," said Roberto, shedding his black cloak to reveal a Spanish colonial style outfit in lush, variegated orange velvets.

"You both look marvelous," I said. "May I take your wraps? I can put them upstairs for safekeeping."

"Thank you," said Gwyneth, handing me a cool armful of white satin.

Roberto gave me his cloak with a smile of thanks, and proceeded to set the box on the floor and withdraw an airy construction of silver and gems, with shimmering, sheer ribbons and tiny white plumes trembling on the ends of wires. Gwyneth stood still while he lowered it onto her head, completing her magical outfit.

I hurried upstairs to lay the cloaks on the couch in my sitting area, and locked the door of my suite while I was there. As I turned back toward the stairs, I heard a low voice and froze.

"At least I'll be right next door, where I can keep an eye on you."

Kris. I looked toward her office. The door was closed, but I could see a light under it. She and Gabriel must be changing in there.

"Don't you trust me?" came Gabriel's voice, confirming my assumption.

"I trust you," Kris answered after a moment.

I trust him to be who he is.

Biting my lip, I tiptoed downstairs, avoiding the fourth step down, which squeaked. I glanced into the dining parlor, empty and silent, waiting for the party. Impulse made me step in and look up at the motionless chandelier, wondering what the captain would think of the pageant that would shortly unfold in his former home.

Julio came in to collect the cauldron. "Time to fill this," he said, offering me a box of matches. "Mind lighting the tea lights?"

"Not at all." I did so, then followed him to the kitchen.

Dee was at the break table, a glass of water with a straw in front of her, reading something on her cell phone. Julio poured the contents of a soup pot into the cauldron. Wine-scented steam, heavily laced with cinnamon and clove, wafted through the kitchen.

"Oh, that smells good!" I said.

"Have some. There's plenty."

"No, I'm being good tonight."

"Well, there's some cider on the stove if you want it," he offered.

He carried the cauldron back to the parlor, placed it on the stand over the tea lights, hung a ladle on its edge, and nodded approval.

"Food's ready," he said. "Should I start putting it out?"

"I think we should wait until the chamber minders are in place."

"You're not still worried about someone messing with food," he said, looking ready to be insulted.

"Just—it's best to be safe. Let me check with Gabriel."

With a small pang of trepidation, I started for the stairs. Kris came down as I reached them, and I waited at the foot, admiring her gown of flowing velvet, vaguely Grecian in style, such a dark violet that it almost looked black except when the light caught it. She wore a tiara of amethyst crystals in silver wire, a necklace of similar design, and her hair was caught back in a net of woven silver and violet thread to reveal earrings of two perfect polished amethyst drops. She carried a violet mask traced with silver filigree designs and glimmering with jewels in shades from lavender to concord grape.

"Wow!" I said. "You look incredible!"

"Thanks." She smiled, blushing slightly as she reached the hall. "Gabriel designed it."

At the sound of his name Gabriel appeared on the stairs, and this time I really gasped. He had answered my musing about the absence of yellow from Poe's color scheme: he was resplendent in gold, head to foot.

A small, golden circlet bound his brow. His honey-colored hair was loose over the shoulders of an amber velvet doublet. His legs looked amazing in…not tights, as I'd thought at first, but period-style hosen, made of knitted jacquard. Having worked on the costume crew of a production of *Romeo and Juliet* whose designer was an authenticity freak, I appreciated the work it took to make hosen fit without sagging. He wore a pair of bejeweled golden slippers and an elaborate, golden mask that I suspected he had sculpted himself. He was supposed to be Prince Prospero, but though the period was different, I couldn't help thinking of the Sun King.

His eyes gleamed through the mask as he came slowly down the steps, watching me take in his glory. "My lady approves?" he said.

"Very much," I answered, dropping a curtsy.

The trace of smugness in his voice diminished his attractiveness, but only slightly, and the sincerity of his "Thank you" made up for it. I was pleased to see him bow deeply over Kris's hand. He couldn't kiss it through the mask, but he made a good pantomime of it.

"Are the chamber guardians all here?" he asked.

"Yes," I said, glancing toward the front door and wondering where Roberto had stashed his box. I could hear him and Gwyneth talking in the main parlor.

"Good," Gabriel said. "Let's get them all together and do the walk-through."

Kris stepped toward the parlor. I went into the gift shop and poked my head into Hyacinth, where Cherie was adjusting the angle of the peacock lamp. "Gabriel wants everyone in the hall," I told her, then fetched Margo and Dale.

Gathered together, the seven chamber guardians made a gaudy display, probably the most colorful group of Goths ever seen. Gwyneth and Gabriel outshone the others, of course, the one white, the other golden. I couldn't help thinking what a stunning couple they must have been.

A lull fell in conversation as Gwyneth came toward Gabriel. Her pale gown and headdress trembled with each slow, small step. She had put on her half mask, so that I could see no facial expression except around her mouth, which was unsmiling. She stopped, facing Gabriel about three feet away, and slowly curtsied.

Gabriel bowed deeply to her. "You shine, White Lady."

She smiled at that, briefly, then turned looking for Roberto, who immediately stepped to her side. He shot a glance at Gabriel, then murmured something into Gwyneth's ear.

"My friends," Gabriel said, raising his voice but not shouting, "thank you for joining me. Let us tour the imperial suite and set the lamps alight!"

He led the way through the gift shop to Hyacinth. I followed at the end of the group, smiling a little at Gabriel's flair for the dramatic. Plainly he was getting into character.

Five people were the most that could fit into Hyacinth. I had to wait in Poppy along with Dale, Margo, and Kris, though we could peek through the curtained passage into the room.

"There should be no lights except the lanterns," Gabriel said, looking at my peacock lamp on the mantel.

"It'll be too dark in here without it," Cherie said.

"But there will be the lanterns, and the firelight." Gabriel leaned toward the passage to look at me. "Ellen? Could you turn out the overhead lights?"

I stepped out to do so. Muted light from the street came through the curtained windows of the gift shop, but as I returned to Poppy I saw that they didn't penetrate the draperies.

A small flame flared up, followed by a blue glow as Gabriel lit the two candle lanterns. He reached up to turn off the peacock lamp.

"I think it will be bright enough," he said. "Our eyes will adjust. Let's continue to the purple chamber."

Those of us waiting in Poppy stood back as they filed out. Margo and Dale gave the blue chamber a cursory glance, then hurried after the others. I stepped into Hyacinth and looked around. Gabriel was right; there was enough light, and though the monochrome lamplight was a bit off-putting, the firelight softened it. I glanced at the peacock, and noticed a sugar skull beside it, decorated with blue icing. Had Gabriel just put that there? I hadn't seen it before.

The others had all packed into Violet. I could have squeezed in, but chose to watch from the passage while Gabriel lit the lamps. Purple light flooded the chamber, casting looming shadows onto the draperies as the people moved. Probably exactly what Gabriel wanted, and at least in the purple light they looked more natural than in the blue. This room was also softened by firelight, and I spotted a sugar skull on the stand of one of the lamps.

Gabriel led the group through a passage along the back wall into Dahlia, now the green chamber. This room was darker, since the draped passage was between it and the fire. As the lamps were lit, everyone was washed in green light, and I suddenly thought of the Bird Woman's witch costume.

"I'll look like the Wizard of Oz," Margo remarked, clearly thinking along similar lines.

Gabriel bowed to her. "Guardian of the Emerald City."

Margo looked as if she didn't know whether to be flattered or offended. Biting my lip to keep from laughing, I followed the group back out through Poppy and into the hall. I remembered to glance over my shoulder and confirm that there was a sugar skull in Dahlia as well: also on a lamp stand.

Curious who was adding the skulls, I looked at Gabriel as I came into the hall, but he wasn't carrying anything but the matchbox. I examined each of the others, and noticed Dale carrying a black shoulder bag.

"Now to the other chambers," Gabriel said. "Lights off, again, please."

I dutifully switched out the lights in the main parlor, but hung back as Gabriel led the group through the short passage into the center of the room. Julio was coming up the hall.

"Are we a go for putting out the food?" he asked. "It's getting close to nine."

"Go ahead and put it out on that side," I said, waving toward the south half of the building.

Julio nodded and turned back toward the kitchen. As he passed the stairs I saw Ramon sit in his chair and pick up the guitar.

I hurried through the passage into the center of the main parlor and stood looking at the four arches, each giving onto one of the alcoves. The group had moved into Jonquil, and Gabriel was lighting the orange lamps. They made the chamber seem very bright, especially compared with the green chamber. This was partly due to a very shiny, metallic brocade that made up part of the draperies. As Gabriel blew out the match, I noticed Dale slide a sugar skull onto one of the stands.

When the party moved along the front of the house into Lily, a couple of them gave quiet exclamations of relief. Even without lighting, Lily glowed. Its drapery walls were all white, and when Gabriel struck a match I blinked at the brightness.

"A fitting setting for the White Lady," he said, and Gwyneth preened, smiling.

Dale waited for the others to leave before slipping a white sugar skull onto the stand beside a lamp. He caught me watching him and grinned. I peered at the skull, confirming that it was indeed decorated, though the icing was white on white.

"Your work?" I asked in a low voice.

He shook his head, still grinning.

We now passed through the center again, this time through two arches into the diagonally opposite Iris, which was the violet chamber. Voices hushed as we moved from the whiteness of Lily into the darker room. The fire crackled softly, concealed from the room but sending flickers of firelight into it from the short drapery passage. Gabriel lit two violet lamps, wakening glints of texture in the brocade walls. The lamps cast a violet glow over the Death's Head skull on the piano, the palest object in the room. I glanced around the group to see if anyone had taken note of it, but if they had they showed no reaction. Dale quietly placed a violet-iced sugar skull next to the Death's Head.

The mantel clock chimed, making me start. The others froze, listening to the three-quarter-hour bells. Exactly as in the story; Gabriel must be pleased by the response.

"It's a little loud," Cherie said into the silence that followed.

"That's necessary," Gabriel said. "People will be talking, and there will be the music."

Gabriel turned to Kris and stood gazing at her while the others murmured together. I watched, unable to see his expression, but sensing his appreciation in his body language. Kris's fair skin glowed in the lamplight, and her jewels glinted softly. She gazed back at him, head held high, regarding him as an equal.

The Dark Lady had won out over the White Lady. Was it because she demanded equality? Gwyneth was as feminine as one could get, but I wouldn't have called her strong. Kris's personality was a better match for Gabriel's.

All merely my opinion, and in fact, none of my business. If they hadn't been so focused on each other, I would have looked away, but they seemed unaware of me.

Behind me, someone coughed. I glanced over my shoulder, but couldn't tell who it had been.

"Come along," Gabriel said, stepping toward the fireplace.

The group moved through the short passage and into the final chamber, Rose. The muted light from the fire had nothing to catch on, here. Through the arch at the inner corner I could see across the center of the main parlor to Jonquil, and I realized that the arch wasn't needed; we would pass from here into the dining parlor. Why, then, had Gabriel included an arch into the black chamber?

To give glimpses of it from the other chambers, was all I could think of. A foreshadowing of what lay ahead. Brilliant, really.

Gabriel lit the two lamps, bathing the group in scarlet light. The velvet walls gave none of it back; we seemed to float in the blackness. Kris's, Dale's, and Margo's costumes all turned black; Roberto's became a dull blood-red, and Gwyneth's and Gabriel's blazed like rubies. I thought of Dee's makeup and sucked a sharp breath. The silver dappling would be bright red in this light, and shine like liquid! Her costume would light up into a red skeleton, and the pink "shroud" would glow scarlet. Gabriel's surprise was going to be even more spectacular than I'd thought.

Dale slowly placed a sugar skull beside the mantel clock. Attracted by his movement, Gabriel turned. "Is the clock's time correct?" he asked.

"I set it this morning," I said.

"Good. From here, I will show the revelers through to the tavern. Ellen, this door should be closed just before midnight. Can you see to it?"

I nodded. "Yes."

"Very good. And you will also welcome the revelers as they arrive at the front door. Only from nine until ten; the door should be locked at ten. "

"What if people are late?" Margo asked.

"They've been told. Ten o'clock, the doors are locked."

"The party starts at nine," Kris added. "An hour should be plenty of time for everyone to get here."

"Those who do not must take their chances outside," Gabriel said. I could hear the smile in his voice, and knew he was thinking of the Red Death. If he ever gave up painting, he would make a brilliant actor. So completely focused.

He led the way through the dining parlor and back to the hall. "Now it is time for us all to take our places. Please remain in your chambers until the last arrivals come through. Ellen, if you would pass through the chambers after you have locked the door at ten, that will be the signal that the guardians may move about freely."

I nodded, adding this to my mental list of duties. Greet guests, show them to Hyacinth (no more than four at a time, I thought), lock the door at ten, go through the chambers and let their guardians know the door was locked.

"Hall lights out, please," Gabriel said.

"I'll turn them out after the food is all in place," I said, as Julio scurried out of the gift shop and back toward the kitchen.

"Ah, yes. Thank you. And thank you, all of you, for making this fantasy a reality," Gabriel added, his voice full of warmth. "This night is one we will never forget."

They dispersed, heading to their chambers, and Julio came up the hall with a tray of deviled eggs. Holding out my hands, I met him between the parlor doorways.

"Which alcove?"

Julio set the tray in my hands with a grateful look. "Lily."

I carried the eggs there while Julio went back for another tray. Gwyneth had put on her silver-white half mask and was stepping back and forth in the alcove, deciding where to stand.

"That drape would make a nice background for you." I nodded toward a piece of jacquarded satin that softened the southwest corner.

"Good idea," she said, stepping in front of it, and thus out of the way of people entering the chamber. The food stand was in the southeast corner, out of the traffic pattern.

"Do you need anything?" I asked. "A glass of water?"

"Oh, thank you! That would be great."

I nodded. "Be right back."

Feeling it was only fair, I offered water to Roberto, Kris, and Gabriel as well, but they all declined. Kris, ever practical, pointed out that she was only a few steps from the dining parlor, where all the drinks were.

In the hall, I passed Julio with another tray of savories on my way to the kitchen, and again coming back with Gwyneth's water. Ramon plinked softly on his guitar, giving the tuning a final check. I offered water to the three in the south side of the house, then relieved Julio of another tray, this one filled with cheese tartlets. The smell made my mouth water.

"Iris," he said.

The food stand was by the northwest corner, and Kris stood next to it in front of the window, which was covered by a particularly luscious swath of brocade. She had donned her mask.

"You look splendid," I told her as I set the tartlets on the stand.

"Thanks." She smiled. "Here we go."

"Have fun," I said, giving her shoulder a squeeze before I went out to take my place by the front door. The bells that normally hung on the handle and warned the tearoom staff whenever someone entered had been removed at Gabriel's request, and were stashed in the gift shop. The lights above and beside the door had been covered with black cloth, leaving the hall in darkness except for the two candles beside Ramon.

Julio came out of the main parlor and joined me. "OK, all the food is out. Let me know when anything runs low."

"Right. Thanks, Julio."

He gave me an airy salute and headed down the hall. Ramon struck up a melody on the guitar. A moment later the front doorbell rang, and I opened it to three pale-faced women in black. I couldn't decide if they reminded me more of vampires, the three Fates, or perhaps the witches from *Macbeth*. I showed them to Hyacinth, where Cherie took them in charge as I returned to the door.

Those first three were the exception; most of the guests I welcomed over the next hour were masked. A few wore face paint instead. I recognized a familiar face—or chin—here and there, and one young man I knew by his gorgeous, waist-length hair. His costume was a splendid Georgian coat, but the mask of leaves made me think of him as a woodland spirit.

There were many amazing costumes. Most of them were black, but there were splashes of color, predominantly red and purple. Some were beautiful, some horrific, and all but a few must have taken many hours of work.

Gradually the house filled with guests, voices, and laughter. Candlelight flickered with the constant movement, and grotesque shadows danced against the walls and draperies. Ramon's music gradually got louder; he must have been nudging his amp. It got more energetic, too. A few people began to dance in the hall by the front door, where there was just enough room.

As I showed a pair of black-winged, corseted, vampire-toothed fairies to Hyacinth, the clock began chiming the top of the hour. Ramon continued playing through the melody, but stopped when the hour began to toll. The abrupt shift caught everyone's attention; conversations died as everyone stood still, perhaps silently counting the ten strikes, as I did.

As the last stroke faded away I felt a little prickle of dread, no doubt in response to how well Poe's Masque had been brought to life. Gabriel must be delighted.

The guitar broke the spell, gently easing back into the music. People began to talk and move. I turned to lock the front door, first opening it slightly to check whether any last minute arrivals were approaching. I saw no one; the street was lined with cars, and a sharp breeze had kicked up, blowing leaves around in the gutter. I shut the door and locked it, then went to Hyacinth.

"You're free," I told Cherie.

"Thank the gods!" she hurried out to the hall.

I paused to build up the fire, took note of the mostly-empty tray of stuffed mushrooms, then went around into Violet, where I found Dale chatting with one of the vampire fairies. I made eye contact with him but didn't interrupt. He nodded, and continued talking while I added wood to the fire.

Moving on to Dahlia, I found Margo frowning as she plucked at an edge of her veil in the light of the green lamps. "You're free to go," I told her.

"Thanks," she said, and walked out. I glanced at the food; a little less than half gone.

Crossing the hall, I saw Margo heading for the dining parlor. In Jonquil, Roberto, wearing a half mask of orange and gold that emphasized his goatee and a matching plumed velvet hat, was talking with the long-haired wood spirit. I smiled at him, glanced at the food, then continued into Lily.

Gwyneth stood sparkling in the center of a cluster of men. She turned to me, exclaiming, "Are we locked in?"

"Yes," I said. "You're free to move now."

"Oh, good! I want a drink so bad!"

"Let me bring you one," said a tall man cloaked in black with a demon-faced mask. "Absinthe?"

Gwyneth unleashed a tinkling laugh. "No, no! Champagne."

Roberto came into the room and stepped right past the demon, the orange ostrich plume of his hat brushing in the demon's face as he offered Gwyneth his arm. She took it, smiling with glee, and they walked out.

The tray that had held the eggs was completely empty. I picked it up and followed Gwyneth's disappointed admirers out. In the crossroads at the center of the parlor they all turned right, heading for the hall, while I passed into Iris.

The woodland spirit was here now, chatting with Kris and a couple of others, one of whom reminded me strongly of Maleficent. Kris looked up as I came in. She had a wine glass in her hand; someone must have brought her a drink.

"We're clear?" she asked.

"Yes."

"Thanks."

She continued her conversation. A few of the tartlets remained on the tray. I snagged one and popped it in my mouth as I passed by, then propped the empty egg tray on the wood rack while I built up the fire.

One other person was in Rose with Gabriel: a slender woman in an outfit that reminded me of Marie Antoinette, except her hair was black. I nodded to Gabriel and went to check the food. There were still quite a few of the salmon mousse puffs, which surprised me. Normally they went fast whenever we served them at an event. I picked one up and sniffed it, to make sure it smelled all right.

"They're fine," Gabriel said. "People just aren't hanging around in here very long."

I turned to look at him. He'd sounded amused.

"Your re-creation is too good," I said, gesturing toward the crimson lamps. "I hope you haven't been lonely." Since I'd touched the salmon puff, I popped it into my mouth, a little defiantly.

Gabriel chuckled. "Well, you're here to release me, right? No, I haven't been lonely, though people's reactions are interesting. I didn't expect that part of the story to be enacted. Normally these guys *like* dark rooms."

The inclination to avoid the black chamber was understandable. Just standing there for a few minutes made me feel a little oppressed.

"Maybe it's the red lights," I said.

He tilted his head, which created an odd illusion of his mask smiling. "Maybe. Or maybe the story is in everyone's head."

"That's what you want, right?" I said brightly. "I need to let Julio know the status of the food," I added, stepping toward the dining parlor.

"Lead on," Gabriel said with a grand gesture.

The "tavern" was full of people chatting and drinking. Great inroads had been made on a large platter of *pan de muerto* on the sideboard. I slipped through the crowd and crossed the hall, heading for the kitchen. Julio was just taking a fresh tray of tartlets out of the oven.

"Great timing," I said. "Iris is almost out of those. And Lily's completely out of eggs. I brought this back."

He took the tray from me, and I reported on the status of the rest of the food, then headed toward the restroom. Two women were waiting, and Cherie emerged as I got there.

"Much better," she said with a smile. "Now I need a drink."

Absinthe, no doubt. Deciding to go upstairs rather than wait in line, I followed her out. Ramon was putting his guitar on its stand as I reached the stairs.

"Break time?" I asked.

He nodded. "The smell of all that food is making me hungry."

"Me too. Julio will save us."

He grinned and headed for the kitchen. Leaving the chatter of the party behind as I went upstairs, I felt relieved. There was tension downstairs; maybe normal for the group, or maybe part of the plan for the evening, but it affected me. I took my time freshening up, and then took a moment to stand by the front window and look out at the street, the view that had been carefully shut out downstairs.

Still windy. Tree branches, mostly bare now, waved and danced in the night air, creating flickering shadows in the light of the streetlights. My tall votive candles burned steadily on the low table that had become my private *ofrenda*. I looked at each of the skulls in turn, silently wishing peace to the people they represented.

Distant music broke into my reverie; Ramon had started playing again. With a small pang of regret I turned toward the stairs. The party was probably all right for now, but I still felt I ought to keep an eye on things, especially the food.

That thought reminded me that I was hungry. I went down to the kitchen, where Julio (who had an uncanny knack for reading my mind about such things) handed me a plate of the savories.

"You missed dinner. I can heat up some soup if you want it."

"No, this will be fine. Did Ramon eat?"

"Yeah. You're the only one who hasn't."

I stuffed a mushroom into my face. "Mmm. Thank you, Julio!"

He smiled. "There's *pan* in the oven, and one more tray of mushrooms to bake. After that I might go home."

"Go now, if you want to. You've been here since the crack of dawn."

He shook his head. "I'll finish this. You've been up almost as long."

Knowing I couldn't win that argument, I slid onto a seat at the break table. Dee glanced up, eyes glinting in the depths of her hood.

"Did you get something to eat?" I asked her.

"I had a bite before I changed."

I nodded and ate a tartlet. Gorgonzola and caramelized onions. I allowed myself a small sigh of pleasure.

"How's it going out there?" Dee asked, putting down her phone.

"Fine so far. You should see the costumes!"

"I watched from the pantry earlier, until it started getting crowded."

"You're very patient."

She shrugged. "I have a good book. And the reaction will be worth the wait!"

"Gabriel did an amazing job," I said, nodding. "This whole thing really is Poe's story brought to life."

A gust of wind slapped at the windows, making everyone look up. Even Mick paused in washing glasses, despite his earbuds.

"Has Captain Dusenberry done anything interesting?" Dee asked.

"I doubt anyone would notice if he did," I said.

The clock, muffled by our distance from the house speakers, chimed. Dee tilted her head, listening.

"Is that the quarter hour?" She reached for her phone.

"Half hour."

"How can you tell?"

"The melody is slightly different each time. The top of the hour is the whole phrase, and the other quarters are parts of it."

Dee chuckled. "You know the most amazing things."

"Well, I grew up with that clock. I think my father taught me about the chimes."

My plate was empty. I stood and picked it up. "Do you want some cider?"

"No, thanks," Dee said. "I don't want to have to take all this off to go to the bathroom."

"I hope Gabriel's paying you."

"He paid me some for modeling," she said, confirming my suspicions. "He doesn't have a ton of money."

"Don't let him shortchange you."

She raised a shoulder in a shrug. "I'm learning stuff. It's interesting."

If she was smitten with the alluring Gabriel, she was hiding it well. I stepped over to hand my plate to Mick, glancing out the south window at the gyrating tree shadows outside before fetching myself a cup of cider and heading back to the party.

The guitar cut through the chatter of the guests, playing a waltz that sounded familiar. I edged my way through the now-crowded hall to get closer to Ramon. Between the shoulders of a tall and scantily-clad fairy and a stocky, bearded gentleman in a tuxedo and goat's horns, I saw a whirl of white near the front door.

The waltz was in a minor key, a classical piece. The white, as I got to where I could see better, turned out to be Gwyneth.

Gwyneth and Gabriel, to be more precise, waltzing in the small clear space near the entrance. They looked ghostly and beautiful.

To get a better view, I went up a couple of steps and sat on the stairs. Ramon glanced at me, but was busy with the waltz, which was fast and complicated. What was it? "Danse Macabre?" No, though that was also a waltz.

From my vantage I could see not only Gabriel and Gwyneth, but the people watching them from the sidelines, including the other "guardians." Kris, leaning against the doorway into the main parlor, was smiling slightly but I couldn't tell the mood behind the smile. Her half-mask hid her feelings from me.

Had Gabriel danced with her? I sure hoped so. If not, he'd better ask her next.

Roberto's mood was more obvious, despite his mask. Body language: he stood with arms crossed, feet planted, at the front of the audience, almost intruding on the dancers' space. Margo hovered in the doorway to the gift shop, swaying from foot to foot in time with the music, hands crossed over her bosom.

Cherie, in a wing chair against the side of the hall not far from Kris, was leaning forward to watch, a glass of something pale green in her hand. Dale lounged against the wall beside her chair, also with arms crossed but looking more relaxed than Roberto. Remembering the sugar skulls he'd added to the décor of the chambers, I resolved to ask him who had made them.

The music slowed to a finish, and Gabriel bowed deeply to

Gwyneth, who sank into a graceful curtsy. I stood and stepped up to Ramon's chair.

"What was that piece?" I asked over the applause.

Ramon flashed me a grin, picking up his water glass. "Masquerade."

Khachaturian, of course. "Perfect choice. Need more?" I asked as he drained the glass. He nodded and handed it to me.

Gabriel rose and, keeping hold of Gwyneth's hand, led her to where Roberto stood. "Lord Orange, I return the White Lady to you," he announced, bowing slightly, and laid Gwyneth's hand in Roberto's. Gwyneth looked both pleased and disappointed; her eyes followed Gabriel as he turned away and headed straight for Kris.

"My lady." He knelt before her, holding out his hands in a beseeching gesture. Kris's smile grew a little warmer as she laid her hands in his. He couldn't kiss them because of the mask; instead, he pressed them to his chest.

"My heart is yours," he said simply.

"Oh! I'm so hot," Gwyneth said, and began edging her way through the crowd toward the dining parlor. Roberto followed, looming over her protectively.

Gabriel stood, keeping hold of Kris's hands. "Not only lovelier, you are by far the wiser."

Roberto's head turned. Gwyneth sped down the hall with swift, small steps, the crowd parting before her. Roberto followed her.

Cherie rose from her chair with lazy grace and handed her empty glass to Dale. "She heard that," she said to Gabriel. "Come to think of it—I've heard it before, too. You really should come up with some new lines, dearest."

She strolled down the hall after the others, her heels clicking on the wood floor. Dale exchanged a long look with Gabriel, then followed.

Ramon struck up another piece on the guitar. Kris crossed the hall and went into Poppy, brushing past Margo in the doorway. Gabriel followed her. The others began to mill and talk. The show was over, so I went to get more water for Ramon, pondering why Gabriel had indulged in that little scene. Maybe he liked playing with fire.

The kitchen smelled like cinnamon, mushrooms and cheese.

Julio looked up from stacking fresh *pan* on a platter. I went to the fridge to fill Ramon's glass with filtered water. A titter of laughter—I suspected Gwyneth—reached us from the hall.

Dee was standing by her brother, talking quietly. Mick had agreed to stay to the end of the party, mainly to wash glassware and serving things (overtime was such an attractive enticement). I was glad that he'd be available to escort Dee home.

"Could you put this in the dining parlor?" Julio said, laying a final *pan* on top of the platter.

The clock started chiming the three-quarter hour. I glanced up, then nodded.

"Sure. Heading home?"

"In a bit. I'll clean up a little first."

I bit back an admonition to leave it. Julio was strict about cleanliness in the kitchen, which was probably why we didn't have a lot of pest problems.

"OK. If I don't see you, have a good night."

He yawned, nodding. I left Ramon's glass on the counter and picked up the tray, carrying it slowly so as not to unleash an avalanche of *pan*. Navigating my way through the pantry and the short hall (where there was still a line for the restroom), I crossed to the dining parlor and set the tray in the empty space on the sideboard.

Cherie and Roberto had their heads together by the fireplace, talking in low voices. Gwyneth was laughing at something the long-haired woodland spirit had just said to her. Smiling, but the muscles in her throat were taut. Her cheeks were high in color, and her eyes looked a little manic.

Having succeeded at being invisible, I retreated to the kitchen and retrieved Ramon's water. He nodded thanks as I set it beside him, but didn't speak as he was concentrating on another waltz. This time it *was* "Danse Macabre."

A tall woman—a dead ringer for Morticia Adams—was dancing with a hunchback who looked suspiciously like Riff Raff. They were nowhere near as graceful as Gwyneth and Gabriel, but they were clearly having a grand time. I watched them for a bit, then decided I should go around and check on the fireplaces and the food again.

Hyacinth was deserted. Only a few mushrooms left, so I fetched the fresh batch from the kitchen, then built up the fire. Heading for Violet, I met Kris coming out, and since the passage was too small for two abreast, I stepped back into Poppy to let her pass. I smiled, but she looked in a hurry and didn't stop.

Peering into Violet, I saw Gabriel by the fireplace, looking down at the coals. I stepped in, picking up a log from the holder to add to the fire.

"Everything all right?"

His head turned toward me, the golden mask hiding whatever he was thinking. Without answering, he stepped past me and out.

Apparently not.

Sighing, I built up the fire, then glanced at the offerings on the mantel. The votive was flickering, burning low. A half-empty glass of wine stood beside the photo of Vi; I left it, not sure whether it was an offering or someone's forgotten drink.

The food was all right. I looked into Dahlia to check the food there. The tray was half-full. Margo stood between the two green candle lanterns, one hand on her stomach.

"You OK?" I asked.sure

She flashed me a smile, nodding. "Fine." As if to prove it, she picked up a glass from one of the lamp stands and drank. Dale's sugar skull grinned beside the lantern.

I crossed the hall to check on the alcoves there. The food was holding up; everyone must be getting sated. Lily and Jonquil were occupied by people talking and nibbling. Kris was back in Iris, conversing intently with Maleficent. She acknowledged me with a brief nod and went on talking.

Bending to tend to the fire, I was surprised by a low voice—Gabriel's, I thought—saying, "What do you want?" I glanced at Kris, but apparently she hadn't heard.

I glanced into Rose and saw Gabriel standing there, but no one else. He wasn't looking at me, so he must not have been talking to me. I slipped through the archway into the dining parlor.

Cherie was trickling water into a glass from the absinthe fountain. Intrigued, I watched her sugar cube dissolve as the water passed through it into the green liquor below. The drink went pale and cloudy, and Cherie shut off the fountain, gave the mixture a stir with the spatula-spoon, and sipped.

"Want some?" she asked.

"No, thanks." I bent to build up the fire. The clock began to chime. When I stood up again, Cherie was watching me.

"You should try it," she said with a languid smile.

"I will, some day." I smiled back, then headed out to the hall.

The back door opened as I arrived, and Roberto and Gwyneth came in. Gwyneth's hair was windblown and her headpiece was a little askew. Roberto straightened it as the clock started tolling the hour.

Everyone fell still; I turned toward the stairs, wanting another break, but waited for the clock so as not to break the mood. On the eleventh toll, a small cry made me look back just in time to see Gwyneth slump to the floor.

12

ROBERTO CAUGHT GWYNETH in time to keep her from cracking her head on the hardwood floor. I rushed to help him, taking one of her hands in mine. It was ice cold.

Everyone in the hall crowded toward us. "Give us some room, please!" I said. Looking up at Roberto, I added, "She's freezing."

"I told her she should wear her cloak!" He sounded panicked.

Cloak—good idea! I grabbed the garment from the nearest coat-hook, which turned out to be a purple velvet cape. Bundling this around Gwyneth, I took the opportunity to check for a pulse. I found it—a bit fast, but reassuring. Glancing over my shoulder, I looked for a familiar face.

"Ramon! Get a cup of that cider from the kitchen, please."

He nodded, eyes wide, and ducked into the pantry. I heard a door bang shut.

"Sit her up," I told Roberto.

By the time we got her propped against Roberto's chest, she showed signs of life, much to my relief. Ramon arrived with the cider and I held it for her.

"Sip this," I said.

She obeyed meekly, and after a couple of sips reached up to take the cup. I wrapped her icy hands around it and steadied them until I was sure she could hold it.

Roberto looked up at me, eyes wide behind the mask. "Thank you."

I nodded and stood, turning to the spectators. "She's all right. Make some room for us to bring her to the fireplace, please."

The crowd obligingly parted, and Ramon picked up one of the

141

smaller chairs from the hallway, carrying it into the dining parlor. I knelt down beside Gwyneth again.

"Can you stand up, or should Roberto carry you?"

"I…um…"

Roberto solved the question by removing the cider from her grasp and handing it to me, then gathering her in his arms and lifting her with apparent ease. I led him into the dining parlor and indicated the chair. He set her there quite tenderly, and arranged the purple cape around her.

"So stupid," she said through chattering teeth. "I just wanted to l-look at the moon."

"You'll be all right," I told her, handing her back the cider. I added another log to the fire and replaced the screen.

Roberto cast me a glance as he stood behind her chair, hands on her shoulders. His eyes showed his gratitude, even through the mask.

A murmur of voices penetrated my awareness. Looking toward the door, I saw Dale standing guard, keeping people out. Beyond him, someone complained, "I just want a drink!"

"Give us a few minutes," Dale said in a calm voice, earning my silent gratitude.

Thinking Gabriel should know about Gwyneth's collapse, I went through the archway into Rose. It was empty. I walked through to the intersection in the middle of the parlor and looked into the other three chambers. They were empty, too.

The hall, on the other hand, was crowded. Everyone had come out there to see what was going on. I checked the south alcoves, but found no one in Hyacinth, Violet, or Dahlia. As I returned to the hall, I looked for Gabriel. He should have been easy to spot, in that golden outfit. The crowd was mostly dark and muted colors.

Maybe he'd gone to the restroom. I worked my way through the throng to the side hall: no one waiting. I continued through the pantry to the kitchen, where I found Mick frowning out the north windows, cell phone to his ear. When he saw me he took it down.

"Where's Dee?" I asked.

He gestured toward the outside door. "She went rushing out a couple minutes ago. She's not answering her cell."

The pit of my stomach started to clench. Something was very

wrong.

"Julio left?"

"About ten minutes ago. He made me swear to stay in here and guard the vodka shots." Mick sounded decidedly unhappy. "Can you watch them while I go after Dee?"

"I'll find her," I said. "Please do stay and guard the drinks. Keep trying to raise Dee. I'll be right back."

Mick nodded, albeit grudgingly, and returned his attention to his phone. I went back to the hall.

The guests were beginning to spread out again. Ramon looked up from his chair as I headed for the stairs. "Should I keep playing?" he asked.

I paused. "Have you seen Gabriel?"

He shook his head. I bit my lip.

"Maybe something quiet? Help calm people down."

He picked up the guitar and I hurried up the stairs. As I reached the top step I heard a small sound, like a sigh. My skin prickled.

"Hello?"

Silence. I didn't see anyone in the hall, and my suite was locked. I stepped toward the doorway into the offices. Moonlight slanted in the window and fell across Kris, standing in the middle of her office. She looked up as I came in, rubbed at her cheek, then swallowed.

"I'm all right," she said before I could ask. Her voice was a little shaky, but she held her head high.

"May I turn on the light?"

"Please don't. I'm OK, really."

I honored her wish, worrying as I stood watching the restless moonlight flicker over her. Her privacy was something I always tried to respect, but right now I needed information.

"Have you seen Gabriel? I can't find him."

She swallowed again. "Not since I left Violet. You saw."

I nodded. "Gwyneth fainted."

Kris's brows rose, then her eyes narrowed. "She did, eh?"

"She's recovering, but I thought Gabriel should know."

"He's not in Rose?"

"No."

She looked around, as if she might spot him hiding somewhere in the office. I realized how ludicrous that idea was, even as I stepped into my own office. Same empty stillness, except for the shadowed moonlight.

"I'll check again," I said, leaving to give Kris some privacy.

As I turned toward the stairs, a gleam of light shone out above the top step, like the glint of a chandelier drop. I caught my breath.

My phone rang. I jumped, nearly dropping it as I tried to fish it out of the sleeve pocket.

"Hello?"

"Ellen—"

"Dee!"

She took a couple of breaths. "It's Gabriel."

"You found him? Where is he?"

"Hidalgo Plaza. Can you come? I think he's—dead."

13

My heart clenched, and I cast a glance toward the office door, worried for Kris. She hadn't come out. I started down the stairs.

"I'll be right there," I told Dee when I reached the landing. "What happened?"

"I don't know—I saw him run past the kitchen so I followed him—"

"Have you called the police?"

"Yes. But I don't have my I.D...."

"I'll vouch for you. I'd better hang up in case they're trying to reach you."

"Oh, Ellen—"

"Hang tight. I'm on my way."

At the foot of the stairs, Ramon was still playing the guitar. I stopped him with a hand on his shoulder.

"Do you have your keys?" I asked in a low voice.

He nodded. "Why?"

"I'm going down the street. Come to the kitchen."

He put down his guitar and followed me. There were a lot of people milling around in the hall, and I was less than courteous about getting past them to the kitchen.

"Mick! Come with me. Ramon, please stay here and don't let anyone go near the fridge or the freezer."

"OK, but what's going on?"

"I'm not sure. Call me if there's trouble."

Mick followed me out back, where his car, a medley of different-colored parts generously dappled with primer gray, was parked next to mine. I headed for the passenger door.

"You drive. Hidalgo Plaza. Dee's there."

His eyes sharpened with swift concern, then he gave a nod and unlocked the car. I climbed in, tossing a couple of car magazines from the shotgun seat into the back.

"Is she OK?" he asked.

"Yes." I buckled myself in. "I'll explain on the way. Don't back over any Goths," I added, glancing behind us down the driveway.

The Mustang's engine rumbled to life and Mick backed all the way out to the street rather than take the time to turn around. A pale face gaped at us in surprise from the garden beyond the fence as we whipped past. Some Goth who'd gone out for a smoke, probably. I realized I was clutching the door handle and forced myself to let go.

I told Mick about Dee's call as he drove the half-block to Palace Avenue and turned east, passing numerous costumed pedestrians as we circled the Plaza. It was almost too short to drive—especially because finding parking would be a pain—but it was the fastest way to get to Dee.

"I'll go in while you park, OK?" I said.

"Yeah. Tell her I'm coming. Did she say how he died?"

"No."

I swallowed, not looking forward to finding out.

Mick dropped me at the entrance to Hidalgo Plaza and drove off. I was on the same spot where I'd first seen the gleam of light a few days before. The muscles between my shoulder blades tightened.

Muffled music came from ahead; the restaurant was probably closed by now, but the bistro might be having a party. I drew a deep breath and walked through the *zaguan* passage, looking for Dee.

The music was indeed coming from the bistro on the east side of the *plazuela*. Laughter and voices came from its open door.

It took me a minute to spot Dee; she was almost invisible in the dark garden in her black hooded robe, standing motionless at the crossing of pathways where I'd seen the second gleam. Clenching my teeth, I joined her and realized she was gazing up toward the west side of the plaza.

"Dee? You all right?"

"Y-yes."

I heard a siren in the distance. Turning to follow her gaze, I saw a familiar, golden figure.

"Oh, God!"

He was hanging from the iron bracket that held a flower basket, below the second story, between two posts.

The spot where I'd seen the third gleam of light.

The first responders arrived before Mick. They came through the *zaguan* on the north side: two uniformed cops, then three paramedics who swarmed up the stairs and went to work getting Gabriel down.

One of the cops went into the bistro while the other—a stocky Latino guy not much older than me—came over and started asking questions, most of which Dee had to answer. I stayed with her, holding her hand, which was chilled. The black robe was just a cover-up; it wasn't warm enough to protect her from the cold breeze. I wished I'd thought to bring something for her. I hadn't even grabbed a coat for myself, but at least my dress was warm.

Mick came running up, winded. The cop bristled.

"Mick, thank you," I said, then turned to the cop. "This is Dee's brother, he drove me here when she called me."

The cop relaxed a little. "You know him?" he said, nodding toward the balcony, where two paramedics were strapping Gabriel into a harness while the third stood in the garden below.

Gabriel's *body*. There was no chance he was still alive. I swallowed, fighting down the part of me that wanted to give way to grief.

"Not really," Mick said, glancing at me. "He's a customer, sort of. I never—"

A piercing scream behind us interrupted him. Looking toward the sound, I saw a woman in a Supergirl costume standing in the doorway of the bistro, watching the paramedics with an expression of horror.

The cop cursed under his breath and started talking into his radio, asking for backup. "Stay here," he told us with a sharp look, then headed for the bistro.

A witch and a figure in a business suit with a really good mask of a leading politician joined Supergirl in the doorway. The cop raised his arms to herd them back inside.

Dee shivered. I hugged her and invited Mick to do the same. "She's freezing. You don't happen to have a blanket in your car?"

"No." He stood behind her, wrapping his arms around her. She shuddered and leaned against him.

Hearing footsteps approaching, I turned to the southwestern *zaguan* and saw Tony Aragón coming toward us, hands shoved in the pockets of his jeans and his leather jacket zipped to his throat. His shoulders were hunched and he was frowning. He stopped a couple of paces away, eyes going wide.

"Ellen?"

I sighed, partly from relief, partly from sadness. "Hi."

He looked from me to the paramedics, who had started lowering Gabriel's body to the ground. "Oh, crap!"

The uniformed cop came jogging up. "Got a bar full of hysterical people in there," he said, gesturing over his shoulder at the bistro door, which was now closed. "They just noticed the deader. This is the one who made the call," he added, indicating Dee.

"OK, I'll handle it from here," Tony said. "You keep a lid on the bar."

"Roger."

The cop jogged away again. Tony turned to me with an incredulous look.

"I did *not* find this body," I blurted. Stupid, defensive remark.

Tony's gaze shifted to Mick. "Your girlfriend?"

"My sister."

"It's Dee," I added. "She's freezing. Could we get her inside?"

Tony glanced toward the bistro and shook his head. "Not in there."

"What about the *zaguan*?" I said, indicating the entrance I had come through. "At least it's out of the wind."

"Yeah, OK, but we might have to get out of the way." He shot a glance toward the balcony. "It's going to get busy here."

We moved into the passage, which was dark but slightly warmer. I could see Tony's bike double-parked a little way down the street, lights flashing. Mick leaned against the wall, hugging Dee to him.

"Mind taking off the hood?" Tony said to her.

She glanced at me, then carefully peeled back her veil and the hood, revealing her skull makeup. Tony blinked, then took out his pocket notebook. He made a note and frowned, turning to me with a somber look.

"Do I need to take myself off this case?"

"What? No! Well...I don't know. I don't think so. I wasn't here."

He sighed. "Better start at the beginning."

I gathered myself, trying to find the nerve to tell Tony about the glints of light I'd seen earlier in the plaza. I couldn't do it. He would think I'd gone nuts.

I swallowed. "The hanged man is Gabriel Rhodes—"

"How do you know?" Tony broke in.

"I doubt there are two costumes like that in the city."

He glanced toward the *plazuela*, where the paramedics now had Gabriel on the ground. "OK, go on."

"Gabriel and his friends hired the tearoom for a private party tonight. A masquerade. There was supposed to be a...dramatic unmasking at midnight. That's why Dee's in costume."

Tony looked again at Dee, made a note, then looked back at me. "Wait a minute. If there's a party at your place, what is he doing here?" He turned his frown on Dee. "And what are *you* doing here?"

"I was in the kitchen, waiting for midnight," she said, "and I saw him run by the window. It seemed wrong; he was running really fast. So I went out the back door and followed him. I saw him turn at the end of the driveway, and when I got there he was turning onto Palace."

"Did you see anyone else?"

"N-no—that is, there were a lot of people walking around on the street. Lot of costumes."

"Anyone else running?"

"Not that I saw."

Tony wrote in his notebook. "So you followed him through the crowd."

"Yes. I couldn't get close to him, but I could see his costume ahead. I think he stopped in front of the Palace of the Governors for a little, under the *portal*, but I didn't catch up. By the time I got there he'd crossed the street. Then he turned in here."

Dee paused and shivered. Mick rubbed her upper arms.

"I didn't see him at first," she said. "It was dark. I heard the music and went over to the bar, but he wasn't there. I started to go in to look for him but they wanted a cover charge, so I came back out. That's when I saw him."

"What did you see?" Tony asked quickly.

"I saw him hanging there. He wasn't trying to get free or anything. Just limp, and swinging back and forth a little." Dee gave a little hiccup and I caught her hand. She gripped mine fiercely.

"How long between when he turned in here and you got here?"

"I'm not sure. I had to wait for traffic before I could cross the street. A couple minutes, maybe?"

A squad car pulled up outside, spilling flashing light into the passage. Two uniformed cops got out. We stood back as Tony directed them through.

"Then what?" he said to Dee.

"I ran in here. There was no one in the garden. I saw a flash of light, probably a reflection from a jewel on the costume, and looked up." Dee paused to swallow and take a breath. "I called 911, and then I called Ellen."

Tony shifted his gaze to me.

"I'd been looking for Gabriel for a few minutes," I said. "One of the guests fainted and I wanted to let him know. I went through the whole house, then into the kitchen. Mick told me that Dee had taken off out the back door, and I knew something was wrong. I left Ramon in charge—Oh! What time is it?"

I glanced at my phone. Quarter to twelve.

"I should get back there."

"Finish first," Tony said. "What next?"

"Dee called and told me she'd found Gabriel and thought he was dead. I asked Mick to drive me here. He dropped me off and I came in and found Dee standing in the garden, looking up at...the balcony. Then two policeman got here, then the paramedics."

Tony finished writing. "OK. How many people are at this party?"

"About fifty," I said, and he winced.

"Great." He glanced toward the paramedics. "Stay here a minute. Be right back."

"Please, can we get Dee inside?" I asked as he walked away. He held up a hand with one finger skyward, telling us to wait.

"He's really dead, isn't he?" Dee said in a small voice, then gave a small, gulping sob.

I hugged her and Mick both, fighting my own tears. A cop started stringing yellow tape across the stairs to the balcony.

Until then, I hadn't had time to think about the gleams of light. Now I remembered, and it all seemed surreal. Had Captain Dusenberry been trying to warn me? If so, how on earth could I have known what he meant?

Tony came back and looked at each of us in turn. "Ellen, come with me. You two, stay here."

He led me into the *plazuela*, toward the paramedics. "I need you to identify him. There's no I.D. on him."

"It's back at the house."

"Any idea why he'd kill himself?"

I looked at him, shocked by the suggestion. "None. I would have sworn he wouldn't!"

Tony gazed back flatly. "How well do you know him?"

"Not that well. I met him a couple of weeks ago. He's—a friend of Kris's."

Tony lowered his chin. "And?"

I swallowed. "They were dating."

"Hm." Tony looked toward the paramedics, then back at me. "You OK to look?"

I cringed inside, but said, "Yes."

We stepped up to where Gabriel lay. His mask was on the ground beside him, and I caught my breath.

Even in the moonlight, I could see that his face was painted like the sun, with golden-white beams and flame-like rays that almost seemed to glow. There was something metallic in the makeup.

His final work of art, that he would have revealed at midnight. The waste of his talent brought up the tears I'd been fighting.

"Need to look closer?" Tony asked.

I didn't, but I knelt beside Gabriel anyway. His face was not bloated, by which I knew that his neck must have broken. The painting was mostly undamaged, though I could see now that it was smudged in a couple of places, probably where the paramedics had handled him. His golden hair splayed beneath his head, continuing the illusion of rays of light.

"Is that him?" Tony said, standing over me.

"Yes," I whispered. I drew a shuddering breath, then leaned back on my heels and spoke louder. "Yes. That's Gabriel Rhodes."

"OK. Let's go."

Tony helped me up and we turned away as the paramedics closed in again. He talked briefly to one of the cops, who nodded.

"It sounds like I have around fifty people to interview," Tony said bitterly as we walked back to the passage. "I hope none of them have left."

I wiped at my eyes. "I'm sure there's a guest list."

"You didn't make it yourself?"

"It's not my party. Kris will have a list."

God. Poor Kris.

His eyes narrowed and he opened his mouth as if to ask a question, then looked at Dee and shifted gears. "Where's your car?" he asked Mick.

"On Otero Street," Mick said.

"I'm going to escort you to it, then follow you to Ellen's. Got it?"

"Yes, sir."

Tony threw me a wry glance, then walked out to his motorcycle, talking on his phone. He fired up the bike and turned it around in the street, then paced us as Mick led me and Dee to his car, parked on a side street.

"You get in front," I told Dee, and was grateful when Mick turned the heater on full blast. Even in my velvet dress, my hands were getting cold.

We cruised sedately to the house, Tony right behind us. As we turned into the driveway, my phone rang. It was Kris.

"Where are you?" she said in a panicked voice. "Where's Gabriel?"

"I'm here," I said as Mick parked and turned off the engine. "Go upstairs, I'll talk to you there."

I hung up before she could answer. Better to have that conversation in person.

A couple of Goths were on the bench on the back *portal*,

smoking. The coals of their cigarettes glowed in the shadows.

Tony opened the car door for Dee. "I want you to go upstairs and not talk to anyone, OK?"

She nodded. "OK."

"You, too," he said to Mick.

"I'll take them up," I said.

"No, you stay here. I need your help."

Dee was shivering, but looked calm otherwise, as much as I could tell through the makeup. I turned to Mick.

"There's a throw on the chaise longue in my office. Tell Kris I'll be up as soon as I—"

"There you are!" Kris's shout cut in.

She was standing in the hall doorway, her violet diadem glinting in the moonlight. She reminded me of the Queen of the Night from *The Magic Flute*, glorious in her outrage.

"Where's Gabriel?" she demanded. "What's going on?"

I looked to Tony, who had his cop face on. "Everybody inside," he said. "You, too," he told the smokers.

They grumbled and stubbed out their cigarettes. I couldn't help wrinkling my nose at the smell as we went in.

The clock began striking twelve.

 *14*

THE GUESTS FELL SILENT. Kris's eyes widened as Dee passed her, going through the door.

Tony took my arm and murmured in my ear. "I've got backup coming but until then I need you to help me keep everyone together."

He flipped on the hall lights, which evoked a gasp from the crowd. Mysterious shadows turned into people in costumes and winced at the light. They stared at Dee as Tony pushed through to the stairs, directing Mick and Dee to go up with a gesture as the final stroke of midnight rang through the house.

"OK, everyone in the main room," he said, gesturing to the north parlor.

"That won't work," I said quickly. "They should stay in the hall."

Tony shot me a look, then took a step toward the main parlor and stopped when he saw the drapery walls. "What *is* this?"

"It's for the party. Edgar Allen Poe's 'Masque of the Red Death.'"

He gave me a long, hard stare. "All right, lock the front door and stand in front of it. No one goes out."

I obeyed. Kris came to stand beside me as Tony went into the gift shop. He turned on the light and dove through Poppy to the back alcoves, shooing people out.

"What's going on?" Kris whispered.

"I'd better let Tony tell you."

Her frown deepened. Cherie came and joined us.

"Did you find Gabriel?" she asked.

Kris shook her head, then looked at me. I felt like a traitor, but I knew Tony'd be furious if I told them anything. I watched the people coming out of the gift shop instead. Two fairies, a vampire, and a goblin who was almost as green as the Bird Woman had been —God, was it just that afternoon? It seemed an eternity ago.

Tony went through the whole ground floor, turning on lights and chasing everyone into the hall. Roberto and Gwyneth sat on one of the love seats against the wall, with Gwyneth's admirers clustered around them. Margo sat in a wing chair, nodding absently as Maleficent, in the neighboring chair, talked to her. Dale and the leaf-masked nature spirit, whose costume was much more elaborate than I'd been able to tell in candlelight, stood by the foot of the stairs with Ramon.

Tony came out of the dining parlor, closed the door behind him, and walked up to me. "Anyone outside?"

"Possibly."

He pressed his lips together, then pulled out his phone and made a call as he walked to the back door. I saw him throw the deadbolt before he came back to the edge of the group now clustered in the hall.

"OK, I need everyone's attention," he bellowed in a voice that would have been beautiful onstage. I'd never heard him do that before.

The guests all looked at him, waiting. He took out a small, black leather case and held it up, displaying his badge.

"I'm Detective Aragón. There's been a mishap involving one of the guests. I need to talk to each of you before you leave. It's going to take a while, so just be patient."

He came toward me, Goths parting before him like the Red Sea even as they started to murmur. "I need the guest list."

"It's in my desk," Kris said. "I'll go get it."

"No," he said as she took a step toward the stairs. "You stay here. Ellen will get it."

Kris looked at me, going pale. "In the file drawer. The folder labeled 'Masque'."

I nodded and hurried up the stairs. Mick and Dee were sitting by the front window, talking quietly. I fetched the list and went back down, handing it to Tony. No one had moved.

"OK," he said, looking at Kris. "You first. Come with me."

The clock tolled the quarter hour as Tony led Kris to the dining parlor, ushered her in, and shut the door. The guests began talking louder.

Cherie turned to me. "What happened?"

I shook my head. "Sorry. I shouldn't say anything."

"Is Gabriel all right?"

The whoop of a siren outside saved me from having to reply. I peeked around the black fabric covering the lights by the door, and saw a squad car double-parked out front, red lights flashing. A second one pulled up behind it. I unlocked the door and waited for them to ring the bell, which they did while simultaneously pounding on the door.

"Where's Detective Aragón?" said a man with light brown hair in a buzz-cut and a mustache. Behind him stood a frowning middle-aged Hispanic cop, and I saw two more uniforms starting to search the garden.

"He's interviewing my business manager. I'm the owner, Ellen Rosings."

The buzz-cut guy traded a look and a sideways nod with the Hispanic guy, who took up a stance guarding the door. "Take me to him."

I led the officer down the hall, which swiftly fell silent. At the dining parlor, the buzz-cut cop rapped sharply on the door.

"Officer Finch," he said.

Tony opened the door and had a quick consultation with Finch. Kris was standing by the French doors, gazing out. I tried to catch her eye, but she didn't notice me.

"You got a fingerprint reader?" Tony asked.

Finch fished a device smaller than a cell phone from a pouch on his belt and handed it to Tony, who looked at me. "I'm going to need a notepad or something."

I nodded. "I'll get you one."

Officer Finch took up a stand outside the door when Tony closed it. I went through the side hall and pantry to the kitchen, passing Ramon near the side hall entrance.

"They wouldn't let me stay," he said.

"It's OK." I smiled briefly to reassure him.

The kitchen smelled of cider and spice. I turned off the burner under the cider and added some hot water to the thickening brew, then rummaged through Julio's cupboard and found a legal pad. I ladled cider into five mugs and put them on a tray, tucked the pad under my arm, and returned to the hall.

Officer Finch shot a frowning look at me, but softened when he saw the mugs.

"This is hot cider. Coffee's coming. I have the paper T— Detective Aragón wanted."

Finch knocked on the door. Tony came to it and accepted a mug and the pad. Looking past him, I saw Kris standing by the fireplace. Her face was tear-streaked.

"Thanks," Tony said, and started to pull the door shut.

"OK if I take some cider upstairs?" I asked.

"Yeah."

He shut the door. I offered the tray to Finch, who took a mug and nodded thanks. I gave a mug to the Hispanic cop at the front door, then took the other two upstairs for Mick and Dee. They were by the front window, lit only by the moon and my two candles, a pretty scene, but the lights were on downstairs and I thought it best to turn on the chandelier.

Mick looked around at me. Dee, wrapped in my office throw, was no longer shivering but looked pretty glum. She took a mug with whispered thanks.

"The police are here," I told them. "Detective Aragón is interviewing people. I'm afraid you're going to be here a while. Can I get you anything?"

Dee shook her head, hands wrapped around the mug.

"I guess not," Mick said. "Thanks."

"I'll check back."

Returning to the kitchen, I fired up Julio's coffee maker. While it started to drip, I put a splash of cider into a mug for myself and drank it, thinking of Gabriel.

Why? Why would he kill himself? I just couldn't believe it.

And that was worse. If he hadn't killed himself, who had killed him?

And why?

My phone goosed me: a text from Kris.

I'm leaving.

My heart sank. I texted back.

Where are you?

In my car. He wouldn't let me
back in. Doesn't want me to talk
to anyone.

Are you all right?

No.

Wait. Let me drive you home.

Don't worry, I won't do anything
stupid. I want to know who did
this.

Poor Kris. My heart ached for her.

Call me if you need anything. Or
if you just want to talk.

OK.

I waited to see if she'd say more, then put the phone back in my
pocket. A door banged shut; I went out to the hall and saw three
cops at the front door, talking together.

The Goths looked sullen. A woman in a red-and-black striped
corset turned to me.

"When can we get to the drinks?"

"Not for a while, I imagine."

"Damn. Can't drink, can't smoke. What do we do?"

I saw her point. Heading back to the kitchen, I turned the
mulled cider on again and dumped a fresh gallon of cider into the
pot, then dug a jumbo bag of paper cups left over from a previous
event out of storage and filled a half-dozen pitchers with ice water. I
put the cups and one pitcher out on one of the low tables in the hall,
where they were swooped upon by the Goths. The rest of the
pitchers I distributed on the other tables.

The guests were now chattering, which was an improvement
over sullen muttering. I collected an empty pitcher and went back to
the kitchen. The coffee was done, so I poured it into a carafe and

started another pot.

Poor Julio. I was raiding his stash again. I should just put his coffee on the tearoom's grocery list and be done with it.

I took mugs of coffee to the cops, earning resentful stares from the Goths. Officer Finch gave me a nod in exchange for his mug, and I knocked on the dining parlor door. Tony answered, with Dale Whittier beside him, looking alarmed.

Tony grabbed the last coffee mug and took a deep swig. "Thanks. You can go," he told Dale. "Don't talk to anyone."

"Wait—my coat," Dale said.

"I'll get it," I said. "What does it look like?"

"It's black."

Impossible not to answer that with a stare.

"Black wool, knee-length, with a scarf tucked in one sleeve," Dale added. "On a hook by the stairs."

It took me a minute to find his coat amid the myriad black garments. Carrying it back to the dining parlor, I handed it to Dale. Officer Finch escorted him out the back door.

"Need anything else?" I asked Tony. "Food?"

"Maybe later." He gave me a forlorn smile and consulted the guest list. "OK, send in Cherry Legrand," he said to Finch.

"Che*rie*," I corrected, earning glares from both of them.

"Whatever," Tony said, and shut the door.

Biting back a response that was unworthy of a disciple of Miss Manners, I went into the main parlor, collected the tray of eggs from Lily, and set it on a table in the hall. Again, the Goths swooped.

I fetched the rest of the food from the chambers and put it where they could reach it. It was theirs, and they had nothing else to do except whip themselves into a state of discontent. Food might at least delay that.

I set down the tray of tartlets, thinking it ironic that I had been so worried that someone would poison the food. Now, in the full glare of artificial light, the Goths looked like ordinary people whose party had been disrupted.

Well, maybe not quite ordinary.

As I went into Rose, the clock tolled again—the half-hour—and I couldn't help freezing. It was still dark in there; the black draperies blocked the chandelier. The red candle lanterns perpetuated the uncomfortable atmosphere, and the clock reminded me of Gabriel's planned finale, which now would never take place.

Gabriel had dressed himself as Prospero, who was struck down by the Red Death. A shiver went through me.

The mantel clock subsided, quietly ticking its way toward the next tolling. I noticed that the door between Rose and the dining parlor was shut. Muffled voices came through it.

Straightening my shoulders, I picked up the tray of salmon mousse puffs, then turned my back on the black chamber and tried to shake off the gloom. Keep being the hostess, I decided.

It was a defensive approach, and it served me well. It permitted me to continue functioning and avoid thinking about the disaster. As long as I had guests to care for, I could make them my priority and postpone having to deal with the elephant.

I took coffee to the cops, made a pass through the hall collecting empty food trays and pitchers, then put out filled pitchers and tried to decide what to do about the cider. I ended up enlisting Ramon's help to carry the pot out and set it on top of a trio of trivets on one of the low tables, with an industrial-sized ladle. The Goths descended on it as we stepped back, and Ramon looked at me.

"Can I pack up?"

"Sure. Yes. Do you need help?"

"Nah. Want me to disconnect the mic on the clock?"

"Yes, *please!*"

"OK if I change first? These sleeves…" He raised his arms, demonstrating the awkwardness of the heavy sleeves of his tunic.

"Go ahead."

Returning to the kitchen, I started another pot of coffee and took stock of the food. The Goths had gone through most of what Julio had made for them. A bowl of leftover salmon mousse was in the fridge. I put it on a tray with some crackers and set it out in the hall, then turned on the oven to preheat.

A commotion in the hall drew me back there. I heard the front door open as I reached the hallway, and saw the Hispanic officer waving some new arrivals in.

One of them looked familiar: slim and sandy-haired, with wire-framed glasses. An evidence tech; I remembered him from previous occasions.

"Hi," he said, grinning. "We meet again."

I gave him a rueful smile in return. A Latino woman came after him, carrying a large camera bag. They stood in the middle of the hall between the gift shop and the main parlor, looking around.

"Hey, Marcos, where's Aragón?" asked the sandy-haired guy.

"He's interviewing," said the Hispanic cop at the door as he closed it behind a third tech, a short, stocky Asian guy carrying an equipment case.

"He say where he wanted us to start?"

Officer Marcos shrugged.

"You might start in here." I said, stepping to the entrance of the main parlor.

"Interesting decorations," the tech said, looking at the draperies.

"It's intended to represent 'The Masque of the Red Death.'"

His face lit up. "Oh, cool! That's a great story! So where's the black chamber?"

"Right ahead of you, on the right. I think you'll want to begin there."

"Yeah, definitely." He led the other techs through the drapery passage and into Rose. "Is there a clock, too?"

"Just the mantel clock," I said, gesturing toward it.

He stood in the center of the alcove, taking in the candle lanterns and the now-empty food stand.

"Awesome!" He set his case down on the floor and opened it.

"I'll get out of your way," I said. "Do you need anything."

"Nah. Thanks!"

"Oh—I should tell you—Gabriel Rhodes was in this chamber most of the evening."

The tech looked up at me and tilted his head to one side. "He was Prospero?"

I swallowed. "Yes."

"Was someone supposed to be the intruder?"

"One of my staff. She's the one who found—" I lowered my voice. "—who found Gabriel."

The tech gave a slow, thoughtful nod. "OK. Thanks. She still here?"

"Yes. Upstairs."

"I'd like to talk to her before she goes."

"I'll tell her."

The other two techs began taking out their equipment. I got out of their way, and went back to the kitchen to throw together some sandwiches. I gave one to Ramon when he came in the pantry to disconnect the mics from the stereo, and he flashed me a grateful grin.

Mick and Dee were still on the sofa upstairs. Mick had his earbuds in, but took them out when I set a plate of sandwiches on the table.

"I figured you were probably hungry," I said.

Dee shook her head. "I don't want to mess up the makeup."

"Oh, honey—"

"No," she said firmly. "We need to document it. I need to go down to Rose in the costume. Mick is going to take photos."

I traded a glance with Mick, who was clearly prepared to humor his sister.

"It's Gabriel's last work," Dee said. "We *have* to document it."

Not quite the last, I thought, remembering his sun face paint, but I didn't contradict her. She was right; Gabriel deserved that his intentions should be honored.

"There are technicians downstairs now," I said. "It could be a while."

"I'll wait."

"You want some soup?" I offered. "Or cider?"

She turned her head to look at me. The skull makeup made her look fragile, vulnerable.

"Could I have some tea? I can make it—"

Tea! I almost moaned aloud at the thought.

"No, I will. Back in a bit."

I gave her shoulder a squeeze, smiled sadly at Mick, who was eating a sandwich, and went downstairs.

I put the kettle on in the pantry on my way to the kitchen. Coffee was done and the oven was hot. I tossed three dozen frozen scones onto baking sheets and put them in, loaded up the coffee carafe, and started another pot. By that time the kettle had boiled. I set a pot of Irish Breakfast steeping and made a round with the coffee and sandwiches for the cops.

The crowd of Goths was noticeably thinner. They had eaten

everything off the trays and were working their way through the last of the salmon mousse. I glanced at the cider pot, which was down to the dregs. Might have to ramp up the tea; Julio's coffee wouldn't last if I started giving it to the guests.

In the pantry, the Irish Breakfast was done. I poured a cup for myself, then put the pot and two more cups on a tray with sugar and milk and took it up to Dee and Mick. Dee thanked me with the first real smile I'd seen from her since Gabriel had painted her face.

Back downstairs to indulge in my own tea and check on the scones. My calves were getting tired from all the up and down.

Ramon was in the kitchen, dressed more normally in black T-shirt and jeans, eating his sandwich by the work table. His guitar case and sound gear stood against the wall by the break table.

"Hey, boss," he said. "How you holding up?"

"Marginally," I said, sitting at the break table with my tea. I closed my eyes to savor the first mouthful. Strong, black, with a hint of maltiness from the Assam, Irish Breakfast was the perfect choice for an after-midnight pick-me-up on what was probably going to be an all-nighter.

"Is it true what the guests are saying?" he asked, carrying his sandwich plate over to join me.

"What are they saying?"

"That Gabriel's in trouble. Some of them think he's in jail, some think he was in some kind of accident."

I swallowed. "He's not in jail."

Ramon gave me a sharp look. "But he is in trouble."

"I shouldn't talk to you about it," I said. "Detective Aragón will want to interview you, too."

He looked disgruntled, but didn't say anything. Instead he attacked his sandwich.

"Sorry it turned out to be such a mess," I said.

He shrugged and swallowed a bite. "Not your fault."

I sighed, wondering if Gabriel had paid him in advance for the music. If he hadn't, I would pay Ramon myself, as well as Mick and Dee. Gabriel had put down a sizable deposit on the party, but I'd be lucky if it would cover the cost of the food, and I might not get any more. If so, I was looking at a substantial loss on this hellish night.

Unexpectedly, that thought brought tears to my eyes. It wasn't about the bills; I was plenty used to living on the edge of financial disaster by now. It had something to do with all Gabriel's effort going to waste.

The timer rang. It took me a second to remember what it was for: the scones.

I got up, brushing at my face, and took the tray out of the oven, leaving the heat on in case I'd need to bake another batch. While they cooled, I got out lemon curd and clotted cream, and set up three trays: one for the Goths, one for the cops, and a small one for Dee and Mick. I fed the Goths first, then took scones around to the cops.

Officer Marcos broke into a smile. "*That's* what I've been smelling. Thanks!"

Officer Finch looked at the scones with suspicion. "Biscuits?"

The parlor door opened and a vampire slunk out, headed for the back door. "They're scones," Tony said from the parlor doorway. "Thanks, Ellen," he added as he helped himself to one.

"How's it going?" I asked.

"Mmph," he said through a mouthful. He handed the list to Finch, who looked at the remaining Goths and called, "Gwyneth Bancroft."

She rose from a love seat where she'd been sitting with Roberto. He stood, too, and escorted her to the dining parlor like an attendant knight, her pale hand on his arm. They had both removed their masks, which made me glance at the others in the hall and realize that all the guests were unmasked. A tiny ping of sadness went through me at this further deconstruction of Gabriel's planned moment.

Roberto looked at me as he returned to his seat. "Kris was looking for you after Gabriel disappeared," he said. "Do you know what happened?"

Feeling a dozen pairs of eyes on me, I grabbed an empty pitcher. "Let me get you some more water," I said, and escaped to the kitchen.

In a blatant act of cowardice, I sent Ramon out with the full pitcher. I ducked upstairs with the scones for Dee and Mick, taking my teacup with me, and hid with them while I drank another cup.

When I came down again, Roberto was gone and I heard

muffled crying. Looking toward the dining parlor, I saw Finch with his arms crossed, staring at the back door. The crying was coming from *outside*, I realized. I went to the back door and opened it before Finch could react.

Gwyneth stood on the back *portal*, softly weeping. A frowning female cop stood with her.

"Hey!" Finch said behind me.

"Is there a problem?" I asked Gwyneth.

"They won't let me back in, but Roberto's my ride home," she said.

I took her hands in mine. They were cold.

"She's too lightly dressed to wait outside," I said to the female cop. "May I take her in the kitchen?"

I indicated the kitchen door. The cop looked through the window.

"Who's that in there?" she demanded.

"One of my staff. Ramon Garcia."

"Has he talked to the detective?"

"Not yet."

The cop opened the door and went in, shooting a glance around the room. Ramon looked up from washing his sandwich plate.

"Wait out in the hall," the cop told him with a jerk of the head.

He glanced at me, then at Gwyneth, then headed for the pantry. The cop followed him out.

I drew Gwyneth into the kitchen and closed the door. "Would you like a hot drink? Coffee, or tea?"

She shook her head, looking forlorn, then a shiver went through her and she began to cry in earnest.

"Come and sit down," I said, gently putting an arm around her and steering her to the break table.

There was a box of tissue there; I pushed it toward her. While she was mopping her face, I ducked into the pantry and put the kettle on, wondering what Tony had said to her. When he was in cop mode he could be pretty ruthless.

I darted upstairs to fetch her white satin cloak and Roberto's black velvet, then returned to find Gwyneth making a valiant attempt to compose herself. I sat beside her and took her hand again, just holding it to steady her.

"Gabriel's dead," she whispered, and I felt a tremor go through her hand.

"Yes," I said softly.

She turned wide, green eyes on me. "Why?"

"I don't know."

A tear slid down her cheek. She dabbed at it absently with the wad of tissue in her other hand.

We sat in silence for a while. Distant voices reached us from the hall, unintelligible but present, reminding us we were not alone. Eventually Officer Finch called out a name. Shortly afterward, Roberto came through the outside door.

Gwyneth released my hand and stood as he hurried toward us. She gave a small gasp as they embraced, and I instinctively moved away. At that moment the kettle in the pantry whistled, so I busied myself setting tea to steep. When that was done, I turned back to the kitchen. Roberto met me at the pantry door, his cloak over his arm.

"We're going," he said. "Thank you for bringing her inside."

Gwyneth, standing a few feet away in her own cloak, looked much more composed. I nodded to Roberto. "Take care," I said. An inadequate wish, but it would do to represent the stronger feelings that were still too raw to be articulated.

I saw them out through the back door, then started more coffee and tea. There were still paper cups in the hall, so I put the teapot on a tray with sugar, milk, and spoons, and took it out.

A half-dozen scones were left. As I debated whether to make more, a purple-corseted fairy left the dining parlor and Officer Finch called out, "Margo Foss."

This surprised me; I hadn't noticed Margo in a while and had assumed she was gone. The reason, I realized, as she rose from her chair, was that she had removed not only her mask, but her hennin, and she'd taken her hair down. It was longer than I'd thought: straight and dark, ending well below her shoulders. Her emerald gown was dark enough to look black in the shadow of the stairs, where she'd been seated. She walked silently down the hall to the parlor, and Finch waved her in.

What next? I stood in the center of the hall, going through the options: coffee, tea, water, scones. I was caught up.

Oh, no.

"Excuse me, Ms. Rosings?" said a gentle, masculine voice.

Turning, I saw the long-haired nature spirit rising from a chair. He held his mask of leaves in his hand. His costume—a vaguely Georgian coat and knee-breeches of tapestry-like fabric, rich with dark greens and crusted with silver braid, embroidery, and a sprinkling of glinting gems—was almost as glorious as Gabriel's had been, although more subtle. Without the mask, he might have stepped out of some historic painting, except that no Georgian gentleman would wear his hair loose and waist-length. It was a perfect, dark waterfall that I admired every time I saw it.

"Yes?" I said.

"May I have a word with you?"

He stepped toward the foot of the stairs, a little apart from the others. Under the watchful eyes of Officer Marcos, I joined him there.

He'd been to the tearoom before, on several occasions. He was one of Kris's friends, and I really ought to remember his name.

"Owen Hughes," he said disconcertingly, with a slight bow. He then lowered his voice. "We've all deduced that something's happened with Gabriel."

"I really shouldn't discuss it. I'm sorry."

"I won't ask you to, but I thought you should know that he asked me to photograph the chambers throughout the evening."

"And did you?"

"Yes." He reached into a capacious pocket in the skirt of his coat and withdrew a slim digital camera. "I'd prefer that the police not confiscate this. Do you have a way to download a copy of the photos for them?"

He had interposed his body between me and the officer at the door, shielding his hand from view.

"I won't withhold anything from them," I said.

"I'm not asking you to. Exactly the opposite; I want you to give them the photos. I'd just rather keep possession of my camera."

"All right. May I keep copies for myself?"

"Of course."

I slipped the camera into my pocket, then went upstairs. Dee had her phone out and was reading her book, which I took to be a good sign. Mick was zoning on his music. I waved to get his attention, and he disconnected.

"Could you help me with something?"

I led him into my office. "I'm going to download the photos from this," I said, showing him Owen's camera. "I want you to watch, so you can confirm that I'm not deleting anything."

He looked puzzled. "OK."

"The photographer wants to keep his camera," I explained. "The pictures were taken here, tonight. I'm going to burn them onto a disk for the police."

"Ah." Mick nodded.

I turned on my computer and invited Mick to bring one of the guest chairs around behind the desk. Meanwhile I dug around in Kris's office until I found a package of disks and another of paper sleeves. The camera's port was compatible with my phone cable, and it connected cheerfully with my computer. I copied the photos onto my hard drive, then burned them onto the three disks, labeling them with a marker and sliding them into sleeves.

"Thanks," I said to Mick as I disconnected the camera.

"Sure thing. Easiest job I ever had." He smiled, which reassured me.

We went out to the hall, where Mick resumed his seat and I collected the scones tray, the teapot, and the empty sandwich plate from the sitting area.

Downstairs, the company of Goths was growing sparse. There were fewer than a dozen left. The nature spirit—Owen—hovered near the foot of the stairs, and looked up with relief as I came down.

"They've called my name," he said.

I nodded, and led him back to the dining parlor, leaving my tray on an empty table. He gave me a troubled glance, but followed.

Tony was waiting in the doorway, tired and grouchy. I caught his eye.

"May I come in for a moment? I have something for you."

His eyes went alert, then he nodded and stepped back. I gestured to Owen to join us, gently closing the door after he came in.

"Gabriel asked Owen to take pictures during the party," I said, producing the camera and the disks. "Owen would like to keep his camera, so he asked me to download them for you. Mick watched; he can verify that I didn't delete anything." I offered two disks to

Tony, and one to Owen along with his camera.

Tony gave me a long look. "Thanks," he said, accepting the CDs.

Owen received his camera and the third disk with another small bow. "Thank you very much," he said.

"Do you need more coffee?" I asked Tony. "Something to eat?"

He shook his head. "Glass of water?"

I nodded and left them together, returning to the kitchen where I found Ramon washing trays and pitchers.

"You don't have to do that," I said.

"Passes the time," he replied.

I filled a clean pitcher with water and put it on a tray with a stack of paper cups, then took it to the dining parlor. Officer Finch knocked on the door and opened it for me.

Tony was seated in the chair I'd taken in for Gwyneth, but he'd moved it to the north wall, between the two windows. The candles on their pillar stands to either side were guttering. He looked like a king holding court.

I paused, taking in the scene he had staged. Who knew that Tony had such a flair for the dramatic?

Owen stood before the fireplace. They watched me set the water on the sideboard, next to the impressive array of alcohol.

"Owen, may I talk to you before you leave?" I said.

"He can't go back to the waiting area," Tony said.

"May I take him upstairs?"

Tony gave a grudging nod. I looked to Owen, who also nodded.

"Thanks. Let me know if you need anything else," I said to Tony, and got out.

I should have taken another chair into that room hours before, I realized. Except that if Tony had wanted one, he would have asked for it. I pressed my lips together, disliking the subtle intimidation of making people stand while they were questioned. If I'd thought of it, I'd have sent a chair in anyway, but it was too late now.

Back to the kitchen, where the timer was beeping and Ramon was taking the scones out of the oven. I took them out to the remaining Goths and got back to the dining parlor just as Owen was emerging.

"Straight upstairs," Tony told me, "and straight out when you're done."

I nodded, and led Owen up to my office. He accepted a chair and set his leaf mask on my desk, then sat gazing absently at the print of Monet's "Water Lilies" on my wall.

"Would you like tea, or a scone?" I offered.

He shook his head and smiled. "I'm fine, thanks. You've worked hard to make us comfortable. What did you want to talk about?"

"Photography," I said. "Are you a professional?"

"Semi-pro. I freelance. Gabriel is—was—a client. He had me document all his work."

"Oh! Well, then, what I have to ask is a continuation of that. And I'll pay, since Gabriel isn't able to."

Owen raised an intrigued eyebrow. "You have some of Gabriel's work? I assume you mean besides the chambers downstairs."

"Yes. His finale. Come and see."

We went out to the sitting area, where I introduced Owen to Dee and asked her to stand up. Owen took a step toward her and peered at her face, marveling.

"Wow. Yes, of course I'd be glad to photograph it."

"It should be downstairs, in the black chamber," Dee said.

"Downstairs will have to wait until the technicians are finished," I said. "And that reminds me—Dee, they want to talk to you."

Her eyes widened. "Me?"

"Yes. Don't worry—I think it's about the costume."

"Oh."

"Since we have to wait," Owen said, "I'd like start up here, if you don't mind."

Dee glanced at me. "I don't mind. Should I take off the cover?"

"There's more?" Owen's face lit with excitement, and he took out his camera. "Let me get this first."

He took a few minutes to decide where the best lighting was. In the end, I brought out a table lamp from my suite to supplement the hall chandelier, and Owen had Dee stand in front of a blank patch of wall. Mick was sufficiently interested in the proceedings to withdraw from his musical reverie and watch with a critical eye.

After taking what seemed like a hundred photos, Owen told Dee to remove the black cover-up. I helped her to take it off, avoiding brushing it against her makeup. She rearranged the lacy shroud and looked expectantly at Owen.

"Wow!" he said. "This was going to be the midnight reveal."

"Yes," Dee said.

"That's not body paint."

"It's a bodysuit. He painted it in three sessions. He did the makeup and the hands tonight."

"Magnificent! OK, let's start with a profile."

For the next half hour, Owen took pictures from every angle. Full body shots, half-body shots, details. He didn't pose Dee much, but occasionally asked her to shift a limb or change her position, and I could see that these subtle changes made a difference. The whole process was so fascinating I forgot about the Goths and the cops until a heavy tread approached on the stairs.

Officer Finch appeared on the landing. "Detective's talking with your cook now. We need the rest of you down here."

Owen put away his camera, and Dee draped the black cover-up around her shoulders. We trooped downstairs after Officer Finch and found Tony standing in the hall, leafing through his notes on the legal pad. Officer Marcos was gone.

Ramon came out of the pantry, carrying his guitar and sound gear. "I'm going home, unless you need me to stay."

"No, go ahead. I'll talk to you on Monday." I locked the door behind him, then returned to the others.

Tony glanced at Owen. "You can go."

"Actually, I've asked him to stay and take some photos for me," I said.

Tony gave me a skeptical look. I gestured to Dee.

"This is Gabriel's last work of art," I said.

Last *surviving* work; his own face paint was damaged, and while the ghoulish might still consider it art, I had no wish to record it even if I could have. The police photos would have to stand as documentation for that.

Dee lifted the cover-up to show her costume. Tony stared at it.

"Oh," he said.

"It was going to be revealed at midnight, in the black chamber," Dee said.

"That was supposed to be the highlight of the evening," I added. "Everyone was going to unmask, and there was going to be a toast—ohmigod. The vodka. It's probably still in the kitchen."

Tony turned to me. "Vodka?"

"Cinnamon vodka. To symbolize the Red Death."

He frowned. "I want you to explain this whole Red Death thing to me," he said.

"Yes, of course. It's a story by Edgar Allen Poe—"

"Not now."

Silenced, I waited. Tony seemed lost in thought.

"Could we take the photos?" Dee said. "It's cold."

With a shrug, Tony gestured toward the front of the house, which we took for permission. The technicians were now on the south side, so we went into the main parlor. It was warmer there, though the fire was down to coals. The candles in Rose were burning low, but still lit the black chamber with a red glare.

"I should turn off the lights," I said, glancing at Owen, who had his camera ready.

He nodded, and while everyone else clustered at the entrance of Rose, Dee removed the cover-up and took her place between the two candle lanterns. I turned off the overhead lights, and the others gasped.

Dee looked ethereal, a pale skeleton with a glowing red shroud. The silver paint dappled in patches on her face—and also on the bodysuit, the shroud, and even the tips of the wig, I noted— reflected the light from the candle lanterns in a brilliant red gleam, while the rest of the costume was shadowy. The effect was of tiny droplets of liquid blood, dappled all over her body.

15

"MAGNIFICENT," OWEN SAID SOFTLY, breaking the silence. He went to work taking photos of Dee, asking her to change position slightly so that he could get every angle.

The sandy-haired tech came across the hall to look. "Oh, that is *awesome!*" he declared, and summoned the police photographer to take photos of Dee.

I moved out of the way, into the center of the parlor where the draped archways gave onto the other chambers. Tony touched my arm and nodded for me to follow him out to the hall.

"We'll need that vodka," he said to me. "No one actually drank it?"

"No. You don't think—"

"I don't want to find out the hard way."

I swallowed. "OK. Yes, you're right—though I don't think Gabriel would do that."

Tony gave me his flat cop stare.

"And besides, Julio prepared the drinks."

"Let's go see what you've got," Tony said. He glanced at Officer Finch, who was watching through the draped archway. "Keep an eye on that."

Finch nodded and folded his arms across his chest. I led Tony to the kitchen.

"God, what a night," he said, suddenly looking exhausted.

"Want some coffee? I think there's some left."

"Yeah."

I poured him a mug and held it out to him. He put his notepad on the work table and wrapped his hands around mine. For a

173

heartbeat we stood, gazes locked. Then he pulled the mug away and drank.

"The vodka," he said.

"It's not in the fridge; I was in there earlier. I bet Julio put it in the freezer."

I opened the door of the walk-in, and saw the tray immediately. It stopped me short.

The large, oval serving tray was lined with white velvet. Around the outer edge, plain sugar skulls made a ring that tightly enclosed dozens of tall, straight shot glasses half-filled with red liquor.

"Damn," Tony muttered.

"We ought to take it to the parlor to be photographed," I said. "Dee was supposed to distribute them."

Tony frowned, but said nothing. I carefully picked up the tray and brought it out, realizing too late that my fingers were freezing to the metal.

It was heavy. Julio had been smart to fill the glasses only halfway; one slip and the red would have sloshed onto the white velvet. Gritting my teeth, I set the tray on the work table and carefully unstuck my fingers. They had gotten cold so fast that they ached, and I shook my hands in an attempt to warm them up again.

I closed the freezer, then joined Tony. We both stared at the tray.

"Yeah," he said slowly. "OK. Let's take it in. Don't touch the glasses."

I got some potholders to protect my skin, and picked the tray up again. Tony retrieved his notepad and went ahead to hold the draperies aside for me when we reached the parlor. Officer Finch's eyes went wide and he moved back.

"Coming through," Tony said, pushing back the drapery from Rose's entrance.

The others stepped aside. Dee gave a little gasp as I entered the chamber.

The sugar skulls' eyes lit up gleaming red. More of the silver paint; I hadn't noticed it in the kitchen. The vodka glasses lit up, too, with tiny motes of silver-red floating in the glasses.

"What the hell is that?" Tony said.

"Edible glitter. We use it for specialty items."

I set the tray on the stand where the salmon mousse puffs had been, and stepped back to get a better look at it. The skull eyes were not completely filled with silver; only pinpoints of brightness gleamed out from the center of the sockets. The effect was unnerving.

The clock began striking the hour. It was no longer amplified, but even so, we all stood still to listen. I glanced toward the mantel for the time. Three o'clock, and the night was not yet over.

"Oh, yeah!" Owen said, when the chimes stopped. "Dee, could you stand next to the tray?"

"Don't touch it," Tony warned, and looked at the sandy-haired tech. "Process that tray when you're done taking pictures. It all goes to the lab."

The tech nodded. Dee took her place, and Owen and the police photographer started taking photos.

Tony stepped out to say something to Finch, who went out to the hall. I heard the front door close and suddenly wanted to check that all the entrances were secured. I had locked the hall's back door, but what about the kitchen?

Leaving Tony watching the proceedings in Rose, I made sure everything was locked, including the French doors in the dining parlor. Returning to the main parlor, I found the lights on, Dee bundled in the cover-up again, and two of the techs swarming over the tray of vodka shots while the sandy-haired guy stood talking with Tony.

"You get the dining room?" Tony asked.

"Yeah. Looks a lot like the other time, except for the body. And the booze."

"Check the fireplaces?"

"Nothing in the ashes."

I felt a touch on my arm and turned to see Owen beside me. "Could you download photos again?" he said. "I said I'd share mine with the police."

"Sure," I replied, then looked at Dee. "And Dee, if you'd like to shower and change, you're welcome to use my suite."

"Yeah," she said, nodding. "I'm cold."

Leaving the police to wrap up their business downstairs, the rest of us trooped up, Mick and Owen to watch the file transfer while Dee showered. I marked the disks of photos and gave them to

Owen, and we drifted out to the upper hall to wait for Dee.

I sank into a chair in the sitting area, inviting Owen and Mick to join me with a wave of my hand. Without hostessing tasks to keep me busy, exhaustion was setting in. My eyelids felt heavy. Thoughts of Gabriel's body in Hidalgo Plaza rose up to haunt me.

Owen took an interest in my *ofrenda*. "May I photograph this?"

My instinct was to say no, though I could think of no logical reason. "It's private," I said finally.

Owen nodded and put away his camera. I liked him the better for it. He gazed at the table with the skulls and candles, smiling slightly. Taking pictures in his mind, perhaps.

Tony came upstairs with a heavy tread. "We're done," he said. "They're packing up. Thanks for the coffee and scones."

"Those two words really don't belong together," I remarked, "but you're welcome."

Tony walked over to us, gazed at Owen with a slight frown, then turned to me. "So. The Red Death. Want to tell me about it?"

"You might as well read the story. It's short. I'll go get my copy." I started to get up.

"It's online," Mick said.

Tony took out his phone and punched up a search. "I take it the gay erotic graphic novel is not what I'm looking for?"

"What? No!" I said.

Owen chuckled.

Flustered, I added, "It's Edgar Allen Poe. It's a classic."

Tony poked the phone again. "'Masque of the Red Death.'" He showed the phone to Mick, who nodded.

While Tony read, I stared out the front window and realized that the street outside was beginning to be less dark. Glancing toward the east window, I saw that the sky was taking on a blue tinge.

"OK, that's pretty weird," Tony said, putting away his phone and sitting on an arm of the couch. "At least now I get the colored rooms. So Gabriel was supposed to be Prospero?"

"It was a work of art," I said, overwhelmed by sadness. "Performance art, I guess."

"Maybe. But I don't like the Jonestown overtones."

I turned to look at him. "I'm *sure* Gabriel wouldn't do that!"

"How can you be sure?"

"This was a *party!*"

"Just because Goths have a taste for the macabre doesn't mean we're into mass suicide," Owen said. "There'd be a lot fewer Goths if we were."

Tony stared at him briefly. "Would Gabriel kill himself, though?"

"Gabriel's the last person I'd expect to do that."

"He had everything to live for," I put in. "He just got into a gallery in Canyon Road!"

"Mm." Tony looked at his notepad and scrawled a note on it, then tossed it onto the low table in front of us and rubbed his forehead. "I think my brain just shut down."

Dee (looking almost too normal in jeans and a sweater), came out of my suite, fluffing slightly damp hair.

"Here's the bodysuit," she said, offering a small, neatly folded bit of silvery fabric to me.

"Thank you. I'll deal with it."

"Felt kind of sad, washing off the paint."

I stood and tucked a wisp of blond hair behind her ear. "Thanks for hanging on to get the photos. It was important."

"Yeah. That's what I thought. Well, good night, I guess."

"Good night. Thank you, Mick," I told her brother as he stood.

"Want me to come in tomorrow to help clean up?" he asked.

"Maybe. Get some sleep first. I'll call you."

They headed downstairs, leaving me and Tony alone with the ever-patient Owen. "How much do I owe you for the photos?" I asked him.

"I wouldn't dream of charging you," Owen said, making a warding-off gesture with one hand. "It was a privilege to document Gabriel's final work." A shadow of sadness crossed his face, then he rose and made one of his quaint bows. "Good night, or good morning, rather. May tomorrow be a brighter day."

It could hardly be darker, I thought, but I merely gave him a weary smile and followed him downstairs, with Tony on our heels. Owen collected his cloak from the hall and headed for the front door, flinging the velvet around his shoulders with easy grace. I let him out and watched him walked down the path toward the gate. Closing the door, I leaned against it and looked at Tony.

"Alone at last," I said.

"Yeah. About that dinner date... you want breakfast instead?"

"How about a rain check? Really all I want now is my bed."

"That sounds good."

He came over to me, leaning a hand against the door on either side of me. A possessive gesture, but I didn't mind it, especially since he looked so tired. I reached a hand up and stroked his stubbled cheek.

He caught my hand in his and planted a kiss into my palm. A shimmer of anticipation went through my loins. He kissed me, long and deeply, then drew back.

"I really shouldn't see you during this investigation," he said, his voice rough.

I wanted to protest, but common sense told me he was right. Disappointment flooded my veins.

"Maybe you should take yourself off the case after all."

He shook his head. "We'd lose too much time bringing a new investigator up to speed. I don't want to have to explain..." He gestured toward the parlors.

"Right," I said.

"The first twenty-four hours are our best shot at catching the killer. After that the odds start dropping fast."

"So you don't believe it's suicide either."

He fixed me with a stare. It was not the cop stare; his dark eyes were full of longing and weariness.

"I trust your judgment," he said.

"Why, Tony Aragón. You're going to make me cry."

He sighed and planted another kiss on my forehead. "Gotta go. Call you in the morning."

"It *is* morning."

"Fine. I'll call you later, then."

"OK."

I let him out and watched until his bike roared out of sight around the corner. Locking the door, I thought of one more task I needed to do before crashing. Between the insurance company and the fire marshal, I'd had candle safety thoroughly drummed into me.

I chose to begin with the black chamber. Even though the overhead lights were on, the red glare of the lanterns made the back of my neck prickle. The colored glass was smudged with fingerprint powder. I stood between the lanterns and carefully extinguished them both. The black chamber was now merely black, no longer sinister.

Going through the narrow passage into Iris, I checked to make sure the fireplace was safe as I passed it. I put out the candles in each chamber as I worked my way back through them, from the violet to the white to the orange, then across the hall to the green and into the purple—my Violet alcove—where I paused. The lanterns were guttering there. I extinguished them, then looked at the *ofrenda*. Three votives, each in glass and each on a fireproof coaster, lit the offerings and Vi's painting. I left them burning, checked the fireplace, and went out to Hyacinth, the blue chamber, in time to watch the second of the two lanterns flicker out. I double-checked them just in case, verified the fireplace was safe, and went to the dining parlor.

A pale light was growing over the mountains, shining dimly in through the curtained French doors. The drinks table gleamed softly, waiting to serve revelers who would not be returning. A few bits of ice still floated in the half-full absinthe fountain. The candles that had warmed the cider had long since gone out. I glanced up at the chandelier, but it was still.

What did the captain think of all this? Perhaps the Goths had offended him.

Had he really known what would happen to Gabriel? Had he tried to warn me?

I needed to talk to Willow. We'd agreed to talk on the second, which was Monday. Tomorrow. Thank God it wasn't today.

All at once, I felt unspeakably weary. I checked the fireplace, then went upstairs. Dee's bodysuit sat folded neatly on the corner of the table in the sitting area with the candlelight of my tall votives flickering over it. They were safe; everything was safe, and I needed sleep, but I paused by the *ofrenda* for a moment to think of Gabriel.

Beautiful Gabriel. So talented, so *vivid*, and he'd been on the brink of success. It reminded me of Vi, the loss of such a shining soul. Wherever he was, I hoped he was free of suffering.

Normally I liked my phone's Chopin "Impromptu" ringtone, but it was too energetic for me just now. Groaning, I groped for it to shut it up, and peered groggily at the caller ID.

Gina.

"H'lo?"

"*Hola*, girlfriend! Happy November! It's time to finalize your holiday ad campaign. How about eggs Benedict? My treat."

I squeezed my eyes shut. Too many ideas at once, all things I didn't have room for in my brain right now.

"Um, I dunno. I think I need to stay here today."

"Why? Party too hard? A bloody Mary and some protein are just what you need."

"No…Gina…lemme get some tea in me and call you back."

"OK. If I don't hear from you in half an hour I'm coming over."

"I'll call you. Promise."

I disconnected, then looked at the time. Eight-seventeen; she'd let me sleep in a little.

Not enough, though. It had been after four when I crashed.

Memories of the hellish night rushed in on me. I dragged myself out of bed, stumbled over my costume from the night before which was lying on the floor, and slunk into my kitchenette to put the kettle on. I showered while it was heating, all the while remembering moments of horror from the previous evening.

Bundled in my robe, I made tea and toast. Protein would be a good idea, but I wasn't up to cooking eggs. As a gesture of good intention, I poured a dollop of milk into my tea mug. This was definitely a mug day, not a fine china day.

Sipping tea in my favorite chair, I watched the mostly-leafless tree branches waving outside my window. Breezy, though the sun was out. I tried to summon some enthusiasm for getting dressed. My feet ached and my calves were sore from going up and down the stairs. Emotionally, I was wrung out. Mentally, I felt like my brain was filled with cotton.

As I munched the last bite of my toast, I picked up my phone and called Gina. She answered on the second ring.

"Caffeinated now?" she asked.

"Partially. I'm going to have to ask for a rain check on the ad planning session. I'm probably going to be busy all day."

"Don't tell me the Goths trashed the place."

"N-no. Well, there's some cleanup, but that's not the problem." I winced and closed my eyes, not wanting to say the next words aloud. "One of them died last night."

"Crap! In the tearoom?"

"No, thank God, but it was during the party. So the police were here most of the night, talking to all the guests.

"Ellen, was this person murdered?"

"Maybe." Probably.

"Oh, honey—"

"Don't worry, I didn't find him."

"But still. God, is it someone we know?"

"You don't know him. One of Kris's friends."

"Have you called Tony?"

"He's investigating the case."

"Ay, yi. yi. Well, better him than a stranger."

I thought about that, wondering whether I agreed. Complicated question. My brain wasn't up to it yet.

"Tell you what," Gina said. "I'll bring calzones over for lunch. We don't have to talk business today, but I think you're gonna need a hug."

"I'll take all the hugs I can get. Thanks."

We said goodbye, and I put the phone down and finished my tea, then got up to refill the mug. I was halfway through dragging on sweat pants and a long-sleeved sweater when the phone rang again. This time the ringtone was the "1812 Overture" and I grabbed the phone with one leg in my pants.

"Tony," I said. "Did you get some sleep?"

"Nah. Espresso and a couple of energy drinks."

Ouch. "Have you eaten?"

"I'm about to. Then I'll be over to ask you some questions. Just wanted to make sure you were awake."

"I am. Sort of."

"Good."

I finished donning my sweat pants, drank a second mug of tea while I tidied, then went into my bedroom to collect my costume. The gown could be laundered; the belt and headpiece could not.

Feeling a sudden urge to call Kris, I retrieved my phone and entered her number. Got voicemail, for which I hardly blamed her.

"Kris, this is Ellen. Please call if you want to talk, or just come have some tea. I'm thinking of you."

I took the gown downstairs to wash it. As I reached the foot of the stairs, I found the hall in semi-darkness, because the windows at either end were still covered. Switching on the lights, I realized what I'd been too tired and stressed to see the night before.

The place was a wreck.

Paper cups were scattered everywhere, on the low tables and on the floor, interspersed with glassware. About a dozen capes and coats hung on the hooks that lined the hall. One of them was probably Gabriel's, but I was surprised that so many of the other guests had left their belongings. Of course, the police had pretty much thrown them out right after interviewing them.

"Don't get mad," I told myself. "Get busy."

This called for Mozart, I decided. I went into the butler's pantry to turn on the stereo, and found a tray loaded with a teapot, plates, two cups with saucers, an empty lemon curd bowl, and assorted silverware. When I carried this into the kitchen, I saw more trays and an array of coffee mugs, carafes, and pitchers.

I needed help, I decided. Mick. Too early to call, though. I'd let him sleep another couple of hours. Meanwhile, I'd start getting the mess under control.

Returning to the pantry, I loaded Kris's costume into the washer and started it. The mess had distracted me from my need for music. I dug out *Eine kleine Nachtmusik* and plugged it in. Hard to get more cheerful than that.

With Mozart bursting through the house, I fetched a trash bag and began going around the downstairs collecting paper cups and napkins. We hadn't provided plates for the food, wanting people to nibble and keep moving through the chambers rather than load up. When I'd filled the bag, I took it to the kitchen and swapped it for a tray, then made the rounds again, this time collecting stemware and mugs. I was in Lily when the front doorbell rang.

Leaving the tray on a table in the hall, I pulled aside the black cloth covering the lights around the front door. Tony was outside, in the same clothes he'd had on the previous night, and looking the worse for wear. I unlocked the door.

"Tea?" I offered.

"No thanks, I'm stuffed. Where do you want to talk?"

I opened the door wider, inviting him in. "Let's go upstairs. I'm a bit tired of...." I waved my hands at the parlors. If it hadn't been for Gabriel's death, I'd have made a joke about Prospero's abbey.

We went up to my office, where I invited Tony to make himself comfortable while I put the kettle on for tea. When I returned, I found him in a guest chair, holding the leaf mask in his hand. He looked up at me with a raised eyebrow as I went to my chair and set my phone on the desk.

"That's Owen's," I said.

"What was he doing in your office?"

"Talking about photography. And downloading pictures for you. What do you think he was doing?"

I hadn't meant to challenge, but I was in no mood for dog-with-bone behavior. Tony gazed at me with narrowed eyes for a moment, then let it drop. He put the mask back on my desk. I moved it to the credenza.

"Let's just get that out of our way," I said briskly, then returned to my seat. "Now, how can I help you?"

He dug a much-folded wad of paper from his pocket, and I recognized the pages as having been torn from the legal pad I'd given him. Next he pulled out the guest-list, also much abused and adorned with check marks and scribbles, which he offered to me.

"Help me narrow this down. Who should I be looking at?"

"So it's murder."

He laid the list in front of me. "Who should I look at?" he repeated softly.

"Good grief, how should I know? I never saw most of these people before last night!"

"Most of them. Which ones did you see before? Besides Kris. And Gabriel."

"Kris didn't do it."

"That's not what I asked."

"She *couldn't* have!"

"Look, if you're not going to help—"

"Sorry. Sorry. All right." I looked at the guest list, reluctant to pick it up. "There was a planning meeting for the party a couple of weeks ago."

"Here?"

I nodded. "In the dining parlor."

"Who was at it?"

"Kris and Gabriel, myself, Ramon." I frowned at the guest list, which was alphabetical. "Gwyneth Bancroft and Roberto Chavez. Margo Foss. Cherie Legrand. And…Dale Whittier. I think that's it. Let me check."

I fired up my computer. The kettle whistled, and I went across the hall to make tea. Tony was making notes when I returned with my kitchen timer. The computer had booted, so I brought up my calendar to check the planning party.

"Yes, that's everyone."

"What about Mr. Leaf-face?" he asked, gesturing toward Owen's mask.

"He wasn't there," I said firmly. "Julio was in the kitchen, and Dee was serving. Oh, and Mick was here too."

"Dee?"

"Yes. But she didn't do it."

Tony gave me a skeptical look. I shrugged.

"She's the one who *found* Gabriel. She called me right away."

"When? What time?"

I checked my phone. "Eleven seventeen."

"M.E. says time of death was between eleven and eleven-thirty."

"Well, that fits."

He leafed through his papers and read from one. "Mick saw Dee leave a couple minutes after eleven."

"Dee did *not* kill Gabriel! She hardly knew him. She only met him the night of the meeting, like me."

"But then she let him paint that body suit while she was wearing it. Said it took three sessions."

I swallowed, not wanting to believe that Dee could betray Kris. There *had* been a connection between Dee and Gabriel, though. I had sensed it, but I'd assumed it was confined to his art. Was that wishful thinking?

"Even if there was something going on there," I said slowly, "and I'm not convinced there was…that wouldn't give Dee any reason to kill Gabriel."

"Let's get back to the meeting," Tony said. "What do you know about the people who were there?"

They all slept with Gabriel.

Or maybe just all the women.

I swallowed. "Roberto's an artist. Gwyneth modeled for both him and Gabriel. She was with Gabriel before she hooked up with Roberto."

"Why did she switch?"

"I don't know. I think…maybe Roberto was more inclined to put her on a pedestal. I could be wrong, though. I don't really know them."

"What makes you think that, though?"

"Well—I saw their art at the exhibition. Gabriel's was pretty stark, not always flattering to Gwyneth. Roberto's…well, he painted her as Titania."

"Who?"

"The queen of the fairies. From Shakespeare's *Midsummer Night's Dream*."

Tony looked through his notes, and scrawled something on one of the pages.

"Do you want some fresh paper?"

"Nah. So Roberto loves Gwyneth. Think he stole her from Gabriel?"

"Possibly. I think they were…rivals…in more ways than one."

Tony tilted his head, gazing at me. "You mean professional rivals."

I nodded. "Gabriel just got into a gallery on Canyon Road. I think Roberto was trying to do the same. Well, all artists want that, right?"

"Think Roberto would kill over that? Professional jealousy?"

An appalling suggestion. I made myself consider it before answering. "It seems rather a stretch. Roberto had won Gwyneth. Couldn't that be revenge enough?"

"You said they were rivals. Lot of money in Canyon Road." Tony gazed steadily at me and I sensed his intensity go up a notch.

"Yes," I said slowly, "but killing Gabriel wouldn't improve Roberto's chances of showing there."

"How do you know?"

I bit my lip. "I'm not a professional critic, but I think Gabriel's work was a few notches above Roberto's."

My timer went off. I picked it up and stood. "Change your mind about tea?"

Tony shook his head. I fetched a fresh mug for myself, indulged in sugar and milk (a little more protein), and settled back behind my desk.

"What about Gwyneth?" Tony said.

"She didn't kill Gabriel."

He dropped his notes in his lap and treated me to the Cop Stare.

"No, I'm *sure* she didn't. She was distraught after you talked to her last night. I found her crying outside, waiting for Roberto."

"Could be an act. She strikes me as a drama queen."

"I don't think so. I mean—yes, she's a drama queen, but I don't think she's that good an actor. When I brought her in the kitchen, she asked me *why* Gabriel was dead. She seemed genuinely bewildered."

"Oh." Tony grimaced and made a note. "It's never the easy answer."

"The easy answer would have been Roberto. But I don't think he did it either."

Tony's eyes narrowed and I thought he might be about to contradict me, but instead he said, "Do *you* have someone in mind?"

"No." I thought about it, frowning. "No. I'm sorry. There were so many people here…"

"What about these others from the meeting?"

"Ramon would have no reason to kill Gabriel. None of my staff would."

"Except Kris. And maybe Dee."

"I don't think Kris did it, and I don't know why Dee would," I said loftily.

He made another note, and looked through the pages. He wanted me to get defensive on behalf of Dee, or Kris. Probably both. Determined not to let him push me, I picked up my mug and drank.

"Several people mentioned that Gabriel danced with Gwyneth right before eleven," Tony said.

"Yes. He did." I put down my mug, remembering that dance,

how everyone watched. "It was probably a bad idea, but I totally get why he did it."

"Why's that?"

"He…reveled in his attractiveness to women."

"You mean he dug being sexy."

"It's more than that. He wasn't just sexy, he was magnetic. Charismatic. I felt it myself."

"Did you kill him?"

"Tony!"

He hunched a shoulder and busied himself with his notes. "Sorry. Gotta ask."

"No, I did not! He was my *client*. I had no reason at all to kill him. Every reason not to, in fact, because now—" I stopped myself before I went over the cliff of self-pity.

"Because…?"

"I'll probably lose money on that party. It isn't important."

"He didn't pay you?"

"He paid a deposit. Tony, it doesn't matter."

"It could matter. How much was it going to cost him?"

"Not enough to kill for, if that's where you're going."

"You'd be surprised what people will kill for."

That was one of the more chilling things Tony had ever said to me. I stared at him, trying to convince myself he was just being dramatic, but the straight gaze he gave me seemed to confirm his words.

My throat felt dry, suddenly. I picked up my mug. Sometimes it was hard to feel good about the world.

"I wonder who's Gabriel's heir?" I mused. "If he even had a will."

"I can answer that one. He did."

I waited, curious, but not willing to push. It might be that Tony wouldn't divulge that bit of information.

He stared back at me. Unwilling to get into such a game, I yielded, turning to my computer.

"I know less about the other people at the meeting, except for Dale Whittier. He's applied for a job here, so I know a good deal about him, but not really anything to do with Gabriel. Except…." I frowned. Something was niggling at my memory. "There's a connection."

"With Gabriel?"

"No," I said slowly. "Not Gabriel. Someone else."

Whatever it was slipped away. I rubbed my forehead. "I'm sorry. I can't remember."

"If you remember it later, write it down."

"Yes."

"What about Cherie Legrand?"

I shrugged. "I met her the night of the meeting, and didn't see her again until the party. Same with Margo. No—that's not true. I saw them at the art exhibition. Briefly."

"Were all of them at the exhibition?"

"I think so. Yes, Dale was there, too."

Silence made me look up at Tony. He was watching me with narrowed eyes.

"What?"

If he intended to bring Loren into the conversation, I just might blow my cool. I leaned back in my chair, waiting.

Tony reached into his jacket and pulled out an evidence bag. Inside it was something flat and black. He tossed it on my desk.

"Don't open the bag. Ever seen that before?"

I looked at the bag, poking it gingerly to rotate it. There was a black cord and a flat, black, rectangular object attached to one end of it. It rang a bell. I turned the bag over and recognized the black rectangle, because on this side it was clear and contained a map.

"It's a badge from the exhibition," I said. "That's a map of the booths."

"Did you get one?" Tony asked, leaning forward and staring intently at me.

"Yes. Everyone did."

"Do you still have yours?"

"I think so…" I started digging through my "to file" pile. About two thirds of the way down I found my badge and pulled it out.

Tony gave an audible sigh and collapsed back in his chair. "Thank God."

"Why?"

He pointed to the evidence bag. "Because that's the murder weapon."

16

I STARED AT THE BADGE INSIDE ITS PLASTIC BAG, twin to the one in my hand...or almost. Now I registered a detail I hadn't noted before: the cord of the bagged badge had been cut. By the paramedics, I assumed.

My eyes filled with tears. "Oh, God."

I dropped my badge and pushed my chair back from the desk, weeping. It was stress, lack of sleep—and deep sadness for Gabriel, who mattered to me much more than I'd expected.

"Ellen. Ellen, I'm sorry," Tony said as I blubbered.

I waved a hand helplessly, wiping at my streaming eyes with the other, wanting him to know I didn't blame him. Fumbling toward my desk, I tried to find the box of tissue, then felt it pushed into my hands.

"I'm sorry," Tony said again, his voice gentle. "I had to—"

"I know, I know," I said soggily.

A hug would have been nice. Instead I heard his footsteps leaving the office. Struggling to get control of myself, I coughed and hiccuped.

One hiccup. *One.*

I straightened and pushed my shoulders back, drawing a deep, ragged breath. Tony came in, carrying my teapot carefully with both hands.

"Will this help?" he said.

I nodded and pushed my mug toward him. He put the teapot on the credenza and carried the mug over to it. Watching him pour tea for me, my heart relaxed a little and all my former annoyance left me.

189

He put the pot down and brought me the mug. "Thanks," I said, and took a sip.

"You want to take a break?"

"Uh-huh."

I got up and walked out to the hall and over to my sitting area, standing by the window and looking down at the street as I drank my tea. A breezy, sunny day.

"What's all this?" Tony asked. "Did you make these?"

Turning, I saw him looking at my sugar skulls. "Yes. Julio had a skull-decorating party, remember?"

"You make the ones downstairs, too?"

"There's one that I made in Violet, on the mantel."

"I mean the ones in all the colored rooms."

"Oh—actually, I don't know who made those. Dale put them there right before the party began, but he said he didn't make them."

"Dale put them there? Why?"

"I don't know. You might ask him."

Tony shoved his hands in his pockets, frowning in thought. I looked out the window again. Leaves blowing around on the lawn. I'd have to rake them up. Maybe next weekend I'd have time.

"Feeling better?" Tony asked.

"Yes. Thanks."

"Can I show you something else?"

I felt the muscles between my shoulder blades tighten. "If you must," I said, turning to face him.

"It's not bad. It's just a scrap of fabric. We found it at the scene."

He produced another, smaller evidence bag and held it out to me. Inside was a small shred of black tulle.

"Could any of your guests have been wearing that?"

"Probably at least half of them," I said.

"Yeah, I kind of figured. Thanks."

"Plus, it was Halloween. Any black costume could have included this kind of fabric. There was a witch in the bar at Hidalgo Plaza."

"You're right."

"I don't suppose anyone there saw anything."

"Not until after you and Dee arrived."

"Hm. And you think the killer left this?"

He met my gaze as he held out his hand. "Yeah, I think so."

"Well," I said, turning the bag around. "That lets out Kris and Dee, then. Neither of their costumes included tulle."

"Tool?"

"Tulle. T-u-l-l-e." I waved the bag. "That's what this is. It's a kind of fabric. Used in ballet costumes a lot."

"How do you know Kris and Dee weren't wearing it? Could've been underneath."

"Tulle isn't used for linings or undergarments. It would be too itchy. And I know about Dee's costume because I helped her dress. There was no tulle in it."

He took the bag back. "Did you help Kris dress?"

"No, but her gown was silk velvet, not tulle. And it wasn't black. In fact, none of the party planners were wearing black. They were all dressed in the colors of the chambers."

"There was a black chamber."

"That was Gabriel's. Kris's was next door, the violet one. Do you need a copy of the map?"

"There's a map?"

"Yes. Gabriel planned it all. It's in my office."

"I want to see it." He met my gaze and added, "In a minute."

"Thanks," I said, and took another swallow of tea.

Tony looked at the tulle. "So I'm looking for a ballerina."

"Not necessarily. There were some fairies at the party wearing black tulle. What you're looking for is a torn costume. If you're lucky, it wasn't intended to look torn."

"Let me guess. There were people wearing torn tulle at the party."

"Wouldn't surprise me, though I don't recall offhand."

Tony nodded, looking depressed. "Another roadblock. I've got a lot of them on this case."

"Can I help with any of them?"

"I doubt it."

"Worth a try?"

He sighed, and sat on the sofa. "OK, here's one. Nobody saw Gabriel leave the house."

"Dee saw him go by the kitchen window."

"Right. The hall was full of people, and none of *them* saw him. I figure he went out the front door right after Gwyneth fainted, when everyone was looking the other way."

"So he went out the front, and along the side to the back. And Dee said he was running. Why?"

"Good question."

I sat beside him and put my mug on the table.

"Maybe he saw Gwyneth faint, and got upset..." I shook my head. "That doesn't make sense. I'd expect him to go *toward* her, not away."

"Even though she was with Roberto?"

"Yes. He was kind, despite the artist's ego. So either he got an urgent message that made him leave, or..."

"He was chasing someone."

"Which would mean someone else left the party before him."

"Right. But nobody has fessed up to that."

I met his gaze. "Somebody's lying."

He nodded. "Or Gabriel was killed by someone who wasn't a party guest. But I think that's not likely."

"What happened to suicide?"

"We're pretty sure it wasn't."

I leaned back, absorbing the fact that the killer had been a guest in my house. I didn't want to believe it.

"Most murder victims are killed by someone they know," Tony said.

"You think it was Kris."

"I haven't ruled her out."

I bit my lip. I knew in my heart that she hadn't killed Gabriel. Even when he danced with Gwyneth, she'd been calm. She'd forgiven him.

But they *had* disagreed about something that night. I'd overheard them talking, here upstairs. I rubbed my head, trying to remember.

I heard my phone, which I'd left on my desk, ring, dispelling the memory like a puff of smoke. I fetched it and came back out.

"It's Gina," I told Tony. "Please excuse me."

He nodded, looking amused, and took out his own phone.

"Special delivery!" Gina said when I answered. "Come and let me in."

I met her at the back door. She looked smart in a red coat over a floral dress, crowned with a red pillbox hat with a little net veil. Her cheeks were rosy from the chill and she had a large paper carry-out bag in one hand.

"Sweetie," she said, folding me into a perfumed, one-armed hug. I closed my eyes, enjoying the comfort, wordlessly grateful.

She released me, took one look at the state of the hallway, and said, "Let's go upstairs."

Tony put his phone away as we reached the upper hall. "Hi, Tony," Gina said as she opened her bag. "Good thing I brought extras! You want pepperoni and mushroom, veggie feta, or green chile sausage?"

"Oh, no thanks," said Tony, patting his stomach. "Big breakfast."

She arched an eyebrow at him, then turned to me.

"Pepperoni, please," I said. "And thanks for bringing them."

"So *you* did *not* have a big breakfast." She flashed a grin at Tony. "I'm practicing to be Sherlock Holmes."

"Nice outfit," he countered. "Do you always dress up to buy take-out?"

"I came straight from church," she said, and there the subject died.

Gina was not the most devout person I knew, but she was arguably the most faithful church-goer. She went every week, often in the company of her *nonna*. I took credit for getting her to wear hats. At first she protested that it was old fashioned, but once she started wearing them she loved the attention they got.

She looked at the sitting area, where the sugar skulls took up half the table. "Hm."

"Let's eat in my suite," I said. "I can make coffee."

"Bless you, darling."

Tony followed us in and joined us at the small dining table. I started my seldom-used coffee-maker while Gina shed her coat and dug out plates and silverware. The smell of garlic and spices had set my stomach growling; I dug into my calzone without ceremony.

"Radio had a story about a Halloween hanging," Gina said, looking at Tony as she opened a container of marinara. "That your case?"

Tony grimaced. "Probably."

"Can we not talk about it over lunch?" I said.

"Sorry. What would you like to talk about? Not the holiday ads, I assume."

"No."

Gina looked from me to Tony and back again. "What are you guys doing for Thanksgiving?" she said.

"I'm not sure," I said, glancing at Tony. "Usually I get together with Nat, but she might have other plans this year."

"Well, you're always welcome at our dinner. You too, Tony. It's a big, Italian family meal with lots of wine and antipasto and cannoli along with the turkey and all that."

"Thanks," Tony said, "but we have our own family meal."

"Where do you have yours?" I asked Gina. "Not at your apartment."

"Mama's place. She's got a table that seats twenty. We all dress up. I know you can manage that," she said, grinning.

Gina kept up a flow of chatter about her family and holiday meals while we ate. Not feeling chatty myself, I was grateful. Tony watched and listened and drank coffee.

When I'd finished my calzone, Gina produced a container of cannoli. "Chocolate chip or raspberry almond?"

"Oh, gosh," I said, looking at Tony. "Want to split one?"

Shrug, nod. I chose the chocolate chip, figuring he'd like it better than the raspberry. Gina took a raspberry and snuck about a third of it onto my plate. I smiled my thanks.

"Well, I've got to run, darlings," she said when the sweets were gone. She bustled around putting lids back on containers. "Now, let's see if this'll all fit in your fridge."

I started to get up, but Tony jumped up faster and took my plate away. Our gazes met and I smiled my thanks. He smiled back, with a look in his eyes that made my pulse accelerate, then turned to the kitchenette.

"This is so you don't have to worry about dinner," Gina said, rearranging the contents of my mini-fridge. "But if you want something different, just call and I'll take you out."

"Thanks."

"Now, you take care of yourself! Go out for a walk or something. Don't spend the whole day in here. Tony, you make sure she gets out."

"Yes, ma'am."

Gina put on her coat and gave me another big hug. "Love you, honey."

"Love you too. Thanks."

I saw her out, and realized on my way back up the stairs that I felt better. Tony was waiting for me in the hall.

"Can I see that map now?" he asked. "And can you stand to look at the badge again? I have a question about it."

"OK."

We went back in my office, and I returned to my desk. My badge had fallen on the floor, so I picked it up.

"Can I see that?" Tony asked.

I handed it to him and he examined it, then looked at the one in the evidence bag. "What are the circles?"

"Circles?"

"On the map. Some of the numbers are circled."

"Oh, Gabriel did that. I asked him to recommend other artists to look at."

"Did he do it for anyone else?"

"Yeah, Dale, and Margo, I think. And that's just who I saw."

"So he could have done it all weekend."

I nodded. "Kris will know. She was with him in the booth."

He handed my badge back to me. I shouldn't have felt relieved, but I did. I slipped it into my desk drawer, and while I was in there I pulled out my file for the party and extracted Gabriel's map of the chambers. I held it out it to Tony, who stared at it.

"Who else saw this?"

"Gabriel handed out copies at the planning meeting."

"Could I keep this one?" he said.

"May I scan it first?"

He gave it back. I fed it to my all-in-one printer, saved the file, then gave him the original. He gazed dejectedly at it.

"So Gabriel was here, and Kris was here," he said, pointing to the map.

"Right."

"Who were in these two?"

"Roberto in the orange, and Gwyneth in the white."

Tony grabbed a pen from my desk and wrote in the names. "But they were both at the back of the house when Gabriel left."

"Yes. They'd been outside, and had just come in the back door, and then she fainted."

He tilted his head, looking at the map. "I wonder if that was an act. They could have been cooperating with the killer."

"I really doubt it. I saw her collapse. It looked real, and Roberto was truly upset."

Tony sighed. "OK. Who was in these other chambers?"

"Cherie in blue, Margo in green, and Dale in purple."

He filled in the names, then frowned. "Why is there both purple and violet?"

"Got me. Ask Poe."

He shot me a glance.

"Sorry. The answer is nobody knows. Poe never explained the color choices."

"So…any one of the three on the south side could have seen Gabriel leave. But they all denied it."

"It was after ten, so they weren't necessarily in their chambers. Gabriel said they could move around after the first hour. And in fact…" I frowned, chasing the memories. "I saw Cherie right before Gwyneth and Roberto came in."

"Saw her where?"

"In the dining parlor. She was getting a glass of absinthe."

"Who else did you see?"

I closed my eyes, thinking back. "I'd just gone around to check the fireplaces. There wasn't anyone in the blue, green, and purple chambers."

"All the ones on the south side of the house."

"Right. I saw Kris in her chamber, then I checked the fire, then I saw Gabriel in his. Oh!"

Opening my eyes, I saw Tony watching me, waiting. He had his notes spread open on his knee and a pen in one hand.

"Gabriel said something, but when I glanced into his chamber I didn't see anybody but him," I said. "It was odd."

"Talking to himself?"

"I don't think so. It was something like, 'What do you want?' and I assumed he was on the phone."

"Couldn't have been. We found his phone with his street clothes." Tony made another note. "Maybe it was Kris. Her chamber was right next door. She could have stepped into his."

I frowned. "She would have had to pass me, or go the long way around."

Tony shrugged. "Feasible."

"But I would have seen her when I looked in!"

"Her dress was violet, right? Pretty dark in that black chamber."

"She had on a silver crown, and silver trim on the dress, and her mask was silver," I said, trying not to sound angry. "You saw how those red lights lit up the silver paint on Dee's costume."

Tony sighed and looked back at his notes. "What about Cherie? She was next door, in the dining room. Was there silver on her outfit?"

"No. It was all blue." I frowned. "And I'm not sure exactly when she came into the dining parlor."

"So she's a possibility. Gwyneth and Roberto were at the back door, so it wasn't either of them. That leaves Dale and Margo. Crap," he said as his phone rang.

He folded the map and stuffed it in his pocket, then walked out into the hall. That pleased me; he wouldn't have bothered a few months ago. Maybe I was actually influencing him a little.

I glanced at the clock on my computer: after one. Kris hadn't called me back. I picked up my phone and sent her a text.

> You OK? Need anything?

> No.

I grimaced, but was glad to see that she was alive, at least. Alive, and in pain, and ready to take it out on the world.

> Call if you want to talk.

She didn't respond. I was about to get up when the desk phone rang, making me jump.

"We're closed," I said to it as it continued to ring. Specters of news reporters rose in my imagination, then the voicemail kicked in.

"Hi, Ellen, it's Dale. I was wondering if—"

I grabbed the handset. "Hello?"

"Oh. Hi. Um, is it OK if we come pick up the absinthe fountain?"

"Of course," I said.

"Thanks. Half an hour OK?"

"I'll be here."

I put down the phone. Not wanting to sit alone and stare at the murder weapon, I got up and went out to join Tony, who was just stashing his phone. "That was the lab," he said. "Nothing in the vodka besides food coloring and that glitter."

I was glad to be right on that point. The thought of Gabriel using his magnetism to get people to poison themselves made me shiver, the more so because I believed he could have done it, if he'd wanted to.

"Who called you?" Tony asked.

"Dale. He's coming to get the absinthe fountain."

"The what?"

"That big water-cooler thing in the dining parlor."

"Oh. Dale's the one that put the skulls around, right? Did you ever figure that out?"

"No."

Tony frowned. "Can we go look at them again?"

"Sure."

He stepped past me into my office, stuffed the evidence bags with the badge and the tulle into his jacket pockets, then led the way downstairs. Following Gabriel's map, he began walking through the chambers in order, starting with the blue chamber. He picked up the sugar skull, turned it over, then shrugged and put it back.

We both went into the purple chamber, Violet. Tony paused to gaze at Vi's portrait.

"You're right, it needs better light."

The candles on the mantel had burned out overnight, and I felt an urge to light at least one new one. Later, I told myself, and turned to the lamp stand with a sugar skull decorated in purple on it. "This is the one Dale put here."

Tony looked at it, then back at the skulls on the mantel. "Who did these?"

I pointed them out. "Me, Julio, Kris, Gabriel, Dee."

"Did Gabriel know Vi?"

"I don't think so. Kris probably told him about her."

"And these were up here before the party started?"

"A week before. We made them at Julio's decorating party."

Tony leaned his hands against the mantel, tapping one thumb on the wood. "Anyone at that party who *didn't* make a skull for Vi?"

"Sure. Your sister, for one."

Tony shot me a glance. "Who else?"

"Andre, Julio's roommate. And by the way, I don't think Vi has anything to do with this."

"Humor me."

"Dale. Margo. Cherie." I paused, thinking. "Mick, but he didn't decorate any skulls."

"Not Roberto? Or Gwyneth?"

"They weren't there. I don't think Julio knew them. It was his party."

"But Dale and Cherie and Margo were all there. Does Julio know them?"

"N-no. I guess Gabriel invited them."

"But he didn't ask Roberto and Gwyneth."

"No. Do you blame him? He and Roberto were rivals, remember?"

"And Gwyneth was his ex."

"Y-yes," I said slowly.

Tony turned his head to look at me. "What?"

I swallowed. "Kris told me that Gabriel had…slept with the others at the planning meeting. I think she meant just the women."

Tony's eyes went wide. "*All* of them?"

"That's what she said."

He paced around the room, which only took a few steps. "So not just Gwyneth, but Margo and Cherie…in what order?"

"I don't know."

He took out a pen and his wad of notes. "Thanks."

After making a note, he consulted the map and went through the passage at the back into the green chamber. I stood still, staring at the purple brocade draperies, feeling like a betrayer of womankind. How awful to think that Gabriel might have been killed by a jealous lover—so cliché! Worse, the most likely candidate in that case was Kris.

No tulle, my heart shouted. But that wasn't conclusive. The tulle could have come from anywhere; it could be completely unrelated.

Maybe it was!

I hurried through the green chamber and caught up with Tony in the hall. "Tony, where was that scrap of tulle found?"

He paused and gave me an appraising look. "You remember where Gabriel ended up?"

I swallowed and nodded. "The flower basket."

"The scrap was between the strap of the badge and the basket hook."

"Oh."

Not unrelated, then. That scrap of tulle would convict its owner, if she could be found.

Not necessarily "she," I told myself. But tulle was mostly used for women's costumes. Ballet tutus, wedding veils…

I tried to imagine how a tutu could get caught between the badge lanyard and the flower hook, and failed completely.

"Why Hidalgo Plaza?" I mused.

"I've been wondering that, too," Tony said, following the map into the orange chamber and pausing to look at the sugar skull there. "The badge tells me the killer knew Gabriel, and he left the party in a hurry. That makes it probable that the killer was someone at the party. But if so, why go a quarter-mile away? Why not hang him in the yard here—"

"Bite your tongue!" I said, outraged.

"—where the intended audience would see him?"

"Maybe the killer didn't want him to be seen."

"In that case, there are much better places than Hidalgo Plaza."

That was true.

"Or maybe it was an accident," I offered.

"Possible, but not our top theory. He was—do you want to hear this?"

I hesitated, then nodded.

"We found damage to the railing on the second story, above the basket hook. He was pushed."

And that gave me the picture of how it happened. He chased the killer, they ran into the plaza and up the stairs. Argument, push.

"But how did the lanyard get around his neck?" I asked.

"And why?" Tony said.

"Around his neck..." I frowned. Something was tickling at my memory. Something about the sugar skull party.

Gabriel by the lilac bushes, putting something into Cherie's hands. Kris pretending not to notice as she decorated a skull. Gabriel returning to the table, his collar framing his neckline.

And no ankh. No ankh, when he'd been wearing it before!

Quickly I told Tony what I had remembered. "He must have given the ankh to Cherie!"

"In front of his current girlfriend?" Tony said skeptically.

"Maybe it was a gift from Cherie, and he was returning it. She wasn't happy about it, I remember that!"

"What happened next?"

I shrugged. "People decorated skulls. I...don't think I saw Cherie again. She might have slipped away."

"You don't have any of the skulls she decorated, do you?"

"No, but I took pictures of all the skulls."

He looked up from the map, gaze intent. "Show me!"

We went upstairs, and I brought up the skull pictures. There were a lot of them. Tony blinked at the screen full of thumbnails. It was a wild medley of color. Seeing them all at once reminded me how creative everyone had been.

"Oh, man," Tony said, sounding tired. "Do you know who did which skulls?"

"Some of them. Not all."

"Show me the ones Cherie made."

"I'm not sure about them. I can eliminate a lot of the others."

"Do that."

I copied the folder, then deleted all the photos of skulls decorated by me, Angela, Kris, Gabriel, Julio, and Andre. That left about thirty skulls.

"Dee did that one. Rosa did those," I said, deleting them. "Dale did these two. I'm not sure about the rest."

Tony enlarged the remaining thumbnails and looked through them. "That one," he said, pointing to an Egyptian looking one. "Who made that?"

"I'm not sure."

"Look at the forehead."

I zoomed the photo and gasped. The skull had an upside-down

ankh on the forehead.

"Oh, my...."

"Bet it was Cherie," Tony said. "Who would know for sure?"

"Um. Rosa and Dee were at the table with her. They might remember."

Tony made another note. "Want to save me the trouble of looking up their numbers? And could you text me that photo, please?"

I did as he asked, and browsed through the remaining skull photos. There was another Egyptian one, but it didn't have an ankh. I enlarged it anyway, and Tony leaned closer to the screen to look.

I became conscious of his smell, of leather and weariness and his own distinctive Tony-ness. Instinct made me turn my head to catch a better whiff. He met my gaze.

"You smell good," I said.

His mouth dropped open, then he pushed his phone and notes onto my desk and reached for me.

Blood fired through my tired veins with sudden thunder. I returned his hungry kiss with equal enthusiasm. I was tired of skulls, puzzles, and sadness.

In the distance, the front doorbell ring downstairs rang. Tony raised his head, muttering a curse.

"You expecting someone?"

"It's probably Dale, coming to get that fountain." I shifted in his arms, regretting necessity. "Um. Will you excuse me?"

Tony kissed me again hotly, then gently, then let me go. I stood, straightened my clothing, took a deep breath, and went downstairs. At the front door I pushed aside the black fabric that still covered the lights

Not Dale, but Margo stood outside, looking pale in a black sweater and jeans. But then, Goths liked to look pale.

I opened the door. "Hi, Margo."

"Hi," she said in a near-whisper. "Sorry to bother you." She took a breath. "I left my cloak."

I stepped back. "Come on in."

She hesitated a split second, as if returning to the scene of the party brought bad memories, then headed for a row of hooks near the back of the house, several of which held cloaks or coats. Reaching for one, she hesitated, then took down its neighbor and folded it over her arm. They were both black; everything on the hooks was black.

Margo stood staring at the cloak in her arms, one hand stroking the velvet. I noticed it had a pretty silver clasp, a triangular Celtic knot.

Tony came down the stairs. "Margo! Got a minute?"

She jumped slightly and looked up at him. "You scared me!"

"Sorry. I have a couple more questions if you don't mind."

Taking pity on her, I gestured to the chairs that still lined the hall. "Have a seat. Would you like some tea?"

Margo shook her head, hugging her cloak as she sank into a wing chair. "It's just so awful," she whispered, brushing aside a tear.

Tony pulled another chair out from the wall and set it at right angles to Margo's. I hovered, unsure whether I should stay.

"First of all, do you remember who made this?" He turned his phone toward her, displaying my photo of the skull with the ankh on it.

Margo stared at it for a few seconds. "I'm not sure. Sorry. Maybe Cherie."

"OK." Tony put away his phone and took out his wad of notes. "Are you sure you didn't see Gabriel leave the house last night?"

She nodded, staring blankly.

"Where were you when Gwyneth fainted?"

"In the hall."

"What did you do?"

"I...nothing. I just watched. Roberto was helping her."

"How well did you know Gabriel?"

Margo's head jerked up as she met Tony's gaze. "I've known him for a couple of years."

"Did you date him?"

"Yes," she whispered, and a tear slid down her cheek.

"How recently?"

I frowned, trying to catch Tony's eye. This seemed cruel.

"Midsummer," she said. "We got together then. Right after he broke up with Gwyneth."

"Why'd they break up?"

Her face darkened into a scowl. "She's such an airhead." She shot a glance at me. "Sorry. But it's true. Gabriel's so much smarter than her. She drove him crazy."

"When did you stop dating him?"

She winced a little. "About a month ago."

"When he hooked up with Kris."

Margo nodded.

"What happened?"

"Nothing." She shook her head. "Nothing happened."

"He just changed partners? Or were you still seeing him?"

She looked at Tony, then shook her head again. "No."

"What about Cherie?"

A shrug. "Cherie was before Gwyneth."

"Did she and Gabriel part on friendly terms?"

Margo laughed softly. "No. They had a spectacular fight."

Tony glanced at me, then made a note. "Anyone else see it?"

"Everyone. It was at Beltane. Gabriel was flirting with Gwyneth and Cherie blew up at him."

That surprised me. Cherie had always struck me as calm and collected, though she did have a sharp tongue.

"She'd had a bit too much," Margo added, with evident satisfaction.

"Too much what?" Tony asked.

She leveled a flat gaze at him. "Booze. She's not into drugs."

"OK, thanks," Tony said, making another note. "That's all."

Margo sat still for a moment, then slowly rose, smoothing the cloak over her arm. She met my gaze and turned toward the front door. I followed and closed it behind her. The glimpse of sunlight dazzled me; I looked at the black drapes, but they were on a rod that was secured above the door. I'd need a step ladder. Or better yet, Mick.

Time to call in the reserves. My phone was upstairs, so I stepped into the gift shop to use the house phone. Mick's voicemail answered, and I left a message asking him to come in as soon as he was available.

"What's Beltane?" Tony asked as I came back out.

"It's a pagan holiday," I said, remembering Kris telling me about it. "May Day."

"So Gabriel was with Cherie before May, then with Gwyneth

until Midsummer—I assume that's June or July."

"June. The solstice."

"Then with Margo, then with Kris. Whew."

"He was very charismatic."

"Sorry I didn't get to see him in action."

I grimaced at this tactless remark. The suggestion arose in my mind that Gabriel could have given Tony a few pointers, but I dismissed it as unworthy.

"I need to put some laundry in the dryer," I said, and headed for the pantry.

Tony started upstairs, but the back doorbell rang and his foot-steps stopped, then came down again.

I opened the door and found Dale and Cherie outside. In an olive green sweater and jeans, Dale looked more like a preppie than a Goth. He also looked a bit embarrassed. Cherie was draped in black: a black broomstick skirt under a top with long, dripping sleeves and a plunging neckline that showed off a familiar silver ankh. No makeup, just an expression of wounded woe.

"Hi," I said, and Cherie winced. I lowered my voice and added, "Come in."

"Sorry," Dale whispered to me as we went into the dining parlor. "I couldn't talk her into letting me come alone."

Cherie slunk into the parlor and stood staring at the absinthe fountain. I glanced at Tony, who had remained in the hall.

"We'll need to empty it out," Dale said, stepping toward the fountain. "Where's the nearest sink?"

"The restroom," I said, "but the kitchen sink is bigger."

"Kitchen, then," he said, and started moving crystal goblets away from the fountain. "There should be a box for these."

"Yes, it's in the gift shop," I said. "And some of those goblets are in the kitchen waiting to be washed."

"We can wash them later." Dale glanced at Cherie, who was slowly walking around the table, her feet shuffling, her drooping demeanor putting me strongly in mind of Ophelia. She spotted one of the goblets on the sideboard and picked it up, staring at it as she turned it in her hands.

"I'll get that box," I said, starting toward the hall. Tony came to the door before I reached it, and I stepped back.

"Hi, Dale," he said.

Dale shot him a wary look. "Hi."

"Got a minute for a couple of questions?"

"Sure."

Tony paged through his notes. Cherie, goblet in hand, resumed her slow circuit. I hesitated, feeling tension between the two men.

"I was wondering if you made those sugar skulls you put in the chambers," Tony said.

Dale set down a goblet and turned to face Tony. "No, I just put them there."

"Who made them?" Tony asked.

"Roberto."

"Why'd he ask you to put them in the chambers?"

"It was just a joke." Dale said, watching Cherie glide slowly through the draped doorway into the main parlor. When she was gone, he relaxed and took a step toward Tony.

"Roberto found out about the skull decorating party, and was mad that he wasn't invited. So he made his own skulls and had me put them in the chambers."

"Pissing on Gabriel's territory," Tony said.

"Kinda, yeah. But I don't think Gabriel even noticed."

"Why didn't Roberto place them himself?"

"*That* Gabriel would have noticed."

"They didn't get along?"

Dale sighed, moving a goblet away from the fountain. "They had a friendly rivalry."

"Sometimes friendlier than other times?"

"Look, I'm not going to say anything bad about either of them. They're both my friends."

"And you thought it would be funny to help one friend mark the other one's territory?"

Dale frowned, then took a breath and steadied himself, meeting Tony's gaze. "I knew it would make Roberto feel better, and Gabriel probably wouldn't care. I figured it would defuse things some."

"Uh-huh."

They stared off, and I held my breath. To his credit, Dale didn't flinch from the patented Aragón Cop Stare.

A tinkle of breaking glass cascaded into the silence.

Dale looked toward the doorway into Rose. "Cherie? You all right?"

A sob followed. We all rushed for the doorway.

Dale got through first, and Tony and I squeezed through together, arms tangling briefly. My heart pounded as I tried to see. The black drapes masked the overhead lights, and at first all I understood was that Dale had grabbed Cherie.

"Give it to me!" he demanded, one arm around her waist, the other reaching for her flailing arm.

Cherie gave a louder sob. "No! I want to die!"

She tried to wrench away, and bumped into a lantern stand. The lantern toppled, crashing to the floor, the red glass shattering. I yelped as I hopped back.

Tony stepped in and caught Cherie's wrist in both hands. A gleam of light on a jagged edge of glass and I suddenly understood: Cherie had broken the goblet.

17

TONY SHIFTED HIS WEIGHT, changing the angle of Cherie's wrist, and as she cried out, the jagged goblet was in his hand instead of hers.

At the same time, Dale grabbed the black cloth off the empty food stand and caught Cherie's other hand in it. I saw a dark streak down her arm a second before Dale swathed it in the cloth.

"Ellen, take this!" Tony called, holding the broken goblet out toward me. "Careful."

With shaking hands, I took it by the stem. There was blood on the sharp edges, and dripping down what was left of the filigreed bowl.

Tony reached into his pocket, produced a pair of handcuffs, and snicked one onto Cherie's wrist. He pulled it behind her and reached for her other wrist, still held by Dale.

"Is that necessary?" I asked in a small voice, my heart going out to her.

"Keep her from hurting herself more," Tony said as he snapped the second cuff into place. Cherie's knees buckled and she sobbed. Tony and Dale both supported her, keeping her from collapsing onto the floor covered with broken lantern glass. I had a flash of memory: Gabriel's painting, "Calculation," of Gwyneth surrounded by shards of red glass.

"Call an ambulance," Tony said to me over his shoulder, then he looked at Dale. "Let's get her out of here."

I backed into the dining parlor, glass crunching underfoot, and set the broken goblet on the table, then ran for the kitchen and the nearest phone. I struggled to catch my breath as I dialed 911.

While I was giving my address to the dispatcher, a car came up the driveway and parked next to mine. My heart sank.

It was Kris's Scion.

All black was not unusual for Kris's wardrobe, but the T-shirt and jeans with her hair pulled back in a ponytail was. It made her look young and vulnerable.

"What is your emergency?" the dispatcher said.

"Uh—we need an ambulance. A woman is injured—broken glass."

I waved at Kris through the window, hoping to divert her to the kitchen. She didn't notice.

"Are you with her?"

"What?" I said. "Oh—no. Detective Tony Aragón is. She's—not exactly rational."

"Is she violent?"

Another wail from Cherie. Kris paused at the back door, frowning.

"Sorry, I've got to go," I said, and hung up the phone, then opened the kitchen's back door.

"Kris! In here."

She came in. "What's going on?"

"What are you doing here?" I said simultaneously.

"I—we need to take down the chambers today," she said, looking miserable.

That had been the original plan, before the world had turned upside down. "You didn't have to come," I said. "I called Mick. He can help me."

Distant sobbing. I winced. Kris frowned.

"Stay here," I said. "I'll be right back."

I headed for the hall. Kris followed. Not wanting to waste time arguing, I let her.

Cherie was on a love seat, still handcuffed and weeping quietly, with Dale's arm around her shoulders. I could see part of the black tablecloth still swathed around her forearm. It looked wet.

Tony stood nearby, talking on his phone. He glanced up at me, then his eyes widened as he saw Kris. He turned away, still talking.

"God!" Kris said, staring at Cherie. "What happened?"

"She cut herself," I said.

"Cherie!" Kris stepped toward her.

Cherie looked up, focused on Kris, and let out a wail of despair. A siren howled a harmony in the distance, from the west.

"That's the ambulance," I said. "Kris, could you let them in?"

I gestured toward the front door. To my great relief, Kris obeyed, stepping past Tony, who glanced over his shoulder at her. Cherie subsided into muffled sobs.

The ambulance crew soon had Cherie bandaged and strapped to a gurney. Dale stood watching with an expression of pity as they rolled her down the hall toward the door.

"Gabriel," Cherie moaned. "Gabriel."

The EMTs took her to the waiting ambulance. Kris watched from the doorway. I turned, looking for Tony, but he had disappeared somewhere. Dale stood by the love seat, his sweater smeared with blood.

"Thank you for your quick thinking," I said to him.

"I shouldn't have let her come. I didn't think she'd...well."

"None of us guessed her intentions."

He sighed. "I don't know if anyone's said this to you, but I'm sorry our party turned into this—" He gestured helplessly toward the wreckage.

"It's hardly your fault," I said.

A sad smile curved his mouth briefly. "I'd better follow them to the hospital. Mind if I come back later for the fountain?"

"Not at all. Would you like to clean up in the restroom?"

Dale looked at his hands, smeared with Cherie's blood. "Yeah. Thanks."

"Cold water on bloodstains," I called after him.

The ambulance pulled away. Kris closed the front door and turned to me.

"How did she get cut?"

I took a careful breath. "She broke a goblet."

Kris frowned, then her eyes widened. "Deliberately?"

"I think so."

"She tried to commit *suicide*? In the *tearoom*?"

"In Rose."

"God *dammit*, Cherie!" she yelled, slapping a hand against the wall.

She stormed into the main parlor. I followed, catching her arm as she reached the arch into Rose. "Don't go in! There's glass all over the floor."

She stood staring in at the mess. I could feel her trembling with rage.

"Damn you, Cherie!" she said. "You selfish *bitch!*"

"Come upstairs," I said softly. "Please."

Kris turned to me, scowling and breathing hard. My heart skipped as I wondered whether she'd loose her fury on me. I gave her arm a gentle squeeze.

"Please, Kris."

Her eyes narrowed, then her breathing slowed. Uttering a contemptuous curse, she strode back to the hall and up the stairs. I hurried after, following her into her office where she threw herself into her chair and commenced gnawing on a violet thumbnail.

"I'm going to make some tea," I said from the doorway. "Be right back."

She shot me a malevolent glance, then looked at her computer screen, ignoring me. I slipped away downstairs to put a kettle on and look for Tony. I found him in the dining room, an empty evidence bag in one hand, frowning at the broken goblet Cherie had used to cut herself.

"Do you want a box for that?" I offered.

He looked at me. "Yeah. Thanks."

I fetched him a sturdy box from the gift shop, and some tissue for good measure, and watched him carefully pack the goblet. "Does this move Cherie to the top of your list?" I asked quietly.

"Hell, yeah. She proved she's unstable enough."

"I...." I bit my lip.

Tony finished scribbling on the box and put away his black marker, then looked at me. "Don't tell me. You don't think she killed Gabriel."

I shrugged. "It's just a feeling."

"Looks like a pretty good case to me. That whole thing with the necklace."

I shook my head, unable to articulate my misgivings. Yes, Cherie was hurt by Gabriel's returning the ankh. Yes, she aimed a couple of snide comments at him during the party. I just didn't see that adding up to murder.

The front doorbell rang, followed by a brisk knock. I stifled a groan.

"That'll be Phillips. Send him back here," Tony said.

"Phillips?"

"Investigator."

I went to the door and discovered that "investigator" meant my favorite sandy-haired evidence technician, who was apparently named Phillips.

"Hello, again," he said, grinning. "Get any sleep?"

"Not much," I admitted, waving him in. "You?"

His grin widened. "Nah, this case is too interesting!"

"Well, it just got more so. Come on back."

I turned him and the photographer following him—a different one, young white male—over to Tony. The kettle began to whistle. I got to the butler's pantry just in time to catch it before it started shrieking, and started a pot of Assam. Returning to the hall, I met Dale coming out of the bathroom. His sweater was still a little stained, but looked better.

"Thanks for the tip," he said, brushing at it.

I nodded. "Soak it in cold water when you get home, then rub soap into the stain and wash it in cold."

"Will do." He rubbed his hands together, looking chilled and self-conscious. "Guess you'll give the job to someone else. You'd probably rather not see me again after this."

"Not necessarily," I said. "You were indispensable when Cherie lost her head."

His cheeks reddened. "If I hadn't brought her here, she wouldn't have done it."

"You don't know that."

He shook his head. "She only does things like that when she has an audience."

"Are you...close?"

His eyes widened. "Not like that, no. Just friends. But I've known her a long time."

"Well, you were a good friend to her today." A stray memory

came to me, of Roberto's painting of Puck, for which Dale had clearly been the model. "Is Roberto a better friend to you than Gabriel was?" I asked.

Dale looked at me in surprise, as if the question hadn't occurred to him. "Apples and oranges," he said. "They're very different people." He sighed. "I'll really miss Gabriel. We all will....Is that a timer going off?"

"Yes. Thanks." I started for the pantry.

"When do you need the fountain out of your way?" Dale asked, following me.

"By late Monday, if you can. Would you like a cup of tea before you go?" I offered, removing the infuser from the pot. I inhaled a deep, comforting breath of Assam-scented steam.

"That's tempting, but I'd better get over to the hospital," he said. "I'll call."

"All right. Thanks."

I saw him out, then put together a tea tray, adding a couple of tartlets and two slices of leftover wedding cake. As I carried it toward the stairs, I heard Tony's voice from the dining parlor. Looking in, I saw him pacing, talking not into his phone but into a hand-held recorder, describing Cherie's suicide attempt. He glanced up at me, but kept talking. I eased away and went upstairs.

Kris was where I'd left her. Anger had subsided into sullenness. She accepted a cup of tea, a hopeful sign.

"The cops'll think Cherie killed Gabriel now," she said.

"I'm afraid you're right."

Kris looked out the window, frowning. "She couldn't have."

In my heart, I agreed, but I had no proof. I lifted my cup and sipped tea.

"Did you see those heels she was wearing?" Kris said.

"This morning?"

"No, at the party. She couldn't have run in them. She could barely walk."

"Why would she need to run?"

Kris gave me a look. "Gabriel took off running after someone. After the person who..." Her voice hitched, and she took a gulp of tea. "It couldn't have been Cherie."

I nodded, thinking Tony should hear this. Picking up one of the cake plates, I offered it to her. She stared at it.

"Yeah," she said, reaching for it. "It's a cake day."

The tearoom phone rang, and we both looked at it. "Let it go to voicemail," I said.

"It might be important." She picked up the handset and had a brief conversation, apparently with someone she knew. "Hold on," she said, and covered the phone. "It's Owen Hughes. He says he left his mask."

"Yes, it's in my office."

Kris gave me the phone, and I told Owen he could come get the mask any time. "He's coming over now," I said, handing the phone back to Kris. "There are some coats and cloaks left, too."

"I may be able to tell whose they are," Kris said. "If not, I'll get them out of your way."

"Who gets the liquor?"

Kris grimaced. "I guess I'll take that, too. We can put it out for the wake."

"Oh, Kris."

She took a bite of cake, then put down her fork and swallowed. "I've got to deal with it."

"Tell me how I can help," I said, knowing that platitudes would be useless.

She turned her head toward me with a shadowed smile. "Keep me busy."

"OK."

I knew firsthand how the distraction of simple work could keep one from teetering over the cliff of depression. "Tony said Gabriel had a will," I added, thinking that his family might provide some support.

She nodded. "He left everything to me, except for a few gifts."

"Oh. No family?"

"Not here."

Thinking of Gabriel's artwork, I wondered if this could be good news for her. But the material gain, whatever it amounted to, was nothing compared with her loss.

"You might talk to Loren Jackson," I suggested gently.

"Maybe." She picked up the cake again.

"You'll think about it?"

"Yes."

We were out of tea. To give her some space, I went downstairs to brew more, and to keep her from following I asked her to make a to-do list for the coming week.

While I was in the pantry, I heard the rumble of a car engine and the crunch of gravel in the driveway. A minute later the kitchen's back door opened. I went through and found Mick signing in, looking fresher than I thought was fair.

"Thanks for coming," I said. "How's Dee?"

"Haven't talked to her today. She was OK when I dropped her at her place. Pretty tired, though."

"No surprise. You're getting overtime for this, by the way."

"Where should I start?" he asked. "Dishes or decorations?"

"Decorations," I said. "You'll need the stepladder. Please take down the black fabric around the doors, then work on the south side. The police are in Rose."

His brows went up. "Thought they finished last night."

"Well, there was a new development. Just stay out of the main parlor until they're done."

"OK."

Lingering in the pantry, waiting for the kettle to boil, I opened the lace curtains over the window, revealing the rosebushes dancing in the breeze out in the garden.

How beautiful they were. I watched, silently grateful, until the kettle was ready.

Leaving a fresh pot of tea steeping, I went to check on Tony, who emerged from the dining parlor as I approached. "I'm going," he said.

"To arrest Cherie?"

He shook his head. "She'll be given a psych eval, once she's stable. Then we'll see."

I nodded, swallowing. Poor Cherie.

"How's Kris?" he asked.

Surprised, I looked up into his eyes. "Coping. She doesn't think Cherie did it, either."

He sighed. "There's only so much credit I can give to women's intuition."

"It isn't intuition," I said. "Kris remembered that Cherie was wearing high heels at the party. *Really* high heels. She wouldn't have been able to run in them."

Tony frowned. "Got a picture of them?"

"Maybe Owen took one."

"Text it to me?"

"Sure."

"Phillips will let you know when they're finished." He kissed my forehead. "I'll call you."

"Thanks."

I leaned against him, grateful for the contact. His arm slid around me.

"Hey, Ellen?" he said softly.

"Yes?"

"Thanks for putting up with me."

I looked up and saw weariness in his eyes, tinged with worry. "I'm not the most charming guy on the planet when I'm working," he added.

I smiled and touched his cheek. "As long as you remember to wipe your feet, it's OK."

He glanced at his shoes, and we both laughed. I walked with him to the front door, where Mick was taking down the black fabric. Sunlight streamed in, filling me with relief and a tiny spark of hope. There would be an end to this. Life would go on.

Through the lights, I saw a dark shape outside. It was Owen, looking unexpectedly normal, but still striking, in a gray cable-knit sweater and jeans. He smiled when I opened the door.

"Thanks for letting me come by. Hi, Detective Aragón."

"Hi," Tony said, and added, "Bye." His fingers brushed mine, then he was striding down the path toward the curb where his bike was parked.

"Come in," I told Owen. "We're just taking down the decorations. Your mask is upstairs."

We went up to my office, where the mask still lay on my credenza. I handed it to him, and he gave a sigh of relief.

"Did you make it?" I asked.

"No, Gabriel did. In trade for photography."

"I see."

"It's all I have now, besides the photos, to remember him by."

"You were close, then?"

"Not terribly, but I've always admired him. He's—he was—an artistic genius."

I nodded, glancing toward Kris's office. "Such a dreadful loss."

"It really is," Owen said, cradling the mask carefully. "I was hoping to buy one of his paintings one day. Now I guess I won't have the chance."

Prompted by impulse, I stepped to my desk and took out my badge from the art show. "Have you ever seen one of these?"

He stepped closer to look at it. "Sure. It's from the exhibition last week."

"Did you go?"

"Yes."

"Does your badge look like this?" I said, showing him the map side.

He laughed. "Yes, I asked Gabriel who else I should look at. I have to say, I didn't care for what I saw in most of those booths."

"Neither did I. Do you still have yours?" I waggled the badge.

Owen nodded. "I liked the holder, so I kept it."

"What about the map?"

"Yes, I kept that, too. Gabriel wrote a message on the back of it."

"He did?" I slid the map out of my holder, and found a few words scrawled across the back. Gabriel must have done it when I wasn't looking.

> *Thanks for your support! Looking forward to All Hallows -*
>
> *Gabriel*

"I hadn't noticed," I said softly.

"He was good at that sort of thing," Owen said. "He was good with people."

I slid the map back in and returned the badge to my desk drawer. "Keep yours safe," I advised Owen.

He smiled wistfully. "I think I'll keep it with the mask."

"Do you have a card?" I asked him as we went downstairs. "For your photography?"

He took out a metal wallet and handed me a business card. It was black and white, a striking photo of a yucca plant in front of the entrance to a cave.

"Thanks. I may be calling you."

"Thank *you*. And thanks for keeping this safe."

He hefted the mask, then went out. I looked into the gift shop. The blue drapes were all down, and Mick was working on Dahlia. I headed back upstairs and turned on my computer, then took out the case where I kept collected business cards and found a spot for Owen's next to Gabriel's.

Something about Gabriel's card caught my attention. The design was simple: besides the text, there was just a Celtic knot, no doubt Gabriel's work. I'd seen it before, I was sure. I fingered the card, trying to remember.

Giving up, I fetched my phone and sent Tony a text:

> Check back of badge
> map for message from G

I slid Owen's card into the case. The image was deceptively simple. The darkness of the cave was the perfect background to set off the yucca, bright in sunlight. It confirmed what I'd suspected watching Owen take photos of Dee: he was a professional, in skill level if not in actual fact.

I brought up the photos I had downloaded from his camera and began looking through them for a picture of Cherie's heels. Owen had a genius for capturing interpersonal moments. I became acquainted with the guests in a way I'd never imagined. People who had been costumed strangers became living, laughing, sultry or sinister beings. Fascinated, I kept going through the images.

Ramon frowning in concentration as he played the guitar, looking darkly romantic in his blue tunic.

Cherie smiling as she talked with the two Goth fairies. Shoes not visible in that photo, unfortunately.

Gabriel in the black chamber, caught nodding in conversation. The mask concealed his face, but his stance was somehow both regal and humble.

Gwyneth in a moment of unexpected stillness. Alone in Lily, no one to impress, she was gazing into the distance, looking hopeful and a little afraid. An extraordinary image.

Dale and Margo flirting by the mulled wine cauldron. Dale was bowing over Margo's hand, and she was feigning shyness by drawing her veil over her face, while simultaneously sending him a coquettish glance. I hadn't seen her smile like that very often.

I gazed at the photo, wondering what had led to it. Was it staged for Owen's benefit? The others didn't seem so. If not, he'd been lucky to catch the shot.

Something niggled at me. I enlarged the image until it nearly filled my screen. The candlelight was soft and warm. Reflections glinted off of Margo's eyes, the chandelier, and the absinthe fountain in the background.

I paused, feeling a chill down my back. Owen had captured one large gleam of light shining out from the chandelier, right above Dale and Margo.

Peering closer, I looked for some unusual detail. The purple feather on Dale's hat partially obscured his face, but Margo's veil did little to hide hers.

Margo's veil.

I drew a sharp breath. The hennin, her tall hat, with the stiff black veil floating from its points.

Could it be tulle?

I zoomed in on the hat. Fortunately, the photo's resolution was high and there was no blur from motion. It wasn't visible against the dark green dress, but against Margo's pale skin the veil was clearly made of net.

It looked very much like tulle.

I cropped the image and sent it to the printer, then sent the whole picture as well. I texted both files to Tony and asked him to call me.

While the printer slogged on I rummaged in my desk for a copy of the party guest list and a folder. There were some colored ones. I gave a small cry of triumph as I extracted a green one.

I hurried downstairs, where I found Mick carrying the ladder across to the main parlor. Phillips the Investigator was on his way to the front door, photographer in tow.

"We're done," Phillips told me as I passed.

"Thanks. Mick, hold up, please." I switched off the parlor's overhead lights as the front door closed. "Give me just a minute."

I ducked through the drapery passage and into Rose, walking gingerly as glass crunched underfoot. Leaving the folder on the empty food stand, I fetched the long matches from the fireplace and lit the remaining candle lantern. Red light flared.

"Ellen? What are these?" Kris asked from the archway. She had my printed photos in her hand.

"Wait, please," I said.

I held the folder up between the lanterns and the black drapery. The crimson light from the lanterns turned the green to a dull, dark gray. A darker shade would certainly have appeared black.

Margo's dress would have looked black in there. She would have been hard to see against the black walls, especially at a glance.

What do you want?

Gabriel hadn't been alone when I looked in. I just hadn't seen who was with him.

"Right. Mick, you can do Jonquil and Lily, but leave this side up."

I blew out the candle, grabbed my folder, and brushed past Kris to turn on the lights. She followed, and I took the photos from her and slipped them into the green folder.

"Thanks. I'm going out for a bit."

"What's up?"

I hesitated. She'd suffered enough trauma. I didn't want to add to her pain, but I also felt I owed her the truth.

"I think I know what happened. Kris, I believe it was an accident. I'm going to find out."

"Going where?"

"To—the person I think was there."

"Are you nuts? You can't go alone! What if you're wrong?"

"I don't think I am."

"That's about as safe as 'Hold my beer and watch this'! You should call Tony," Kris said.

"I did. I haven't heard back."

I went upstairs for my purse and keys. Kris trailed after me.

"I thought you were all law-abiding leave-it-to-the-police."

"Usually," I said, "but if this was an accident, it'll go easier on— the other party—if they turn themself in. Do you see?"

"*'Themself'*? From you, the grammar queen?"

"I'm trying to be discreet."

Kris crossed her arms and leaned against the frame of the door to my suite. "If you want to be discreet about gender, you could say 'hirself' or 'zemself.' But being discreet about it at all implies that the person you're protecting is female."

When the mood strikes her, Kris can be an even more annoying pedant than me.

"Fine," I said, stepping past her into the hall. "Yes, you're right. If she turns herself in, the police may go easier on her."

"And you think you can convince her to turn herself in?"

"I have to try."

I moved to lock my suite and she stepped out of the way. "Take me with you," she said, following me back down the stairs.

"No, Kris. You've had enough."

"Then take Mick," she said as we arrived in the hall.

Mick stood before us, fiddling with one of his earbuds. He looked up in response to our staring at him.

"All right," I said. "Yes, that's a good idea. Mick, will you escort me on an errand?"

18

My Google-fu is not the best in the world, but while Mick fired up his patchwork ride I was able to find Margo's address from her phone number on the guest list. Her apartment was on the south side of town, not far from Gina's though in a less pricey complex, a group of blocky buildings in pueblo-brown stucco.

"I think Margo may have been present when Gabriel died," I told him. "I want to convince her to go to the police. You don't need to say anything. You're here to discourage her from doing anything...ill-advised."

He shot me a sober glance. "OK."

"You don't happen to be a martial artist, do you?"

"Sorry, no."

Rats.

"Well, I don't think she is, either."

I hope.

Actually, I didn't know much about Margo. Wishing I'd asked Kris for information, I walked up two flights of stairs with Mick at my back.

A long pause followed my pressing the doorbell. I was about to knock when the door finally opened and Margo looked wearily out. Her expression turned to surprise as she recognized me.

"Hi, Margo. I'd like to talk if you have a minute. This is Mick, he works for me at the tearoom."

She looked at us both, then shrugged and opened the door. We entered a small living room furnished with a black futon couch and two overstuffed armchairs, also black. A television sat on a table under the front window, which was covered with burgundy curtains.

The coffee table in front of the couch was cluttered with books, comics, candlesticks, coffee mugs, and a statuette of a gargoyle.

The cape that Margo had fetched from the tearoom earlier lay over the back of a chair. My gaze snagged on the silver clasp: it was shaped like a Celtic knot. The same knot that was on Gabriel's card.

Margo waved at the couch and sat in one of the chairs. I went to the chair with the cloak instead, and Mick stayed behind me.

"Is this Gabriel's cloak?" I asked gently, laying my hand on the velvet.

Margo looked up at me with the fear of a child caught in mischief. "I made it for him. It's mine, really. He—doesn't need it now."

She crossed her arms and leaned back, refusing to meet my gaze. I wondered how to reach her.

"Do you still have your badge from the art exhibition?" I asked.

She said stiffly, "I lost it."

"What about your hat?"

She froze, then said curtly, "I threw it away. It was ruined."

"Ruined? How?"

She didn't answer. Her chest rose and fell with her breathing; a bit fast, I thought.

"Margo, was there an accident?" I asked gently. "Did you perhaps tear your veil?"

A wave of dismay crossed her face. For a moment I thought she would crumble, but she drew herself up.

"I don't know what you're talking about," she said.

"The police found a scrap of black tulle entangled with the exhibition badge that killed Gabriel."

I took the photos out of my folder and stepped closer to lay them in her lap.

Margo burst into tears.

It took me a while to talk Margo into calling Tony, but at last she did it, after making me promise to stay with her. Mick was plainly uncomfortable, but I knew I'd get a chewing-out from Tony if I sent him away. I'd probably get one anyway. No need to make it worse.

Tony arrived within ten minutes of receiving Margo's call. He shot me an angry glance as he came in, but sat quietly and listened to Margo's halting explanation.

"I was mad, and I pushed him away," she said. "I wasn't trying to push him over the rail."

This was followed by a bout of tears. Tony waited with clenched jaw for her to subside.

"What were you doing up there?"

"Gabriel chased me. We—I—we argued, and I left the party, but he came after me. He wouldn't let it drop. I kept trying to get away from him. I ran into the garden but there were people there so I went up the stairs."

"What was the argument about?" Tony asked.

"H-he dumped me and never told me *why*. I didn't know he'd hooked up with Kris until that meeting to plan the party," she said, looking at me. "Then he writes that he *loves* me! I was mad."

"He wrote you a letter? Do you have it?"

I tried to catch his eye, shaking my head slightly.

"No," Margo said.

"The badge," I said softly.

She turned an incredulous look at me. "How the hell did you know?"

"He wrote a note on the back of mine, too. Not a love note." I turned to Tony. "Did you get my text?"

"Yeah." Tony pulled the evidence bag with the badge out of his jacket and held it up in front of Margo. "This yours?"

More tears.

"You checked the back?" I asked softly.

Tony nodded. "It just says, 'Love always, Gabriel'."

"Why did he write that when it wasn't *true?*" Margo cried, banging her fist on the arm of her chair.

"How did the badge get around his neck?" Tony asked her.

"I p-put it there. I told him I was giving it back. But he didn't understand. He couldn't see what it was because of that mask. He kept after me to go back to the party so I pushed him away. I felt my hat falling off and grabbed it. There was a tug and then it let go."

She paused, giving little short, gasping sobs.

"At first I didn't see him. It was like he just disappeared. Then I saw his mask—the jewels were glinting in the moonlight."

I shivered, thinking of the gleams of light I had seen there. Would Tony even try to understand, if I told him? I tried again to catch his eye, but he wouldn't meet my gaze.

"I thought about jumping after him," Margo added, "but I wasn't sure it was high enough to kill me."

I put a hand on her wrist. "You made the right choice."

"Where's the hat?" Tony said.

"I threw it in a dumpster out back of the plaza. Then I went back to the party. I didn't know what else to do."

"I need you to come to the station and make a statement."

Fear came into Margo's face. "No—"

"They'll have a counselor you can talk to," I put in. "Right?" I added, looking at Tony.

"We'll get you some help," he told her, nodding. His attitude was not quite grudging, but not very enthusiastic.

Tony got up and went into the kitchen where he made some phone calls. I sat with Margo, trying to beam a bit of courage to her. She stopped crying, and sat staring at nothing. I overheard Tony telling someone to look for her hat.

When Tony's backup arrived, we walked Margo out to the parking lot. Mick followed silently, subdued. Once Margo was in the back of the squad car, Tony turned to me.

"Don't ever do that again."

"Would you have arrested her if you'd confronted her before I did?"

"I could arrest *you* right now for interference. I ought to."

"If you must."

He was silent. I could tell he was deeply angry by the flare of his nostrils, by his rapid breathing.

"I apologize for interfering," I said. "But I stand by my action. She didn't mean to kill Gabriel. Berating her won't help."

He took three more sharp breaths, then met my gaze. "I'm not the bastard you think I am," he said, then stalked away.

I watched the squad car pull out and Tony follow on his bike. My sense of accomplishment had turned bitter.

Still in silence, Mick drove me back to the tearoom. When he parked and shut off the engine, I turned to him.

"Thank you. I'm sorry it was so…dramatic. I didn't mean to make you sit through a scene."

"S'OK," he said. "Want me to come in and keep cleaning up?"

"If you're willing."

We went in and found Kris carrying a chair into Dahlia. She put it down and looked at me, half hopeful, half fearful.

"I need tea," I said, sighing.

I offered Kris a week off. She declined, but eventually ended up taking a couple of days to deal with the details of Gabriel's estate. I was prepared to offer the tearoom for the wake, but she wisely chose to have it elsewhere. No need to remind all of Gabriel's friends of his tragic final evening. I, for one, would never forget.

I attended the memorial service, feeling I owed it to Gabriel. It felt to me like a reunion of the Halloween party, except that Margo was not present. Nor were any of Gabriel's family, though Kris had invited them. Perhaps they had felt the trip from New Hampshire was too far.

Cherie, however, was there, looking pale but sane. She wore black, and the infamous ankh, but kept the dramatics to a minimum.

Gabriel's ashes were displayed in an elegant white marble urn at the service. I had expected something more elaborate, dark and Victorian, but the moment I saw it I realized the white was perfect. I also knew that it wouldn't be buried, that Kris would give it a place in her home, at least for now.

The service was brief; testimonials would be shared at the wake, which I did not attend. Instead I went home and lit a candle for Gabriel on the table in the upstairs sitting area.

How do you tell when a Goth is in mourning? No jewelry.

Kris wore black every day now, with minimal makeup. After the memorial she began to wear one necklace, a string of jet Victorian mourning beads with a pendant, that Cherie had given her.

November flew by. Nat returned from her honeymoon in buoyant spirits. I offered Dale the job he'd applied for, and he accepted. Preparations for the holiday season kept me and Kris busy. That was a blessing, for both of us.

Tony had stopped answering my texts, my calls, my emails. I was hurt, but I couldn't be surprised. Apparently I had gone too far. Still, I didn't regret going to Margo's apartment.

She was charged with involuntary manslaughter. I felt pity for her, and sadness. I bought more candles and kept them lit, both for Margo and for Tony.

Just before Thanksgiving, the White Iris Gallery mounted its exhibit of Gabriel's art. Kris invited me to the opening. I went, more to give her moral support than because I wanted to see Gabriel's artwork again.

I sent Tony a text about it for form's sake, but planned on going stag. I suspected that Gina's personality might be a bit too energetic for Kris, yet. Nat agreed to close the tearoom for me so that I could leave early.

The evening was calm and cold. We'd had snow a couple of times, but not enough to stick. I wore a gray knit dress and boots under my long wool coat. Black hat and scarf. I parked in the public lot and walked down Canyon Road to the gallery in twilight.

The street was notoriously narrow, meandering its way east into the foothills of the *Sangre de Cristos*, and lined with quaint, old, adobe houses, some of the most expensive real estate in the city. Most of them were now commercial properties, the majority being galleries. Canyon Road was the art Mecca of Santa Fe.

White Iris Gallery was in an old adobe house, smallish and linear, with rooms obviously added over time. A small fire burned in a brazier outside the front door, a harbinger of the holiday season to come. I paused in the foyer to sign the guest book and enjoy another fire in a corner kiva fireplace. The house had low ceilings, wood floors, white walls, and candles in nichos making it warm and bright inside.

I entered the first room and was met by the sight of "Calculation." I'd been uncomfortable when I first saw the painting; now I was dismayed. The crouching female—Gwyneth—had no good choices, none at all. The shattered red glass took me back to Cherie's suicide attempt. Pain, of all kinds, in all directions. Somehow, in my heart, that tied into Gabriel's tragic death. I felt my throat tightening, then I noticed a small stand to one side holding a single sugar skull, with a card labeled "La Princessa." With a shock, I recognized it as one of the skulls Gabriel had decorated at Julio's party.

Beyond the skull hung another painting, an abstract in shades of cream and pale blue that I remembered from the exhibition. Beside this was another sugar skull on a stand, this one labeled "Night."

Three more paintings hung in the first room, each paired with a skull. I didn't remember all of the skulls, and as I moved to the second room and saw more of them, I began to suspect that Gabriel had made additional skulls after the decorating party.

My attention was arrested by "The Seventh Chamber," Gabriel's visualization of the end of Poe's story. Rather stunned that Kris had included it, I looked from the painting to the paired skull, "Harlequin," the one that Gabriel had made three-dimensional with layers of icing. Why pair a figure of fun with the dark triumph of the Red Death? Was it to point out that Prince Prospero was, in the end, an object of ridicule?

A green diamond on one cheek of the skull triggered a memory from the decorating party:

You are part of the masque.

"There you are!"

I turned to see Kris, sleek and elegant in black velvet with long, close sleeves, the jet beads hanging almost to her waist. She reached for a hug.

"Thank you for coming. Want some champagne?"

"Yes, please."

She led me into the next room, larger than the first two. In one corner a Latina woman perhaps a few years older than I was standing beside a small refreshments table. Her dark hair was nicely coiffed in a French twist, and her black cocktail dress was simple and elegant. Beside her a younger woman, in caterer's attire, filled champagne flutes with Gruet Blanc de Noir. A platter of cheeses, adorned with almonds and a scatter of pomegranate seeds, sat on one end of the table.

"Ellen, this is Theresa Cortez, the gallery's owner. Teri, this is Ellen Rosings, owner of the Wisteria Tearoom."

Teri shook my hand, then put a glass into it. "Nice to meet you. I've been meaning to go by there."

I set down the glass and dug one of our new promotional cards out of my purse. "Bring this. Good for tea and a scone on the house."

She accepted it with a smile and a word of thanks. Kris and I strolled away with our glasses.

"Kris, it's a wonderful show. All the sugar skulls...."

"Yes. Gabriel fell in love with the idea of pairing them with his art. He got Julio to give him a bunch of leftover skulls and spent a couple of days decorating them."

"It's stunning."

She smiled softly. "Fortunately Teri liked the idea. The skulls are for sale, too. They can be preserved, or allowed to go back to dust."

We strolled around the room, Kris giving me time to admire each of the paintings, several of which I'd seen before. I spent a couple of minutes looking at one of Gwyneth, almost nude in a swath of white gauze, standing amid the distinctive dunes of White Sands. Her head was turned to the side, her expression severe. The sky overhead was an intense blue that made me think of Georgia O'Keeffe. It was striking and lovely. The card gave the title as "Venus of the Apocalypse."

"This wasn't in the exhibition," I said.

"No," Kris said. "Gabriel didn't want to show it. They broke up over the photo shoot. Gwyneth got sunburned. That's why she looks so pissed."

"What a shame," I said, hoping that Kris wouldn't take it the wrong way.

"Yes, well. They'd been rocky anyway. And Roberto was waiting in the wings. We all knew it."

The skull paired with "Venus" was decorated in black. I remembered it from the party. Intricate scroll-work, reminding me of the Renaissance. It was titled, "Cara Mia."

"Did Gabriel title the skulls?" I asked.

"Most of them."

We moved on to the next room, where a life-sized painting of Kris from the waist up made me gasp. She stood with her back against a pillar draped in violet satin, light reflecting from the folds in a way that reminded me of water. Kris's head was tilted back, eyes gazing skyward, expression mournful. The painting was unfinished;

the background around Kris and the pillar was lightly sketched in with a few brushstrokes of neutral tones, but the rest of the canvas was blank. The title on the card was "Ophelia," and it was listed as "Not for Sale."

"Gabriel's title?" I asked.

"Yes. He knew I liked the subject."

I slid my arm around her waist for a hug. She reciprocated, and we stood gazing at the painting. Then I noticed the sugar skull and gave a surprised laugh. It was pink with an orange Van Dyke, and titled "Hamlet."

The last room was dark, and at first I thought it wasn't part of the show, but Kris led me toward it. I stopped in the doorway, emotions flooding through me.

The room was draped in black. A mannequin stood in one corner, wearing Dee's "Red Death" costume and wig and a blank white mask. The mannequin was flanked by two red candle lanterns. Kris must have found a replacement for the broken one, because they were exactly as they had looked at the party, once again turning the silver highlights on Dee's costume to blood.

On the opposite wall, subtly lit, a series of concept sketches for the costume were displayed in simple frames, along with several of Owen's photos of Dee in the costume and makeup. On the adjacent wall was a large photo of Gabriel in his golden costume, also Owen's, obviously taken in the tearoom on Halloween night. My mantel clock was visible over his shoulder. Gabriel stood with arms akimbo, Prospero in his prime. Beside the portrait was a card with a short paragraph about his death. The only other thing on the wall was an eight-by-ten photo of Gabriel's face in the sun paint. The slight smudges told me it was one of the police photos.

I gasped. "How did you get hold of that?"

"Dee talked to one of the investigators, and he got a duplicate for me."

"Was his name Phillips, by any chance?"

"I don't know."

I couldn't bear to look at that photo, so I turned back to Owen's portrait. After a moment I looked at to Kris, blinking back tears, my heart full.

"It's a lovely tribute," I whispered.

She smiled. "Thanks."

A couple of thirty-somethings peeked in, their stylish clothes and expensive cowboy boots marking them as tourists. I stepped out to make room for the probably-paying customers.

"You're out of champagne," Kris noted. "Want more?"

"Yes."

I took some cheese and a cracker to keep the wine from shooting straight to my head. The gallery was filling up; the beautiful people of Santa Fe were coming out to see Gabriel's show and mingle with a scattering of Goths, some of whom I didn't recognize. One couple looked almost too perfect: pale-skinned, the woman with straight black hair, the man with white hair brushed straight up. Both of them were dressed entirely in black leather.

Hollywood Goths. Moneyed Goths. Maybe Gabriel's story had gotten around.

Roberto and Gwyneth, both in black, came into the center room, and Kris went immediately to greet them. I stayed behind to nab another piece of cheese and indulge in people-watching.

My wandering gaze stopped and the cheese turned to dust in my mouth as I spotted Tony in the far doorway.

He was wearing his leather jacket over a dark blue shirt and black jeans. He'd been looking over the crowd, but now his head turned and he met my gaze.

I swallowed the cheese dust and tried for a smile. He threaded his way through the mingling art enthusiasts and stopped in front of me.

"Hi," he said.

"Hi. Want some champagne?"

He glanced at the table where the caterer was still pouring. "Sure."

He picked up a flute, and we both stepped aside as a trio of guests moved in on the wine and cheese. I struggled for something to say that would be sincere and not inane.

Tony beat me to it. He looked around the room, then said, "So this is Gabriel's art."

"Yes."

He shook his head. "I don't do art."

"It's OK," I said, then added, "Here's to Gabriel."

He joined my toast, though his expression said he thought it was all crazy. The champagne fizzed in my brain along with a bubbling spring of hope.

"Come and see this," I said, stepping toward the next room.

Tony followed me to "Ophelia," and I watched him take it in, a couple of waves of surprise crossing his face.

"This is good," he said finally. "Too bad it isn't finished."

I thought the painting's state was perfect, given Gabriel's demise, but I didn't say so to Tony. Instead I gestured toward the last room.

"Dee's costume is in there. It was his final work. Do you want to see?"

Tony shook his head. "I spent enough hours staring at that, thanks."

I nodded and sipped my champagne. "I'm glad you came. Does this mean I'm forgiven?"

He leveled his gaze at me and was silent for two breaths, while I took about five.

"I'm working on it," he said.

I swallowed, then managed a smile. "Let me know if I can help."

He knocked back his champagne, and I winced, thinking I'd said the wrong thing. But the next moment he took my free hand.

"Let's get out of here," he said. "You want to go for coffee?"

"Sure," I said, my heart taking wing.

Sugar Skulls

(for el Dia de los Muertos - edible, but I don't)

Ingredients:

    2 c granulated sugar
    2 t meringue powder
    2 t water
    3" skull mold
    4x6" index card
      or stiff plastic card
    cardboard

Preparation: Mix dry ingredients together. Sprinkle water and mix until consistency of moist sand (not soppy). Pack into skull mold, place index card at back and quickly flip over, slide onto cardboard and slide out index card. Tap mold to make sure it's loose, then lift carefully. Let dry for at least 24 hours, then decorate. Makes about four skulls.

Royal Icing

Ingredients:

    2 c powdered sugar
    1-½ T meringue powder
    ¼ t almond, lemon, or vanilla
    ¼-½ c warm water
    food coloring

Preparation: Blend ingredients with mixer until peaks form. Separate into small bowls and add coloring, then spoon into plastic bags and make tiny snips in corners (or use piping bags). Keep sealed and refrigerated until use.

Pan de Muerto

This recipe is for buns (yields approximately twelve). Traditionally, *pan de muerto* is made in larger loaves. If you choose to make loaves, this recipe will yield two.

For the bread

½ c whole milk
5-½ T unsalted butter, chopped
zest of 1 orange
3 large eggs, lightly beaten
1 T orange blossom water (or plain water)

1 ¼-oz. packet active dry yeast
¼ c lukewarm water (90-110°F)

3-½ c unbleached all-purpose flour; more as needed
¼ c granulated sugar
1 t sea salt or kosher salt
Vegetable oil as needed

For the topping

4 T unsalted butter, melted
1 t orange flower water
2 T powdered sugar

granulated sugar for sprinkling (½-1 cup)

In small saucepan, stir milk, butter, and orange zest over medium heat until butter melts, 2-3 minutes. Remove from the heat cool until warm (10 minutes). Add orange blossom water and eggs, whisk until blended.

Dissolve yeast in ¼ c lukewarm water and let stand 5 minutes.

Mix flour, sugar, and salt in large, shallow bowl. Make a well in the center. Mixing gently with your hand or a silicon spatula, gradually alternate adding yeast mixture and milk mixture into the well. Knead about 10 minutes until dough is smooth and slightly sticky. Add more flour if needed.

Round up dough in a large, lightly oiled bowl, cover with plastic wrap or a towel, and leave in a warm place (about 70°F) until doubled in size, 1 to 1-½ hours.

Shape the buns

Preheat oven to 350°F. Cut off a third of the dough and set aside for decorations. Divide the remaining dough in half, divide each half into thirds, and divide each third in half to create twelve buns. Round up on a lightly floured surface and place on two parchment-lined baking sheets. Press down on each bun with your palm to flatten it – about ¾" to 1" thick. Cover both sheets and let the bread start to rise while making decorations.

Note: these are the traditional *Dia de los Muertos* "bone" decorations, which are more stylized than realistic. On a larger loaf, there are usually three strips of "bones" rather than two. The top ball represents a skull.

The dough will be sticky and stretchy. Have a small dish of water on hand and a small pile of flour at the edge of your work surface. Dip fingers into one or the other as needed.

Decorate six buns at a time

From the reserved dough, take twelve pinches each about ½" in diameter. On a lightly floured board, roll each pinch into a ball. Take one ball and press in the center with a finger.

 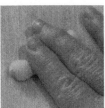 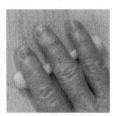

Begin to roll it out, leaving a knob at each end. Add a second finger, then a third, gently stretching as the "bone" elongates. Roll until about 4" long and about ¼" in diameter with knobbed ends.

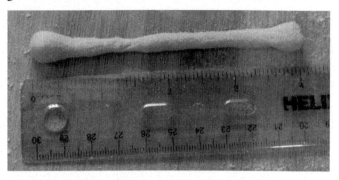

Optional Extra Knobbiness

When all twelve bones are shaped, take a small pinch of reserved dough and roll it thin, to 2 mm thick. Pinch off lengths of about 3/4". With a fingertip, dampen the back of each length with water and wrap around a bone about 1" from the end. Press the outside edge of the small strip with a fingertip to make a dimple. Add another strip to the other end of the bone. Repeat for each bone. (Note: if you are dexterous, you might simply roll extra knobs into the bones as you are stretching them out. However, I've found it easier and faster to do it this way.)

Take 6 pinches of reserved dough each ½" in diameter. Roll into balls for the "skulls."

Uncover one sheet of buns and use fingertips to dampen each bun before decorating it. Lay one bone across bun and press against the bun slightly to make sure it sticks, especially at the ends. If the bone is too long, pinch it together in the middle, which will be covered. If it is too short, stretch it. Dampen the center point of this bone and lay a second bone across it to form a cross shape.

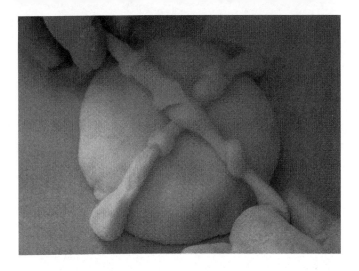

Dampen the point where they cross, and gently press one of the skulls onto that point. Repeat for each bun.

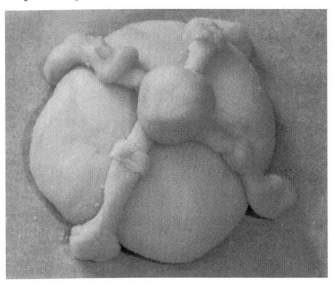

Cover and let rise while decorating second tray (note the time: this tray should rise about 45 minutes).

You may have enough dough left from the reserve to make an extra bun for a total of lucky thirteen!

Baking and Sugaring

With a rack in center of oven, bake the first tray until the loaves have an even golden color, 20 minutes. Cover loosely with foil and bake 5 minutes more. Bottoms should be browned and sound hollow when tapped.

While the bread is baking, melt the 4 T butter in a small saucepan. Add orange flower water and powdered sugar, stir until blended, remove from heat.

Set a wire cooling rack over a shallow pan or baking sheet to catch excess butter and sugar.

When first tray of buns is done, remove from the oven and place second tray in (set timer). Place the baked buns on the wire rack and brush with the melted butter mixture. Sprinkle sugar all over the tops, tilting the buns slightly to coat them evenly. Let cool, then remove to plate. Repeat with the second batch of buns.

The bread is best eaten within a day of baking.

About the Author

photo by Chris Krohn

PATRICE GREENWOOD was born and raised in New Mexico, and remembers when the Santa Fe Plaza was home to more dusty dogs than trendy art galleries. She has been writing fiction longer than she cares to admit, perpetrating over twenty published novels in various genres. She uses a different name for each genre, thus enabling her to pretend she is a Secret Agent.

She loves afternoon tea, old buildings, gourmet tailgating at the opera, ghost stories, costumes, and solving puzzles. Her popular Wisteria Tearoom Mysteries are colored by many of these interests. She is presently collapsed on her chaise longue, sipping Wisteria White tea and planning the next book in the series.

About Book View Café

Book View Café Publishing Cooperative (BVC) is an author-owned cooperative of over fifty professional writers, publishing in a variety of genres such as fantasy, romance, mystery, and science fiction.

BVC authors include *New York Times* and *USA Today* bestsellers; Nebula, Hugo, and Philip K. Dick Award winners; World Fantasy Award, Campbell Award, and Rita Award nominees; and winners and nominees of many other publishing awards.

Since its debut in 2008, BVC has gained a reputation for producing high-quality ebooks, and is now bringing that same quality to its print editions.

Made in the USA
Lexington, KY
21 August 2017